Summit Books
New York   London
Toronto   Sydney
Tokyo   Singapore

Philip F. O'Connor

Finding
Brendan

a novel

SUMMIT BOOKS
Simon & Schuster Building
Rockefeller Center
1230 Avenue of the Americas
New York, New York, 10020

SUMMIT BOOKS and colophon are trademarks of Simon & Schuster Inc.

Designed by Carla Weise/Levavi & Levavi
Manufactured in the United States of America

10 9 8 7 6 5 4 3 2 1

Library of Congress Cataloging in Publication Data

O'Connor, Philip F.
    Finding Brendan : a novel / Philip F. O'Connor.
        p.   cm.
    I. Title.
    PS3565.C64F56   1991
    813'.54—dc20
                                                    91-3956
                                                    CIP

ISBN: 0-671-73155-6

For
Ray Ferguson
Russ Galen
Lisa Kidd
Melanie Kaufman
Doug McVey
Erin O'Connor
Joyce Osterud
and
(especially)
Nicholas

There is, in the sanest hours, a consciousness, a thought that rises, independent, lifted out from all else, calm like the stars, shining eternal.

—Walt Whitman
Democratic Vistas

There are gashes in our understandings of this world.

—Adrienne Rich

∘👄∘ DANA

I don't know who saw them first. They just sort of appeared. We were up on the second level and heard loud mumbling over by the windows and then someone said "God!" and someone else said "What *is* that?" and we all rushed over. Some girls screamed even before they got to the windows. I didn't but almost did when I looked down.

First I have to tell you. There's this square raft about ten feet by ten feet on the other side of some big rocks next to the walkway. Rock bands use it on Saturdays and Sundays and at Spring Festival time. People gather on the walkway around it. But this day no one was on the walkway because the weather was wet and gray. In fact, the only reason we were at Riverside Plaza at all was because some author was supposed to give all the sophomores a talk about drugs or drinking or something and didn't show up. "Probably drunk," Malcolm Frey said. That's Malcolm. Anyway, they decided to make it a field day and took us down to the plaza. We were supposed to write a paper about our impressions of this or that or make price comparisons or find out about the ingredients of stuff in a bakery or deli or salad bar, I'm sure so parents wouldn't think they were letting us goof off, which we basically were. When it was all over, just about everyone did a paper and just about every paper was on guess what?

One body was face up. A man. More like an oversized boy. And he had on this black suit that didn't fit very well because you could see the white shirt sleeves sticking out of the coat sleeves, and the socks sticking out of the pants. They were white too—like tennis socks, even though the shoes were black and shiny. There was a big lavender flower sticking out of the lapel, like a whole flower pulled out of the ground, not one bought in a store. One arm was stretched up like it was waving and the other was loose at the side.

That was the man and he would have scared us enough but there was something else, a girl or woman.

You couldn't tell because she was facedown and not just facedown but facedown on top of him, kind of crossways over him, and had on this white bouffant-type dress and white stockings and pink shoes. You could see way up the legs because of the dress, which nearly blocked the rest of her from our view. It didn't block all of her because I remember seeing her hair. It was dark blonde and curled out at the sides, not the way a hairdresser would do it but like a friend would who wasn't very good. I remember her lips because the lipstick was bright pink and almost matched the shoes but not quite. She had big lips and her face was beautiful but more like a doll's face is beautiful than a person's.

Everyone was by now pressed up against those floor-to-ceiling windows looking out past the balcony that goes around. All of us were totally, I mean totally, silent for a long time and stayed that way until someone said "God!" all strung out like "Gohhhh . . . hahhhh . . . haddd!" Like that. Then we all started buzzing and mumbling. Miss Carroll, who's only a student teacher, sent someone for the coach, Mr. Constanza. He was in charge of the trip and was back at the deli waiting for some kids who were still asking questions. The rest of us kept looking down. "They're dead!" Claire Anthony just had to say. "I'm sure of it!" It started to rain. We all kept watching to see if a hand or foot would twitch or anything would move, but even when the rain got heavy all that happened is their clothes started to stick to them, even the girl's skirt, and shrunk like a wet sheet into her. Then his brown hair, which had been sort of sticking out all over, got darker and kind of pasted back by the rain, making him look older and less like a boy, more like a man, and definitely dead. I never before saw a dead person, ever, and it is totally shocking, so bad I can't describe it. I was backing up and looked around and everyone, like they had a string attached to them, was backing up. It was like an explosion in slow motion. I mean, that was it. The rain was beating down and the river was acting up and the raft was moving and the bodies were sliding to one side like in a second they were going to fall off and sink into the muddy water.

Mr. Constanza came and looked out and said, "Jeesamus

Christmas! Did anyone call Security?" Someone told him Mrs. O'Toole went to get help. I didn't know that. Mr. Constanza kept looking out. By this time I definitely wasn't looking. It was bad enough seeing two dead bodies for the first time in your life. I wasn't about to watch them slip into the river and go under or do something even weirder like bob around with their mouths and eyes open. Someone said, "Maybe they were murdered." I wasn't thinking about how they got there, just what was going to happen next. What did happen next was Mr. Constanza called Billy Titus and Greg Martin over. Billy Titus played right tackle on our nearly all-state JV football team, which Mr. C. coached, and Greg was the tight end, and they are definitely the two biggest sophomores, at least the two biggest who aren't just fat. "We've got to go down and try to get those two off that raft before they fall in." Billy said, "Count me out, coach. I'm just about going to barf." Mr. Constanza said, "Oh, for God sake, Billy," then picked Ellen Frushour which was probably smart because she's strong and definitely a better swimmer than Billy *or* Greg.

Before they even got to the stairs one of the ones who still was looking out said, "The raft is moving!" Mr. Constanza and his helpers started running for the stairs about thirty feet away and the rest of us rushed back to the windows.

Sure enough, the raft had come loose and gone past the boat ramps and was on its way down the river, tilted to one side like the bodies were going to fall off. But they stayed on, almost like they were stuck there. And then it and the bodies started sinking into the mist on the river and they were soon just a little gray silhouette. We kept watching until they disappeared where the river turns.

By then sirens were sounding.

Mr. Constanza and Ellen and Greg and a lot of people were now standing on the walk near where the raft had been.

"All right, all right," said Mrs. O'Toole, coming up behind us. "This is all being taken care of. Let's get on with the work of the field trip.".

Where had *she* been?

Everyone, I mean even Jackie Swan who's straight "A" and never complains, groaned and complained and soon we were saying in one way or another, "We're going after that raft." Mrs. O'Toole *of course* took it personally and got mad. "I suppose if we were outside and a fire engine went by you'd want us to follow it." Malcolm said, "*I* would." In fact, more than one person said something, and her gloomy wet eyes didn't stop us from arguing with her. Which we were still doing when Mr. Constanza came up the stairs with Ellen and Billy. After he talked to Mrs. O'Toole privately, she came over and said, like it was her idea all along, "We're going to take the bus and follow the police cars down the river until they get the raft."

We cheered.

"You'd better remember one thing," she said.

About two people said, "What?"

"This is still a field trip and you'll all have to write down your impressions of what you see."

Just about everybody nodded. No problem.

Definitely *the* smartest person in our class even though she came from the worst junior high is Angela Davenport. At Riverside Plaza she said absolutely nothing, didn't say a word until we were sitting together on the bus on our way to River Road. She turned and said, "Suppose they're not dead."

I had already settled that one for myself. They *were* dead. When Mr. Constanza came up he told us the raft had broken free before they'd gotten to the bottom of the stairs but he'd seen them up close and was now calling them "the bodies." They were surely dead. But Angela is the smartest person in our class. "How could they not be?"

She shrugged.

That bothered me. I said, "I've had a lot of trouble getting myself to, you know, accept they're dead, and now you think they may not be."

"No doctor or medic has checked them yet."

That was true. "So?"

"Why did that raft go away just when people started to go up to it?"

"I don't know."

"And why didn't the bodies fall off when it got all tilted up?"

"Do *you* know?"

"No."

She is my second sometimes maybe first best friend but I

totally wanted to choke her. "You just *think* they might not be dead."

She nodded.

"Well, they are!"

But already I was beginning to wonder.

°⊜° JOSEPH

It didn't matter that I pulled his Stroh's cap tight over his ears. By the time he reached the front of the store it was squatting on his head like a pet squirrel. I called his name but he didn't stop, just opened the door, went out and leap-stepped across Long Avenue without looking either left or right, then disappeared behind the Fetler's garage. I didn't see him again until he came from behind the Friedman's hedge chasing their cat. The cat crossed Elm in three strides and shot into a tree. He waved his fist at it and said something. By the time he turned for the park, his cap was in his back pocket and his jacket was flapping in the wind.

Grace's sister, Cora called late yesterday afternoon and said, "Well, are you still determined to be a martyr?" I didn't answer. Most of her questions don't want answers. "I read about another one yesterday," she went on. "Wandering around in downtown River City and stepped in front of a bus. Thirty-two years old. He suffered spinal injuries and will probably spend the rest of his life in a bed." She paused, giving me time to picture the injured man in his bed. "Maybe there are brothers and sisters to take care of him," I said. "Yes," she replied, "and think of how he's ruined *their* lives." As she went on speaking, Brendan pushed open the door at the front of the store and stumbled in. He stopped by the newspapers and, frowning, said, "Tummy." He came forward, pulling open his jacket. "Listen, Poppa." I put my hand over the phone's mouthpiece and pointed the receiver toward the apartment. "Go in the back. I'll be with you in a few minutes." I removed my hand and raised the receiver. "I must go now, Cora." She wasn't listening. "If they'd put that fellow where he belonged in the first place," she said, "he wouldn't have been out on the street." I hung up, set the punch-bell at the center of the counter and went back to the apartment.

When we were finishing supper last night he said, "Where's Momma?" He's silent about her for days, then asks. "Gone," I told him again. "She won't be back." His bottom lip twisted down the way it does when he's puzzled. Soon his eyes wiggled up. "Back?" he said. "*Won't* be back." He stared at me for a few seconds, then got up from the table, went to the cupboard near the stove, took out the pots and pans and laid them on the floor, side by side, the way he used to do when he was a child. He knelt and took the smaller ones out of the larger ones, putting some over here, some over there, then changing them around. Before I finished my coffee, he got up, clip-clopped to the front bedroom and leaned in, tilting his head one way, then another. Finally he flicked on the light and went in. I didn't hear him move or say anything and soon he came out. "No Momma," he said, as though *he* were informing *me*. "That's right," I told him, "Momma is dead." I got up, took a dishcloth from the sink and wiped off the table. He was shaking his head, as if to say my statement was my opinion, not his. "It's time for you to do your words," I told him. I expected him to resist, but by the time I found a pencil in the junk drawer he was at the table, fingering his workbook and tablet. I watched him work until someone in the store rang the punch-bell.

After a few customers came and went I checked on his work. Sometimes he slips made-up words in among the real ones. I spoke my pleasure about the real ones. "Kettle," I said. "Good." But then I said, "G-o-p-p. It doesn't mean anything." He made fists and squinted up. "Gupp, gupp," he said. "Is big cup." I shook my head. "It's not a real word." Often I want to ask him what this or that word of his means but I never do. Sometimes, like last night, he volunteers. Sarah, his teacher since Grace first got sick, says he's very imaginative. "If you let him, he'll create a vocabulary all his own," she said, "but then no one will know what he means." I put lines through the made-up words and stars beside the real ones. He mumbled something. I couldn't tell what it was and didn't ask, but his frown told me it was no compliment.

Just after he went out this morning I saw his sandwich and orange on the countertop next to the sink. I stopped packing his lunch in a paper bag because he'd lost the bag several times. He's been stuffing the sandwich into one jacket pocket and an orange or apple into the other. It's the second time this week he's forgotten. When his friend Andy stopped in on the way to school, I told Andy about the lunch. "Also, please put his cap on tight. It should be in his pocket and tell him to button his jacket." Andy took the lunch. "I'll button the jacket myself," he said. Andy and Rosa go to Hartsville West Elementary and are Brendan's friends. If Andy puts Brendan's cap on and buttons his jacket for him, Brendan will wear them that way.

The seniors on the Hartsville High football team gave him that jacket the night of this season's first game. Most of them are his age, eighteen and a half, or near it, and have known him for years. He has been in school with them on and off since first grade. The jacket is dark green with light-colored leather sleeves and has the word "Lancers" in yellow script across the chest. He was allowed to sit on the team bench. At the first time-out the coaches let him take the water containers onto the field. It was a mistake. When the whistle blew he wouldn't come off. Fans on the other side hooted at him. The Lancer players pointed him to the sidelines but he still wouldn't leave. Finally a Lancer coach went out and led him off. That was the end of his water-boy work. Later that night he strolled around the neighborhood in the jacket. I had to close the store early and go out to find him. He's worn the jacket ever since, except when he goes to bed. It's full of stains and splotches. I've tried to rub them out when he's asleep but many remain. Unless an all-night cleaners opens in Hartsville, it'll probably never be clean.

He wanted to show Grace his jacket, but she'd been in the hospital for nearly a month by the time he got it and was very weak and turning yellow. Dr. Carroll worried about her becoming too excited and said I should bring Brendan to her room for only a few minutes each time. During most of my visits she slept. One night, about ten minutes after I arrived, I heard his voice from behind: "Boombah, Momma!" Boombah is his made-up name for himself. He'd come up from the waiting area early. I told him to go back. "No, Joseph," said Grace from behind. I turned and saw her trying to sit up. Brendan rushed past me, stumbling to a stop at the edge of the bed. "Oh, darling!" she said. Her eyes opened wide for the first time that night. She reached down and struggled to push away the blanket and sheet. "Don't worry, Joseph," she said. "I want to hold him for a few minutes." I then helped her pull down the blanket and sheet. "Look, Momma." He pointed to his jacket. "It's beautiful," she said. He then climbed awkwardly in beside her. I hurried around the bed in case he accidentally nudged her off on the other side. He reached down and pulled the sheet and blanket up to their chins. He looked at me over the top. "Night, Poppa," he said, then laughed so hard the bed shook. Grace, laughing weakly herself, raised her hand and petted his cheek lightly. "Boombah," he said, using the name he'd given himself when he was seven. She nodded and kept petting him and soon his eyes closed. In his presence Grace had taken on new color. "Let him stay until he wakes up," she said. I told her I would. She then fell asleep. The nurse came in and said, "Oh, my God!" She told us we had to leave. I woke up Brendan. He wouldn't get out of bed until he was sure Grace was asleep. Then he came quietly.

He started speaking gobbledygook at her funeral service. Father Cronin had just talked about her work in the Parents' Guild and was getting to other things when Brendan began a singsong chant: "Bobbedy mombo no go neebadee," or something like that. I turned and said, "Shush," but he kept chanting. I could hardly hear what Father was saying. I got up to take Brendan out, but the priest signaled me to stay. I did. Brendan got up and walked to the casket which was sitting at the top of the main aisle. As Father went on talking, Brendan put his hand on the casket's crucifix, then leaned on the casket itself, crossing one foot over the other. He stayed quiet there until the service ended. He kept quiet in the limousine on the way to the cemetery but really got going when we reached the gravesite. For about twenty minutes he stood beside the casket, bent over, with his hands behind his back, his tie hanging down, and spoke in such a way that, if you didn't know who he was, you might have thought you were hearing an Asian language. I took him back to the limousine before they lowered her into the ground, fearing he'd jump in after her.

For a while after the funeral he spoke very few real words.

Even Sarah had trouble with him. From the counter I heard them at the kitchen table:

"Reng pah deng pah?"

"You may be talking to someone. I hope it's not me."

"Ne ba nu bing dee?"

She ignored him.

"Sa-*rah!*"

"What?"

"Dung day wiss us?"

Silence.

"Sarah?"

"What?"

"Ahm . . ."

"Say it."

"Ahm . . . you come . . . stay wiss . . . us?"

"*With* us."

"With us."

"You mean, live here?"

"Ess."

"Yes!"

"Yah . . . *ess!*"

"I can't, Brendan. I have my own apartment. Anyway, you don't have enough room."

"Sarah?"

"What?"

"Have room."

"Where?"

"In my bed."

She said nothing. He'd caught her by surprise.

In a few seconds his booming laugh thundered through apartment and store.

At about that time he also started getting into scraps with neighborhood children, even the smaller ones. He forgot simple chores like taking the garbage out to the sidewalk on collection days. I tried to bring him back to where he'd been. I couldn't. He began coming home for lunch up to two hours late. I tried using a whistle, then a cowbell. Neither worked. I couldn't leave the store to chase him down. Finally Sarah figured out that he'd forgotten how to tell time. "We have to teach him again." I fixed the strap on my old Timex, positioned the hands straight up and showed them to him. "That's lunch," I said. He took the watch and put it into his mouth. "Lnnphh," he said. "Not funny," I told him. He smiled. "To *Poppa,*" he added. I took back the watch, put it around his wrist, tied it and I pointed to the dials. "That means it's lunchtime." He gazed at the watch, his lower lip going back and forth. I changed the hands to read 11:30 and pointed at them. "That's *not* lunchtime." He pointed to the hands. "*Not* lunchtime." I turned the two hands back to twelve. "What's that?" I said. He looked down, then up at me. "Lunchtime!" I grabbed his hand and shook it. "Right!" He nodded proudly. We did the exercise again. Each time the two hands were straight up he said, "Lunchtime!" Each day after that he took the watch to the park and returned at or near noon. If he returned a little early, he sat on the small stepladder children and short persons use to reach things on the top shelves. He stared at the watch. When the two hands were on twelve, he leaped up and shouted, "Lunchtime!" often scaring a delivery man or customer. One day he returned in what seemed to me a very short time. "Lunchtime!" he said. I looked at the Dr. Pepper clock on the wall behind my counter. It read 10:40. He came to the counter and showed me the watch. Both hands pointed to twelve. "You don't fool me," I said, pointing to the clock on the wall. "Busted, Poppa." I shook my head. "It's not busted." He frowned. "Hungry, Poppa." I opened a bag of peanuts for him but waited until noon before I fixed his lunch. He soon ignored the watch and came back whenever he was hungry. He interrupted me when I was making out orders or talking to delivery men or waiting on customers. I decided then to fix lunches he could take with him. He's been taking them ever since, except, of course, when he forgets.

It's now 2:35. The late winter snow flurries have let up but the wind is still stirring debris. The air has turned so cold I feel it slapping my face every time someone opens the door. Sometimes the weather drives Brendan home. Since noon I've been watching through the window, expecting to see him, but he hasn't appeared. The park has open-sided shelters that give little protection. He may have curled up in the phone booth by the swimming pool and fallen asleep.

Three girls from the junior high come in. They want Snickers bars. They had to pass through the park on their way here. One I recognize, though I don't know her name. I've seen her teasing Brendan in front of the store. I ask if she's seen him.

"No," she says. "Is he lost?"

I tell her I don't think so. "I just want to know what he's doing."

She turns to her friends. All three giggle.

"What's funny?" I say.

"Oh, nothing," says the one I questioned.

They linger at the magazine stand just inside the door.

I open the cash register and count my change, but I also listen.

"Maybe he's the one who turned over that garbage can," says one.

"Probably," says another.

"To have lunch," says the first.

They all laugh. They say other things I don't hear and go on laughing and giggling.

They've probably seen him nosing around trash cans at one time or another. He's a collector, finds old car parts and broken baseball bats and other discarded things and brings them home. I myself eventually put most in our trash. But he doesn't eat out of garbage cans. I want to tell the girls that but decide they already know and are just having their joke about him. There are many Brendan-jokes. (Question: "Why did the chicken cross the road?" Answer: "It saw Brendan coming.") Some even tell *me* the jokes, thinking I'll like them, not knowing how much they hurt. Only a few people are cruel. Most people treat him like a friend, even a brother.

"Expect him to be erratic for a while," Sarah said. "It's part of his adjustment to Grace's death." I know she's right. Since Grace died I've been erratic too, forgetting to pay my distributors on time and losing my watch several times and dozing on my stool by the cash register. Sometimes I wake up in bed and start talking to Grace, thinking she's beside me. At other times I wake up and just feel afraid. I go to Brendan's room, wondering if he's gotten up and gone out to do something crazy, like search for Grace. He's always in bed asleep.

"You've gained weight and taken on an ashen look," Sarah said the last time she visited. "When did you last have a physical?" I couldn't remember. I know it was no less than four years ago. "Four years ago," I said. She shook her head and told me I should have another. Sarah is a bright young woman and senses more than I wish her to. But not everything. I didn't tell her I get pains in my shoulder when I walk more than a block. I walk to the park after Mass every Sunday with Brendan. Lately I have to pause frequently. I move on only when the pain goes away. "Hurry up, slow man," he says. I can't hurry. I tell him to go ahead. I get home fifteen or twenty minutes after him. Lately even little tasks, like arranging items on the fruit and vegetable shelves, bring the pain. "I have Weight Watchers frozen meals in the store," I told Sarah. "I'll use them and try to lose some pounds." She asked me to promise I'd call Doc Grable and schedule a physical. I told her I would, then became suspicious. "Does any of this have to do with Brendan?" I asked. She didn't answer right away. "Tell me," I said.

"You're not a stupid man, Joseph. You know there are people in this community who don't think he should be living at home." I do know but try not to think about them. "Don't give them the excuse of your bad health," she said. There was fear in her voice, and it brought back the fears I had when Brendan was sent away to a special school. That was a nightmare. After she hung up I called Doc Grable's office and made an appointment for next Monday.

Eleven years ago the school psychologist, Dr. Lenore Ogden, gave Brendan tests and told us he was severely retarded. Mr. Reed Stark, the principal at Hartsville West Elementary, filled out a form and told us we had to sign it. We did, not knowing we had a choice.

The special school was in Ambersville, the county seat, thirty miles from Hartsville. Brendan was eight at the time. Every morning he left on one of those yellow minibuses at a quarter to seven and didn't come back until five in the afternoon. His eyes were often red and several times he had bruises on his body. "Stay home, okay Momma?" he said nearly every day. We asked him to tell us what was happening at the school, but he couldn't or didn't want to say. One morning Grace called in sick to the Libertyville Country School, where she taught, and climbed on the bus with Brendan. We'd been given a brief look at the special school before

Brendan started going there, but the tour had been on a Sunday and we saw only the recreation room, a bare place with some wooden toys and coloring books. When she returned home with Brendan after her surprise visit, she told me the principal had tried to prevent her from seeing what went on in the classes. She told him she wouldn't leave until she saw at least Brendan's class. Finally he gave in. There was, in fact, only one classroom. "It's not really a classroom but a large barnlike place where children of all ages are kept, doing what they call crafts," she told me. The teacher left the room frequently and, when he did, older children bullied younger ones. She saw two boys who seemed to be sixteen or seventeen twisting the arms of a boy a couple of years older than Brendan. When the younger one squealed in pain, Mr. Federman, the teacher, returned and made him sit in a chair at the foot of the room. He was being punished for making noise. Brendan, despite her presence, cowered when any of the older ones came near him. She told me about other things she'd learned: A classroom aide was supposed to assist Mr. Federman, but was frequently absent; reading and speech specialists came to the school only once a month; some of the older children had been assigned to the school for having committed petty crimes after they were tested and found to have below-normal IQs. "We just can't let them keep him there," she said.

We petitioned the school board to have Brendan released and returned to Hartsville West. Doctor Ogden and Mr. Reed Stark filed a counterpetition. It said, "We find no evidence that Brendan Flynn's condition has improved." Grace shook her head and said, "How could he have improved at a place like Ambersville?" Weeks passed. There were no special education classes at Hartsville at that time. Only after Grace offered to resign from her job and spend much of each day teaching Brendan did the school board give in, permitting a one-year trial period. If Brendan showed a marked improvement, the board would reconsider our petition. We agreed.

We kept Brendan out of Ambersville. Grace worked with him during the day and went to the public library at night, taking out and bringing back books on teaching the mentally retarded. She used the kitchen as a classroom and concentrated on reading and writing and mathematics in the morning and on lighter subjects in the afternoon. "He'll grow up knowing how to do more than make ashtrays," she said. As rewards for good work we took him to Playworld Amusement Park and movies and the circus. And, being home, he was able to play again with his neighborhood friends. In the quiet of the apartment he learned well and, at the end of the trial period, was tested and found to be improved but not sufficiently. He wasn't sent back to the special school but wasn't re-admitted to Hartsville West.

We pleaded again, on the basis of Public Law 94–142, which was supposed to "normalize" as much as possible conditions for the mentally retarded and developmentally disabled, that Brendan be permitted to attend Hartsville West or any other regular school in the district. "Not as long as we have special schools," we were told. Brendan was permitted to join his former classmates only for social events and athletic activities. Grace continued to teach him until she became ill. Then Sarah took over.

"Now you're stuck with him," said Cora after we called her to tell her about the school board's decision. When she'd first seen Brendan, Cora tried to talk us into having him put into an institution for retarded infants. "You were too old to have that child," she told Grace. "That's why he turned out the way he did." Grace was then thirty-eight. Cora was thirty-two, had been married twice but had never had children. She was now surprised by the school board's opinion but not pleased. "You'll spend the rest of your lives being martyrs!" she said. Cora went on warning her, but Grace was never much affected by her sister's opinion. "That's Cora," she often said. Following Grace's funeral, Cora came back to our apartment for supper and, after Brendan went out to play, said, "He's the one who killed her, you know." I don't get angry often, but that remark made my head throb. Grace was never happier than when she was working with Brendan, even when he wasn't learning well, even after she became sick and had to find Sarah to help. "In my opinion, Brendan helped her live longer." Cora sneered and said, "I saw what it did to her and see what it's doing to you."

Students from Hartsville West Elementary have begun to trickle down Elm. I don't see Brendan. But I don't see Andy or Rosa either. He'll be with them. Surely it's too cold for them to want to stay in the park. Where could they go? Maybe they walked around the reservoir on the far side of the school. Andy said he thought he saw fish jumping around in there. I worry that Brendan will slip under the reservoir fence and fall in while trying to grab a fish. No. It's too cold for the reservoir. But where is he? I shouldn't worry. Everyone observes him. You'd think he was a koala bear or crocodile that had gotten loose. I hope he's not urinating on a bush or . . .

Here comes Andy.

But where's Brendan?

Andy is running past the smaller children. I don't see Rosa. And why is Andy running? He has no shirt. I look behind him. No Brendan. No Rosa. Maybe he only has to go to the bathroom. But he could have done that in school. And where's his shirt? There's something in his hand. A red something. He's crossed Fetler. Not red. Maroon. Maroon and yellow. "God!" The Stroh's cap!

What's happened?

०⊜० SARAH

I felt someone behind me. I turned and there he was, leaning against the doorjamb. Though one of the several offices of this ubiquitous man is at the far end of the building, I rarely encounter him. I and the other teachers see him only when he wants us to see him.

He smiled a cautious smile.

I nodded but didn't smile back or ask him why he'd come. There was no need. Eventually, in his oblique way, he'd tell me what he wanted.

"You're looking perky after a busy day," he said, somehow holding the smile.

"No busier than most."

"Ah, yes." He nodded—he nods constantly—pulled back the flap of his tweed jacket and pressed the palm of his hand against his side in a way that would seem awkward in most men but doesn't somehow in him. "So how are your home students doing?"

Too positive an answer from me would, I sensed, stiffen him. I therefore said softly, "Just fine," picked up the last loose crayon and took it back to my desk.

He tested me with questions as I put my books and papers together to leave, specific questions, even personal ones. I answered spontaneously, not wanting to give him any reason to guard against me. Soon he knew that I was no longer going out with Gerald Keyes, a political science instructor at Midland State University; that my father's arthritis had improved; and that I'd finally purchased the Nissan Sentra I'd been saving for. He nodded more vigorously than usual during my responses, a sign that his need was great. Eventually he approached it:

"About that boy, the older child you visit, the one whose mother died recently."

"Brendan Flynn?"

"Correct." He refers to all students with disabilities as children, no matter what their ages. "I wonder if you have a recent evaluation?"

I didn't, not the kind he wanted, but I shaped an answer I thought might satisfy. "My visits are, in a sense, a continuing evaluation."

"Are they?"

"Yes. Why do you ask? About him? There are, after all, a few other people I teach or tutor at home."

"Well, his situation has changed." Nod nod. "I mean that mother of his did a remarkable job. But now that she's gone we ought to monitor him more closely."

I kept my anger from warming my words. "Don't you think Joseph has been doing just fine?"

"Do *you*?" he said in a surprised tone.

"Yes."

I felt fire in my face and I turned from his gaze.

"You told me he was showing signs of depression after the death of his mother. I believe you said his behavior has been increasingly erratic. The father has even complained about it to you."

He'd read my working notes. A supervisor is expected to inform a teacher before reading her notes. A courtesy. Tucker didn't inform me. What he'd done wasn't illegal or unethical, but it was certainly, to use a word he often employs, unprofessional. I nearly complained but held back, having no desire to let him think he was controlling me. "Brendan is acting much like anyone his age might after the death of a parent."

"That's a matter of interpretation, isn't it?" he said with a forgiving look.

Arguing with him is like trying to run in soft sand. And, truth is, a case can be built. Brendan has been double-clutching. Double-clutching means deviating from the expected behavior pattern. Brendan used to keep his cap on. Brendan used to come back to the store between noon and one. Brendan used to speak in sentences. Brendan used to learn new words every week. Brendan used to make his bed and pick up his clothes. Brendan used to close the door behind him. Brendan used to avoid long periods of solitude. For a time he seemed to know his mother had died. Now Joseph isn't sure.

"And Joseph?"

"What *about* him?"

"How do you find him?"

"I find him attentive but a little weary, as you might expect."

"Interesting," he said. "What's he been feeding the boy for lunch?"

"The usual. Sandwiches. Fruit."

"The mother gave him hot soup too, didn't she?"

"Joseph sometimes serves him soup."

"Only occasionally."

"A person can live without soup."

His eyes had drifted to my hands. "You're tensing," he said, "making little fists." He moved toward me from the doorway like a teasing boy. "I hope my questions aren't intimidating you."

I'd put my coat over my arm and had my books and papers in my hand. I'd been waiting to go, wanting to, but if I did so now he'd pursue me in that marshmallowy but persistent way of his ("We both know, Sarah, that it helps to talk things out") until I'd given him the answer he wanted.

He was appointed director of Cleaver County Mental Retardation and Developmental Disabilities after selling to the board a grand plan called the Sunnyvale Project. In preparing it, he'd conferred with some experts but not with developmentally disabled students and their parents or with those, like me, who have worked with such students. He agreed to lump together people from the existing county home for the poor and indigent with the mentally retarded and developmentally disabled. I think he might have found a way to deliver his perfectly normal mother into the system if that would have helped his case.

In Phase One, now completed, I and two other special education teachers were transferred from the regular school system to the old converted warehouse where he and I now spoke. The warehouse had been owned by the board for twenty-five years and had originally been intended as the second special school in the county, in fact, technically was. It had been used for general county storage until Tucker turned it into three unattractive classrooms and an office for himself, one of several. As in other places, a loophole had been found that undercut recent "normalization" laws and kept the disabled needlessly segregated. The students we once taught in the regular Hartsville schools were transferred here. No longer do they play and intermingle with the so-called normal children, who in general had accepted them. On being drawn away, they've become stigmatized. It doesn't surprise me to see them mocked and ridiculed. ("Hey, Louis! Better get your books ready. Here comes the retard bus.")

Phase Two is populating the newly-expanded community homes. Tucker needs bodies. There exists great demand here and elsewhere for care facilities for the mentally disabled, but laws permit screening in such a way that admission can be made highly selective. Certain kinds of residents are, for one reason or another, preferable to others. I believe one of these is Brendan. As Tucker often and accurately points out, recent laws permit all those not under state or parental guardianship to walk out of a home at will. What he doesn't say is that many are under guardianships who ought not to be, or that those who aren't being prepared for independent living become hopelessly dependent on community home care.

Phase Three is a small industry, called *sheltered workshop,* in which some of the disabled from community homes will work for minuscule wages folding cardboard into boxes or sticking labels on packages. I think, but can't prove even to myself, that Tucker finds Brendan a good prospect for such work, in fact sees him as an eventual foreman. Brendan might be ideal, but he could do better living at home and working elsewhere. Despite problems he's had since the death of his mother, he generally functions well. Tucker knows this and could hardly have missed the unintended sharpness in my tone when I said, "He does not belong in a community home."

"You *are* jumpy. No one's made a decision about him."

"But you have something in mind. Don't you?"

"Really, Sarah, you ought to learn more about my plan before you resist it. I know you're not happy with Phases One and Two, though I believe eventually you will be. Our students and the residents will be well served. It will all, I admit, take time to get used to. To the point. I'd like to join you on your visit to the Flynn household today. I saw it on your schedule. If you don't mind."

I'd planned to stop and see Joseph briefly, without Brendan present, to talk about Brendan. It was certainly not a good time for Tucker to visit. "I'd prefer to . . . give Joseph notice of your coming. He isn't expecting anyone to be with me."

"That would make this a very good time then, wouldn't it? I want to see them all as they are. If everything is as wonderful as you say . . ."

"I didn't say 'wonderful'. Brendan has some problems."

He nodded. "Shall we take my car?"

Refusal, any resistance at all, might make matters worse for Brendan and Joseph. Me, as well. I picked up my notebook and followed him out.

I sat at the Flynn kitchen table about twenty minutes later asking Joseph questions while Tucker poked around the apartment as if it were his own and he were trying to find his keys. Joseph didn't seem troubled by him. As usual, he answered me frankly. "No," he said, "he's not eating well. I waste a lot of food on him. He'll leave his breakfast, then have a couple of candy bars. I think sometimes he throws his sandwiches away." I knew Tucker was hearing some of this. I tried to warn Joseph with my eyes. He just gazed, waiting for the next question. When I was nearly finished, he said, "I think he'll go back to doing things the way he used to after he finally gets it straight that Grace is gone for good." He paused and gave me a hopeful look. "Don't you?" I did, and I nodded. Tucker didn't hear Joseph's perceptive remark, however. He was then in Brendan's bedroom, moving things about. What was he looking for? Anything, I suppose. Anything useful. He was a detective building his case.

When Tucker wasn't listening, I didn't write down things Joseph told me. But Tucker heard much of it. He may have guessed the rest. I again tried to give Joseph warnings with my eyes. A year ago he might have read my signs, but now he simply waited for my next question.

After leaving the apartment we drove to the park.

"I want to observe him firsthand," Tucker said.

I found Brendan on one knee near an oak tree, hand extended with crumbs, trying to entice a gray squirrel. I stopped but Tucker kept advancing. The squirrel, tail twitching, stood about five yards from Brendan. It finally turned, saw Tucker, froze for a few seconds, then scooted toward the tree.

Brendan turned quickly, frowning. "Why you *do* that?"

"It'll come back. We won't stay long."

"Sa-*rah*!" He'd looked past Tucker and seen me. With long clumsy steps he came toward me. "Hug!"

I hugged him tightly, as he was hugging me. "Let's go over to that bench by the tree and talk," I said. "Maybe the squirrel will return."

Tucker tugged at my sleeve and pulled me back. "He'll talk to you if I wait in the car," he said. "He looks overweight and unhealthy. Find out not only what he's been eating but what he's been doing."

"*Not* come back," he said when we were on the bench. He meant the squirrel. "Why you bring that *stupid* man?"

"He works with me. He wanted to see you, to be sure you were eating."

He puzzled over such a foolish intention. "I *eat.*"

I took his hand. Despite the chilly air, it was warm.

He turned.

"You stay and play *wiss* me. Okay?"

"With."

"*With.*"

"I can't stay, but I'll come back soon. Maybe tomorrow. Just me."

"Just Sarah."

"That's right. What are you going to do today? After lunch."

"Play with Andy and other *those.*" He pointed across to the school. He stood abruptly, turned, and bent his knees, facing me. He peered past me, so intensely that I turned around to look.

"No! Me!"

I turned back.

"Heigghhh whan!" He threw his right fist into the air, then flung it to his left, bending even lower, then turned and looked at me over his shoulder. "See that, S*arah?*"

"What are you doing?"

He repeated the action, said, "Heiigghhh whooo!" He turned and grinned. "See?"

I didn't.

"Ump!" He struck his chest. "Boombah!" He laughed loudly.

Before I left the park, the squirrel came out of the tree and squatted a few yards away, I guess waiting for me to depart. Brendan told me—more laughter—he'd get me free tickets to the games he umpired. "First-base? Or third-base?" The games were, of course, open and free. Again he laughed. The squirrel didn't move. We hugged again before I left.

Now, at the cusp of darkness, we sit in Tucker's midnight blue Corvette in the nearly empty parking lot behind the special school. He eases as close to me as the bucket seats will permit and says, whispers, "Do you get the impression I've been preparing you for something?"

He's a man I sometimes fear, but now I'm not afraid. His hand is soft as a baby's bottom. If I draw my own hand away, will his come with it? If I snap open the door and get out, will he regard it as an insult? Will he follow? ("Why do you bolt, Sarah, when I'm only bidding you goodnight?") I'm *not* afraid. But why does he want me to stay? "Well, Sarah, do you?"

"No. I don't."

"Listen. I'm not happy with what I saw. Joseph has the look of a dying man. I'm sorry, but I've spent time working with geriatric cases. Death announces itself in many ways. Its color invades a face. And it causes hands and feet to tremble. Did you see his hands trembling when he spoke to you?"

"No," I say. "I didn't." Since I've known him, Joseph has

developed the habit of occasionally giving his hands a little shake, as though he's drying them off. "What you saw means . . . means nothing."

He nods as if I'd said the hand-shaking was extremely significant, then goes on. "He also seemed very unsure about the behavior of his son. How could he not be? How much time can he spend with Brendan when his store is open seven days a week, fifteen hours a day, except Sunday, when it's twelve hours?"

I slide my hands away, slowly, use one to scratch an imaginary itch on my cheek, then, lowering it to my lap, say, "Brendan spends a lot of time in the store. The time they have together is full of laughter and conversation."

"Is or was? Obviously Brendan's not being very responsive to his father, with his tardiness and . . ."

"What are you leading to?" I say impatiently.

"You seem to be in such a hurry. Is there somewhere you're supposed to be?"

He's invited a lie. I give it. "My father. I'm supposed to call him . . . as soon as I return from work."

"Then I'll be brief. If Joseph dies, guardianship will be sought by Brendan's aunt, a woman named Cora Davis. I've spoken to her. She's adamant about him being in a home."

"And . . ."

"Wouldn't it be much easier on him and his father if he came in voluntarily, now, so that he could leave voluntarily later, when he's more self-reliant. If Cora is eventually made his guardian he might be in the system for a very long time."

Long enough to regress and become dependent on it. Tucker's last screw—I hope his last—has been turned. "What do you expect from me?"

"Nothing."

"Nothing?" I say, loud with surprise.

"Perhaps only a reply to something. You have the respect and attention of the other special ed teachers, the caseworkers, parents, and some of those who staff the homes. On the other hand, you're an opponent of the Sunnyvale Project, of consolidation. I don't mind. I find your views stimulating."

"You expect me to continue to oppose having people like Brendan assigned to community homes?"

"Of course. As long as your mind remains an open one. In fact—and here's the matter to which I hope you'll reply—I'd like you to consider becoming my assistant at the board office. Your pay will be much higher than it is now."

Why? But he's just said why. Yet is that why? I'm not sure he's said why. "I . . . uh . . . I don't, for the moment at least, know . . . what to say." I think I'd like such a job. I'd miss the children, yes, but from his office I might be able to do more for them than I now can. Especially under the circumstances he describes. Yet the idea of it makes me feel like a prostitute. I can't say that. "Um . . ." I can, in fact, say nothing. All in all, I'm pleased by this, the last dip on his roller coaster, the best part of the ride. Should I have expected it? I didn't. I'm wordless.

"Listen. Don't give me an answer now," he says with a reassuring swoop of his hand. "Mull on it. Will you?"

"Yes. I . . . I will."

"God sake. Look at the way the light has disappeared."

I turn and notice that my car, about thirty yards away, the only other one in the parking lot, is a silhouette. The darkness has been sudden. I open the door on my side, climb out and look back to see him leaning over the seat I occupied, nodding.

०⊜० ANDY

Rosa came into the park and told Brendan she was taking him to school to see the Crayola picture she'd made of him. It hangs on the fourth grade wall. She asked Mrs. Dill for permission to take it home and bring it back but Mrs. Dill said no. I had Mrs. Dill last year. She's just like that. I asked Rosa if she forgot Brendan isn't supposed to come to school. "Just for a few seconds won't matter," she said. I knew he'd better be done peeking by the time the buzzer sounded. I told him to stand still until I buttoned his coat. He did. I gave him his lunch but didn't see his cap. Maybe it was stuffed in his pocket. I forgot to look. Rosa grabbed his sleeve and said, "Let's go."

We all wanted Brendan to see his picture. It looks just like him. His mouth is open to one side and his hand is way up like it is when he umpires and calls someone out. When he calls someone out on the bases, he doesn't say "Out!", he says "No way!" His jacket is open and his shirt hangs over his pants the way it really does. Rosa even put some red for catsup on his shirt. She also made his shoelaces untied and showed his cap on the ground in front of him. Along the top she put in big red letters the name he likes, BOOMBAH. She didn't have to. Anyone who ever saw him could tell who it was.

Anyway, someone must have seen us coming and told the principal, Mr. Reed Stark, because he was standing in the hallway when we got there. He stepped between Rosa and Brendan and said to Brendan, "Where do you think you're going?" Brendan pointed to Rosa and said something I couldn't hear. Mr. Reed Stark put his hands on his hips. He weighs about three hundred pounds and when he stands like that even the kindergartners have to squeeze against the wall to get around. Rosa said, "I just wanted him to have a quick look at his picture." Mr. Reed Stark spoke to her without turning around. "What is the rule about bringing visitors?" Rosa said, "You should get permission." He nodded. "You'd better be in your classroom before the buzzer sounds, Miss Guerrero." When he turned back I saw his eyes sliding around. They do that when he's getting mad. "All of you go to your rooms!" Many started moving, even Rosa. Mr. Reed Stark's eyes landed on me. "That includes you, Mr. Harper." Brendan was just standing there watching everyone move. I thought of calling to him and telling him to get out, but Mr. Reed Stark's eyes were stinging me. Anyway, I wouldn't do Brendan any good by staying. I turned and went to class.

Mrs. Potter took roll. I kept looking out the window to see if Brendan was on his way back to the park. He wasn't. I thought I heard his voice from the hallway. I wasn't sure. I kept watching and listening even after Mrs. Potter began a history quiz. She asked me a question I didn't hear. I asked her to repeat it but she wouldn't. She took off two points and asked someone else: "What is the Emancipation Proclamation?" I could have answered that. I hoped she'd asked me another but she didn't. I thought I heard Mr. Reed Stark's voice in the hallway. I wasn't sure. After the quiz we had silent reading. I kept looking out the window. About the third time I looked I saw Brendan. He was walking hunched over. Once before I saw him walk like that. It was when he got sick after eating some of the leftover lunch Sidney Herman gave him. I looked at the clock over Mrs. Potter's desk. It said 9:10. That meant one hour and five minutes until recess, when I could sneak to the park to see if he was okay. I watched him go through the opening in the stone fence. I turned back and saw Mrs. Potter frowning at me. I looked down at my book but soon started peeking sideways through the window. Brendan was gone.

A messenger came with a note that said I had to go to the principal's office. When I got there Mr. Reed Stark was sitting as usual all puffed up in his chair. He pointed to the front of his desk. When I stepped up to it, he said, "How are you today, Mr. Harper?" His voice was chummy the way it sometimes is before he lays trouble on you. I smiled because I wanted him to think I'd be on his side, no matter what he said. I *wanted* to be on his side. "Fine," I said. "Being as bright and informed as you are, you no doubt realize that your companion from the park is not a student here." He often starts with something he knows you know. It's like an easy test. I started to nod but remembered he wants you to speak your answers and said "Yes," pretty loud. His fists came up from his lap and onto his desk. They look like kaiser buns. He said, "Do you know why?" I thought I did. I thought everyone did. "I think so." He shook his head and said, "I doubt it." I nodded and said, "So do I." He closed his eyes. "How would you like to be the same child you were when you left second grade?" Sometimes I wish I were that old again, but I said, "I wouldn't." "Of course not." He leaned forward a little and made the buns smaller. "Because then you'd be classified as retarded or, as we say these days, developmentally disabled. Like your oversized friend out there." He ticked his head toward the window. "When he reached the third grade, he reached the limits of his abilities to learn all but the most fundamental things." I could have told him Brendan has learned things I still don't know, like how to get the right distance from home plate to first base without a measuring stick. How to get a sparrow to eat out of his hand. He even knows things I won't ever know, like the name of every plant, tree, and shrub in City Park. Even the names of everyone he ever met. He just doesn't know the things Mr. Reed Stark and others think he should.

Mr. Reed Stark now pulled his hands back and placed them on his stomach. His knuckles were pointing at the ceiling. "We tried. He was in the special classes until the third grade. Without those classes he couldn't have stayed at Hartsville West as long as he did." He looked down like he wanted to be sure the hands were still there. "I had no choice in the end! I had to recommend he be sent to a special school." He closed his eyes the way my dad does when he's waiting for one of his burps to come up. When he opened them, he shook his head. "Unfortunately, due to actions taken by his offended parents, he was eventually permitted to leave the school." He frowned, letting me know that was the worst thing that could have happened. "He's allowed to spend part of each day in the park, as you know. I find him a disruptive force." He looked up. "Do you know what 'disruptive' means, Mr. Harper?"

I said I wasn't sure.

"It means disorderly. It means damaging. It means destructive. Now, do you now know what it means?"

"I think so."

"Well, that's what he is."

Right after Brendan started going to the park, Mr. Reed Stark began watching him through his principal's window, especially when Brendan came into the schoolyard at lunchtime to referee our soccer games or umpire our softball games. Then he started opening the window and telling Brendan to stop doing certain things. Like shouting. Everyone else shouted, some even louder than Brendan. And we did other things he wouldn't let Brendan do, like go into the little kids part of the yard to get a ball. One day William Flock tried to grab the soccer ball out of Brendan's hands. Brendan was only holding it until William said "please." William always tries to grab something like your pencil or an apple and never says "please." He didn't say it this time either so Brendan pulled the ball away and gave it to Lester Overton. Lester was our goalie that day and was supposed to have it anyway. William is a squealer. Mr. Reed Stark wasn't watching that time, but William ran into the building and told him what Brendan had done. Mr. Reed Stark then sent Brendan out of the schoolyard and said he had to stay in the park not only at lunchtime but after school too. So many of us complained he told us the next one who said anything would have to go to Mr. Swanson's room. We stopped complaining. But a lot of us started going to the park after school instead of staying in the schoolyard.

Mr. Swanson is the custodian and has fat yellow teeth with spaces in between. We call him Halloween. He has the biggest hands I've ever seen. When he leads you to his room, he sinks his fingers into you next to your shoulders and kind of guides you like you're a wheelchair. We call his room Halloween's Dungeon. It's as large as a super-sized closet and has brooms and mops and buckets and a lot of shelves full of tools and bottles and rags and such. He pushes you into the chair at his little table. Above the table is one tiny window that doesn't open. You have to stay at the table until you finish the paper Mr. Reed Stark gives you to write. Halloween bends down and breathes his stinky breath on you while you try to work. Sometimes he pushes the chair against the table until he just about crushes your stomach. He also closes the door and smokes until you cough. Sometimes he makes farts and laughs when you groan. The last time I was there he opened a bottle. A terrible smell came into the room. It started burning my nose and throat. He went out and closed the door behind him. I couldn't stand the smell and burning and got up and found the bottle. It was something used for cleaning. I put the cap on it. The smell stayed but wasn't as bad. My eyes were still burning a little, though. I closed them for a few seconds at a time, then opened them to do my work. When I heard his footsteps, I got up and took the cap off the bottle. He came in and closed the door. When he saw me still working, he bent over me and looked at my face. Even though my eyes hurt I didn't blink. He made a grumbling noise and put the cap back on the bottle. I finished my paper and said I wanted to take it to Mr. Reed Stark. He wouldn't let me. He lit a cigarette and blew smoke all around my head. I breathed in too much and had to cough. When I did, he put out the cigarette and let me go.

"Are you listening to me, Mr. Harper?"

Mr. Reed Stark had caught me in the middle of my thoughts. If I said yes, he might ask me what he'd been saying. I said, "No," and then made up something. "I was just wondering what I was missing in class."

He nodded. "At another time I might find that admirable. But not now. What I've just said is extremely important. I'm going to repeat it once. If you don't repeat it back accurately, you can expect to spend the rest of the day with Mr. Swanson. Do you understand?"

"Yes."

"I said I've made a call to Chief of Police Walters and requested that, beginning today, Brendan Flynn be barred from entering the town park. This restriction includes after-school hours as well as school hours. . . . Sit down!"

I didn't know I'd jumped up until he said that. I said, "Please don't keep Brendan out of the park!"

"Sit down."

I sat down.

"Do not do that again. Do not respond until I tell you to." He waited.

"I said, "Yes, sir."

He squinted and said, "I've observed you and Miss Guerrero and others through the small windows in your classroom doors. I've seen you gazing toward the park, watching your companion instead of doing your schoolwork. One would think he was giving a circus performance over there." He leaned forward, and his chair squeaked like it was going to cry. "Isn't it true?"

"Sometimes." We give each other times to look out to be sure he's safe. I also look out at other times. When Mrs. Potter gives lectures, she picks boogers off the edge of her nose and rolls them into little balls and drops them on the floor. I look out so I don't have to see her doing that. I look when she gives us stupid assignments like making little teepees so we know what it was like to be an Indian. There are a lot of reasons to look out. Today I looked out because I was worried about Brendan. I could have told Mr. Reed Stark all this, but he was squinting, just waiting to jump at me if I said the wrong thing. "Not really very often."

"Well, I am, once and for all, putting an end to his chaotic influence. I'm going to do what I said, and I'm gong to expect your cooperation, and that of Miss Guerrero and others."

It wouldn't have been worse if he'd called up Police Chief Walters and told him to shoot Brendan dead. He spends more time in the park than anywhere else except maybe home. The park is like his other home. He loves everything about it. Once we were watching Mr. Farnsworth, the park workman, put new sides on the sandbox and Brendan said, "I do that . . . someday." He pointed at the slides, then the swimming pool clubhouse. "I fix everything," he said. It was the first time I ever thought about him having a regular job. I was thinking of other things he might be able to do, when Mr. Reed Stark spoke again.

"Repeat what I've just said."

"You mean about Brendan not going into the park?"

"No. What I said after that. What I *just* said." His eyes were wet and sliding back and forth.

I couldn't. I hadn't heard him.

"I see!" After just a few seconds he called out, "Mrs. Wilkens!"

I put my hands between my legs. I tried to sit still but my legs started to wiggle.

"Stop that!" Mr. Reed Stark said.

I tightened my muscles and made myself stop. Mrs. Wilkins came to his door.

"Get Mr. Swanson."

He was looking at my mouth. I was biting my bottom lip to keep from saying anything. When I saw him watching it I pushed my lip out and looked through his window. I wanted to see Brendan. I was still searching when Halloween opened the door.

"Not just yet," said Mr. Reed Stark. He took two sheets of paper from the side of his desk, wrote something on one of the sheets and held up both, wiggling them.

I slid forward and reached out and took them.

He then nodded toward Halloween.

I got up and looked around and saw Halloween's crooked pointing finger aimed at the door. All the way down the hall he hammered his knee into my butt. When we got to his room he shoved me into the chair and pushed the chair against the desk. He stuck his fingers into the muscles by my shoulders and pinched, tighter and tighter until I said, "Ow!" Then he let go and pointed at the desk. I looked at the top sheet. It said, "Write down all the reasons why Brendan Flynn should not be allowed in City Park." Halloween was behind me, pressing against my chair. I wrote, "Mr. Reed Stark doesn't want him to." I tried to think of something else to write. He was standing close, kind of bouncing himself against the back of my chair. I kept looking at the paper, trying to remember Mr. Reed Stark's reason for not wanting Brendan in the park. I'd put anything down to get out of there. I put down: "Brendan is retarded." Halloween came down and put his face real close to mine. I felt his whiskers. They were like needles. The smell of his cigarette breath started to make me sick. I remembered "disruptive." I'd never seen the word written down, but I sounded it out. Mr. Reed Stark wouldn't count it if I didn't spell it right. I wrote, "He is also disruptive." I thought me writing that would make Halloween back away. It didn't. He pressed his face even tighter against mine, then started to move it up and down. The whiskers were cutting my face. He was making humming sounds too. I could have stood his stupid torture the way I'd done before but I kept thinking about Brendan and what Mr. Reed Stark said and I was sure now that today Mr. Reed Stark had told Brendan what he planned to do. That was bad. I got all panicky and slid to the floor and dove past Halloween's feet. "Uhh!" he said. I opened the door and hopped into the hallway. I ran toward the front doors, pushed one open and shot out. I didn't look back until I got near the stone fence. Halloween was coming down the school steps and hobble-walking after me. Lester Overton said he saw him with his ugly wife in River City and he wasn't hobble-walking. I believe Lester. Halloween's hands were waving in the air like flags. The stone fence is about as high as my chest. I didn't go through where the opening is but dove over the nearest part. I felt sharp pieces brush against my pants. I came down in a somersault and flattened out. I was panting out of breath for a few seconds. I could hear his footsteps—buh *phoom*, buh *phoom*. I started moving as fast as I could on hands and knees, so he wouldn't see me. I went toward the line of bushes near the reservoir.

I was soon crawling through a wide place in the bushes. I found a dip behind a grassy mound where I lay down flat for a few seconds, then peeked back. Halloween was limping through the opening in the fence. I stayed very still with my cheek against the ground and my top eye open, so I could see him.

He stood still and looked around, then turned toward me and the hedge but his eyes didn't stop where I was. He kind of stumbled forward, going toward the playground. I hoped Brendan wasn't there. Halloween would beat on him because he was mad at me. I remembered how sick and sad Brendan looked when I saw him through Mrs. Potter's window. I hoped he went home. He's no good at hiding. He breathes too loud and hums to himself.

Halloween went into the trees behind the picnic shelters and I couldn't see him anymore. I guessed he thought I'd climbed into the old Boy Scout shelter which is way up in a locust tree. A boy who was beaten by his father went and lived there for three days. After that the park workers were ordered to take down the wooden ladder boards that were nailed to the tree trunk. But a good climber can still get up.

I turned and looked toward the reservoir. There's a high steel fence around it to keep kids from fishing there. In the reservoir are catfish and carp and crappies. My cousin caught several catfish there. Some kids still fish there. You have to go in at night. In some places the bottom of the fence sticks up from the ground and you can crawl under. I decided to crawl under and hide in there. I wiggled along the hedge until I got to the place where the reservoir is closest to the park. I checked for Halloween but didn't see him. I went low toward the fence. I saw thick bushes on the other side, near the water. I'd climb right into one of them and wait until I was sure Halloween wasn't anywhere around. I found an opening under the fence. I used my elbows to pull myself toward it. I had my head and shoulders under when I felt myself being pulled back. His hands were like big clamps, one on my pants and other on the back of my shirt. I heard my shirt buttons popping off. I shouted. I said, "I'm sick. I have to go home." He picked me up and turned me toward the school, where Mr. Reed Stark was at the bottom of the steps with his hands crossed over his stomach waiting.

"Have . . . go home!"

He lifted me and started carrying me toward Mr. Reed Stark and the school.

I twisted and kicked. I made the last buttons pop off my shirt and fell to the ground. He was still holding my pants. I spun around as fast as I could and made him lose his grip. When I started to stand, he grabbed one of my ankles and turned it hard. I kicked at his hand with my other foot. He tried to grab that foot with his other hand. I kicked and kicked and got free. I stood up and ran. My body was freezing but my hands weren't numb anymore. I started running, past the hedge and into the park. I was going to go home but then I saw Brendan's cap hanging from a low branch on the big oak tree next to the playground. It had a big hole in it like someone had shot a bullet through it. I ran under it and grabbed it and hurried toward Flynn's.

∘◉∘ CARLOTTA

For some reason I was all jumpy when I got home from work and so decided to fix myself a cup of tea. After turning on the kettle I took our pork chops, Herbert's and mine, out of the freezer and put them in the microwave to defrost. When I sat down at the kitchen table and looked at the evening paper, I saw my hands shaking. I'm usually as steady as a log. After the tea was ready I poured myself a cup, had a few sips, then paced about for a while. When I sat I saw my hands were still shaking and also realized I hadn't remembered a thing from the paper. *What's wrong with me?* I wondered. I put the paper down. Herbert would have to let me know later what was happening in the world.

After supper he offered to do the dishes and started picking up in the kitchen. But I said, "No, I need something to keep me busy." I not only did the dishes and the picking up but took out the Spic and Span and scrubbed the counter top, refrigerator and stove. "Come on in here and watch this movie," he said after the news ended. I knew it was something about World War II; those are his favorites. He was an artilleryman during the Korean War but never got over there. Yet he never misses a war movie. I always know if he thinks they're any good or not because, sooner or later, he'll say, "It wasn't really like that at all" or, "I think it was just like that." I told him I didn't care to see shooting tonight, thank you. He said the one he was watching had no shooting.

I went in and looked.

It was in black-and-white. He told me it was called *Judgment at*

Nuremberg. I prefer color but I sat down anyway. He was in the La-Z-Boy with his feet up, as comfortable as a bunny in straw. "I didn't know it was like that," he said. I watched but couldn't make heads nor tails of anything. The people looked grim and weary, which made me feel the same. If Herbert hadn't been enjoying it so much, I'd have asked him to switch on a game show. Those are my favorites.

I went upstairs to my sewing room to work on a sweater I was knitting for his birthday. The one I did for Mr. Reed Stark last Christmas took me nearly two months, but Herbert is smaller and his won't take me half that long. Now and then Mr. Reed Stark wears his to work, which pleases me very much. Though my hands were still, I found I couldn't get my purls right, even when I went back over them. Tonight I was no good for anything but scrubbing. There was nothing left to scrub. "I'm giving up on this day," I called down to Herbert. He called back that I was missing a good one, meaning the movie. By then I couldn't have paid attention even if it was *Gone With the Wind.*

I climbed into bed and tried to read from the latest romance novel I'd taken out of the library, *A New Dawn for Laurie,* but even that wouldn't hold me. I'd say it was about nine o'clock when I fell asleep. It seemed like only minutes later that my eyes popped open. Herbert was in bed, purring away, and I thought it must be time to get ready for work. I was nervous and perspiring. On the way to the bathroom I realized it was still evening. *Good Lord!* I thought. *I haven't gone to bed that early since Herbert was in college after the war.* We used to set the alarm, the two of us rising together so that I could ask him questions. To this day, when people look at his engineering degree on the wall of his den, he says, "Half of that belongs to Carlotta." Anyway, I paced around, wanting to make myself tired, and, while doing so, decided to try to figure out what was causing my jumpiness. I think I wore a groove in the floor going back over the day. Then it came, like a rush of wind, sending me into Herbert's chair. In moments I had it all remembered.

I'd been in my little office outside Mr. Reed Stark's a couple of minutes after the bell rang at nine. No sooner had the children's feet stopped shuffling than I heard him call my name. "Mrs. Wilkins!" He rarely says it urgently like that. I thought he was having a heart attack or something and got up so fast I bumped into the computer table. His back was to me in the middle of the hallway, and he was facing that big retarded boy, Brendan, who used to be around the schoolyard at recess and lunchtime. "Want to see Rosa picture," the boy was saying. Mr. Reed Stark turned to me. "Go find Mr. Swanson," he said.

Vernon Swanson spends much of his time in the boiler room at the far end of the hallway. Many of the children are afraid of him, I think because of the bumps on his face. He was patching a volleyball when I found him. He grumbled when I gave him the message, but then got up and followed me down the hallway to where Mr. Reed Stark, with his arms folded, still faced the retarded boy, who was still talking about Rosa's picture, whatever that was. When Mr. Swanson came up beside him, Mr. Reed Stark turned to me and said, "Go back to your office, Mrs. Wilkins." I did, but for some reason stopped in the doorway and looked back.

Mr. Swanson was standing behind the boy, with his arms locked around him. "I go, I go," the boy said. Mr. Reed Stark stepped forward and slapped him in the face. *Good Lord!* I said to myself, then closed my eyes. "Get out of here and don't come back!" said Mr. Reed Stark. I opened my eyes. The boy had somehow broken Mr. Swanson's hold but was giving Mr. Reed Stark a terrified look. "Lead him to the bottom of the steps and stay there until he's in the park," Mr. Reed Stark instructed. Mr. Swanson nodded and nudged the boy around. The boy was now looking right past Mr. Reed Stark at me but didn't seem to be seeing anything. Only when Mr. Swanson was shoving the boy toward the front doors did I slip quietly into my office. I was at my desk when Mr. Reed Stark came back. He was panting loudly. I didn't want him to know I'd been watching. "What happened?" I said. He paused, squinted past me at the portrait of Thomas Jefferson that hung near my chair, then looked down and said, "Let's just say I had to do a little teaching." He turned to go into his office. I got to typing up yesterday's attendance sheet, knowing I'd have to keep awfully busy so as not to think about what I'd seen and heard.

I'm nudging the bed with my knee. "Herbert? Herbert, wake up. I have to talk to you."

"Keep quiet, Carlotta."

"If I don't tell you something, I won't be able to sleep."

In the light from the hall I see one of his eyes open. "What the heck time is it?"

I glance at the clock, read the time and tell him: "A little after ten."

He raises himself with his elbows. "Are you sick or what?"

"No. I . . . I just won't be able to sleep until I tell you something."

Both his eyes are on me now, giving my face the once-over. He finally decides I haven't gone crazy because he closes his eyes, falls back and rolls to the side. "Sit down, then, and spit it out."

"You won't go to sleep while I'm telling you, will you?"

"Spit it out then, Carlotta."

I tell him everything. As I speak he rises, first to his elbows, little by little, then all the way. By the time I near the end he's sitting up before me with his arms wrapped around his legs.

"I knew I couldn't get back to sleep until I told you."

He shakes his head. "Did you see him slap the boy?"

"Yes. I did."

"What a thing!"

"I wish I hadn't seen anything. You're not supposed to slap people. He doesn't even go to school here. Suppose the boy goes and tells his parents and the police come and question me?"

"I doubt he'll tell anyone. He's retarded. You can be sure Reed Stark thought of that before he struck him." Herbert and Mr. Reed Stark have now and then played poker with other friends on Friday nights. They're not close, but Herbert knows him pretty well.

"But if they do?"

He puts his hand on my shoulder and looks at me straight-on as he does when he doesn't want me to forget something. "No one's going to question you," he says.

"God," I say, "I just hope you're right."

He lowers himself and pulls the blankets up. "Go to sleep now, Carlotta," he says. "It's the best thing."

I stay at the side of the bed. I can't sleep. I want to talk to someone besides Herbert about what happened. I can think of no one.

∘⊜∘ JOSEPH

Darkness comes quickly and brings a fog so thick the street-lamps illuminate only themselves. My flashlight beam shines back at me. The snow has hardened and is slick. I stumble crossing Long, slow my step, not only to keep from falling but to soften the pain that moments ago rose from my ribs. Before I reach the park entrance I stop to catch my breath.

I look in. No lights. People aren't supposed to go in after dark. Brendan doesn't like darkness, but where else would he go? This is the far boundary of his world. He must be in here, or near.

I move from snow patch to snow patch, looking for his prints. There are no prints, his or anyone else's. Few people come to the park in snowy weather. He must have hidden himself somewhere. The old Boy Scout tree house. The storage shed. The reservoir.

Officer Fox brought him into the store a week ago. "Brendan Delivery Service," he said. "No charge." Brendan had climbed under the reservoir fence and was trying to stab fish with a stick. Bill Fox knows that if he fills out a report every time he comes back with Brendan, I'll have to go down to the courthouse to explain. That's one reason I didn't call the police station, though sooner or later I may have to. When Bill or Officer Matthews find him, they just bring him home without filing a report. Also, police reports appear in the paper each day. I'm sure Mr. Reed Stark and others who'd like to see him sent to a home read those. I don't want to give them ammunition. When you have a retarded child, at least around here, you must be very protective.

When some in the state wanted a law which they said would improve the public's perceptions of retarded people, they sent a letter asking experienced parents to give their views at a public hearing. I wrote back saying I didn't like being in public places, even movie houses, but would vote for the bill. One of them came to the store, a pleasant young man with a neatly cut beard, and said, "Your experiences with Brendan would be invaluable." I told him I was sure they would and wished my wife weren't in the hospital because she knew how to speak about them. Grace could speak anywhere. She had not only been a teacher but had given talks at the Lutheran and Methodist churches and to the PTA and one year to the State Teachers' Association. "Why not you?" he said. "I have trouble speaking if my store gets crowded," I told him. He had been smiling but now his mouth fell. "We'll do our best without you," he said.

I visited Grace that evening and told her about the visit. She was by then turning yellow and couldn't open her eyes all the way. But, after I mentioned the visit, she sat up and her eyes opened very wide. In those last weeks they turned the pale blue color of a summer sky. "Oh, Joseph," she said. She spoke in little spurts. "You must challenge yourself . . . as difficult as it will be. Write out what you have to say. Bring what you've written to me and read it and . . . I'll correct anything that needs correcting."

I don't think I would have said yes if I hadn't known she would soon die. Lying there, she looked very calm, like a woman a magician is about to saw in half. But she was stirred up inside. If she had been well, she would have put on her peach dress and worn the imitation pearls I bought her for her fiftieth birthday and gone and spoken without reading anything. She was a tall woman, at five feet nine taller by an inch than me, and looked more elegant than Katharine Hepburn, at least when she was dressed up. What a poor substitute I was! I would rather have cut a hole in the Hartsville Reservoir ice in January and gone swimming than speak in public! But it had to be done. I said I would do it. I kissed her good-by and went to the emergency waiting room where orderlies had been playing with Brendan while I visited. Later, after I heard him snoring in his bed, I started to write my speech.

"Oh my," she said after I read it to her the next night, "it's much more articulate than I thought it would be." She smiled up at me. Her mouth and teeth seemed much bigger lately but also made her seem even prettier than she was. "You're going to have to go through it once again, though. You have a tendency to mash your sentences together. When I say 'stop,' do it and put a period in. All right?" I nodded and read again, making the corrections she wanted. She not only put in periods but changed a few words.

The next night I took Brendan to the Holiday Inn, left him in a side room, where others he'd known from the special school were waiting, and went to the Anthony Wayne Room just in time to read the speech Grace had helped me fix up:

> "We all know our children are different than others' but I came here to tell you I think they are superior in many ways. I can tell you first-hand that the joy you share with them will increase as they grow older. My son, Brendan, is nearly nineteen. I don't see other children his age or even close to it who open their arms and embrace their parents in public. And with Brendan everything is an adventure, even simple tasks like tying shoes or picking out a toothbrush. I don't know of anyone who can melt me out of gloomy thoughts as he does when he stands behind the counter in my store and imitates me trying to help a customer. And I have never seen anyone treat animals or small children more kindly."

On I went, telling them about other ways Brendan and others like him enrich the lives around them in ways they never would have if they'd been normal. I ended this way:

> "If I were you, I wouldn't just ask the legislature for money to keep them out of sight and healthy, I would ask them to support ways to let them do more for themselves than we now let them do and share with us the many gifts, such as love, they have to offer."

The speech took about seven minutes. When I finished they applauded loudly. I took that to be their politeness—until they stood up. Yes, it made me feel good, but I told Grace later it was the hardest thing I'd ever done, ever, including basic training in the Army, and I would never do it again. She said maybe I wouldn't have to.

My beam flashes on a sandwich wrapper by the phone booth. It looks like a Baggie, which is the kind I use for him. I enter the booth and pick up the phone. There's no dial tone. Maybe he stopped and tried to call me. He knows our number, knows how to get an operator to call collect. I step out and look down at the Baggie. It clings to the phone booth. I raise my hand and feel the breeze. It's coming from the southwest corner of the park, where the reservoir lies, from where the Baggie might have blown. I start toward the reservoir but slip on an icy patch. The flashlight has fallen. I start to pick it up but notice something dark and wet and shiny in its beam. I tilt the light as I raise it and see spots, dark red spots.

Oh Lord!

I move cautiously toward them. Brendan's? No spot is bigger than a dime. Maybe he was running, scattering the blood. I follow the drops. They move in an arc toward the reservoir. I go too quickly. The pain under my ribs starts again. I slow down. Yet the pain increases. I must stop. I stand on the road that winds through the park, sucking in air, holding it as long as I can, then heaving it out. The pain lessens. I wait longer, until it completely goes away. I've been pointing the light onto the asphalt. The spots aren't visible there. I move the beam ahead, see them again, on a snowy patch near the basketball court.

I reach the far side of the tennis courts. The spots arc away from the reservoir and toward the stone fence bordering the school-yard. Or are they going from the stone fence to the reservoir, back to the tennis courts? I don't know. I follow the drops around the court, toward the reservoir. Suppose I'm going the wrong way? I don't care. I have to check the worst possibility first. The chain link fence around the reservoir has sharp prongs on the bottom. There are several hilly spots where the fence leaves a space between itself and the grass. That's why Brendan was able to climb under to go fishing. He could have gotten caught going in or out and cut himself. I look toward the reservoir. "Brendan!" I shout.

No answer.

I have only a short distance to go. I move slowly up the first knoll, planning to shine my light along the fence. Within a few yards the spots turn sharply, toward the stone fence bordering the schoolyard.

I feel a knot of pain in my chest and stop to rest once more.

Catching air, I shine the beam across, see that the drops, larger now, lead to the equipment shed. Is he in there asleep? I start toward it. The knot tightens. I stop, send the beam toward the shed, a miniature barn. The light finds the green double door, then the padlock. It's tightly closed. Andy and Rosa didn't mention the shed. Maybe they saw the lock and didn't check. I remember a window at the back. Did they check that? I move ahead, only as fast as my pain will allow, go around to the back. The window is closed. It's chest high, about the size of a bedroom window. I reach forward and try to raise it. It won't budge. Why did I let myself imagine he was in there? Such disappointment! I go around to the front of the shed, see a tree stump a few yards from the door. I must rest. I drag myself to the stump and sit down. The pain has risen to the left side of my neck. Again I stop.

I remember something. Once I saw one of the park workmen go to the shed, which appeared to be locked, and pull open the lock without using a key. I go back to the doors of the shed and reach down. I barely touch the lock when it falls open. I point the flashlight in. I see a four-wheeled mower, a leaf sweeper, tools on hooks along the walls, cans of paint at the back. There's an empty space among the cans. I pull the light my way, see red drops lining the floor from the can to doorway. I go outside and, as quickly as my pain will allow, hurry toward the school.

The wind bites my face, numbing my cheeks. I pull down my cap and wrap my scarf around. I walk very slowly with head down, letting the paint drops lead me. Evidence of Brendan's mischief seems, thank God, evidence that he's not spilling his blood. Though I don't know what he's done, I'm all in all grateful. Cora says I have no life without him. Maybe she's right. My happiness is tied to his. My future. He matters to me more than I matter to myself. That isn't healthy, Cora says. It's what led to Grace's death. Maybe she's right. Tonight he's caused me to rush about and suffer pain. It rises again. I slow even more. It falls. It's my pain, not Brendan's, brought on by my own lethargic ways, the cigarettes I used to smoke, my bad eating habits, who knows what? His pains belong to him, mine to me. I told Cora again I believed Grace would have died sooner had she not had Brendan to care for. "Oh, catch up with the world!" Cora said. And what does *she* live for? Her December vacations to Florida? What do others live for? I've never written a poem or built a bridge. Do I really live only for him?

At the school building the red drops lead me to the front. After flashing the light around, I see the missing paint can, on the broad lawn separating the school from Lincoln Avenue. I shine the light ahead. *Oh God!* It's on the wall! Not just the wall but the windows too! It lies thickest on the windows of the principal's office. Not just splashed, but words, uneven in size, yet clear enough to be read:

Bad Man

I struggle toward them. The paint lid lies on the grass next to the can. Streams of red rush like anger from the can to the wall. As I stand there gazing, yellow security lights pop on all around the building. They come on every night automatically. Because of them all those passing along busy Lincoln can now see the words. Brendan's. Surely his! But why? I pull my muffler to my eyes, not to keep the wind away but to hide myself, then hurry back toward the store, sensing he's there.

The trip should take five minutes but, because of my stopping, it takes nearly ten. Nearing the store I see that the door is open, being pushed and pulled by the wind. Then I see Brendan, or rather his wild hair, just above the vegetable display at the window. He's on the stool behind it. I go panting up the steps. Seeing me he grins. His jacket, face, and hair too, are splattered with red paint. Now he frowns and turns to the clock, then back to me, still frowning. "See what time is *that*, young man?" he says. He holds the frown for a few seconds, then throws his hands up and loses himself in laughter so jolting it drives him off the stool and onto the floor. I stand above him, the door smacking against me, listening to his mad sounds.

°◉° SARAH

Joseph called and asked me to come quickly to the store. It was
nearly ten. Only two days earlier I'd visited him with Tucker, had
spoken to him later that night, telling him of Tucker's designs.
The call surprised me.

"What's up?" I said.

"Brendan," he told me. "Something . . . something's happened."

"I'll be right over."

When I arrived I saw the shades pulled down over the big
window and the door window. I knocked. I thought I heard Brendan say something. In a moment Joseph opened the door a couple
of inches, then all the way. He was stooped and breathing heavily.

"Sa-rah!" Brendan cried out, stepping off Joseph's stool behind
the counter. He rushed toward me, his face covered with red
spots of different sizes. His clothes had the spots on them too and
were mud- and grass-stained. He gave me a hug. Each time he
hugged me recently the hug seemed tighter than the one before. I
hugged him back. "Good to *see* you," he said letting go. You'd think
I'd been away for months.

On the near side of the counter were two plastic milk boxes,
one on top of the other, upside down. A couple of feet away, Joseph
had lowered himself and was sitting stooped on a matching pair.
Now he waved his hand toward the other pair.

I told him I'd stand. "What's happened?"

He glanced wearily from me to Brendan, who was now back on
the stool, finally said calmly, "Will you tell Sarah what happened
. . . from the time you left here this morning until you got back?"

"Mean *again?*"

"Yes, yes. Start with Rosa."

For the next several minutes Brendan reported in his zigzag

way what he'd done and seen that morning. Some of his report made Joseph twitch with impatience like the news that his favorite squirrel, Samuel (which he'd named after a friend who'd died of leukemia two years ago), hadn't been waiting to greet him, and that he'd lost his cap and that, when he'd been talking to Andy and Rosa, he'd seen two birds with purple necks. ("Where they come from *I* don't know.") Despite his twitching, Joseph didn't interrupt, and eventually Brendan came to his encounter with Mr. Reed Stark.

"Stand front of Boombah." He pointed to a place on the floor about two feet away from him. "Show you." He got up, went over to the spot and turned around, pushing his elbows out to the side, then puffing up his mouth and inhaling in a way that made him seem twice his size. "*Stop* Boombah," he said in a complaining tone. He then spoke the words he remembered Reed Stark exchanging with Rosa and others. Finally, he said, he'd been left alone with Mr. Reed Stark and someone else.

"Mr. Swanson," Joseph prompted.

He nodded. "Ugly man."

"Was he there all the time?" I asked.

"Boombah don't know *that*. Was *there*."

"Show Sarah what he did."

"Mister Ree—*eed* Stark?"

"No. Mr. Swanson."

"Snansnun."

"Swanson."

"Swansnun."

Joseph shook his head but didn't try to correct the half-corrected version. "What did Mr. Reed Stark say to him?"

"Say 'Hold him!' Mean Boombah." He looked at Joseph. "Okay?"

Joseph nodded. "Go ahead."

"Show you." He stepped in front of Joseph, stopped, then brought his right hand up, knuckles on top, backhanding them softly into Joseph's chin. "But *he* do hard!" He made his teeth click loudly. "Make Boombah do that."

"You're saying Mr. Reed Stark struck you?" I said.

He rolled his eyes impatiently and let out a sigh. "Yessss," he said, dragging out the s sound until he lost his breath.

I now thought I saw amid the paint splotches a bruise about the size of a nickel on the right side of his chin. "How many times did he strike you?"

"One time."

"What did you do then?"

"Do this." He jerked his elbows upward behind him. He paused, thinking, and added, "Then go." He told us he'd hidden himself somewhere near the park. He didn't say where.

"Why didn't you come home?"

"Was crying," he said.

I've seen him cry in front of Joseph several times. "People are *supposed* to cry. You know that."

He didn't answer for a minute or so, then said, "Crying *mad!*" He finished by telling us how he'd gotten into the tool shed ("Was easy"), found paint and brushes, taken them to the school and painted the wall.

I believed his story, not because he doesn't lie—at times he will—but because of his passionate tone and the vivid details he used.

But Joseph, who was hearing the report or much of it for a second time, had had time to doubt. "Could it have been that Mr. Reed Stark threw up his hand because he thought *you* were going to strike *him?*"

"Poppa!"

"I just want to be sure."

Brendan went behind his father now, took Joseph's wrists and pulled them together behind his back. "Try to hit Sarah. Do that, Poppa. Try *hit* Sarah!"

Joseph struggled to get free but couldn't.

"Ugly man hold Boombah! Like *that*. See!"

Joseph nodded.

Brendan released him. "Boombah *not* hit Mr. Ree—*eed* Stark." He grimaced when he spoke Reed Stark's first name. "No way."

I asked him if anyone else had been there, anyone who might have seen what happened.

He frowned, thinking, finally said, "Ahmmm . . . lady . . . ahmm . . ."

"Mrs. Wilkins?"

"Right, Sarah!"

"What did she see?"

"Boombah don't know *that*." Now he began squeezing his fists together between his legs.

"Do you have to go to the bathroom?" Joseph said.

"Going." He slid off the stool and went to the apartment.

Joseph mentioned that, before I'd arrived at the store, he'd gotten Brendan to agree that he and Joseph should first speak to me, then go to the police station and report what had happened. He wondered if he ought to wait until morning before going in. "I'm exhausted," he said.

"Wait," I told him. No one, after all, had been injured.

"Wonder what the heck they'll do to him," he said.

I wasn't sure. I guessed that, because of Mr. Reed Stark's provoking action, the school might not want to go to court. "Maybe they'll just make Brendan—you, I suppose—pay for the damages."

"If what I saw and what he's told is the whole story."

I said I believed he was telling us everything, then suggested that, after leaving, I call Carlotta Wilkins and try to find out what she'd witnessed.

The toilet flushed in back.

"You think they might put him on trial or something?" Joseph whispered.

"No." But I really wasn't sure.

After I returned to my apartment, I called Carlotta, apologized for reaching her so late (shortly after eleven) but said I had some questions she might be able to answer. "About one of my students." She sounded more relieved than surprised and remarked that we hadn't seen or spoken to each other for months, since the special classes were transferred to the warehouse school. I told her that Brendan had been asked by Mr. Reed Stark to leave the elementary school building today and said, "Is it possible that you witnessed the exchange between the two of them?" She hemmed, then said, "Just . . . a moment." There was a few seconds pause. Finally I was startled to hear not Carlotta but a man who identified himself as Herbert, her husband. "Carlotta has asked me to tell you that she isn't sure it was your patient—" ("Student," I corrected) "—sorry, student. In any case, she merely observed the young man and Mr. Reed Stark in conversation but isn't sure she heard what was said." Would she, I asked, come back to the phone? "I'm afraid she can't," he replied pleasantly. "She's retired for the evening."

If she wouldn't speak up, who would believe Brendan? If he couldn't prove he'd been provoked, would he be allowed only to pay for damages? Or would he also have to go to jail? I had no answers until the next morning, when I accompanied Joseph and Brendan to the police station.

Chief Marvin Walters said, "I heard what happened. Some way Mr. Reed Stark figured it was the young man here, and he says he's recommending that the school board press charges. I didn't expect you'd all be paying me a visit. Sent Sergeant Decker out. He's probably knocking on your door right now, Joe."

Brendan stood between Joseph and me. He showed no anxiety, in fact was grinning. "Fooled him, didn't we, Chief?" he said.

Walters winked at Joseph and said, "Got that right, Brendan." He pressed a button on his desk, gave instructions to the dispatcher to call Decker and have him come back, then pulled his 250-or-so pounds out of his chair and steered them to the coffee machine at the corner of his office. "Any of you want some?"

Joseph and I shook our heads. Brendan, watching us, then shook his.

Each of us, at the chief's invitation, took a chair in front of his desk. He came back with his coffee but didn't sit down. He raised his leg and planted his foot on his desk and leaned toward us, making him seem even larger than he was. "Maybe it'll help you to know something." He looked at me for the first time. "We may or may not book him." He took a sip of the coffee, then lay the cup carefully on the desk and leaned closer. "We could. There was a bike rack broken and some plants damaged and a window cracked and such. The cost of repairs is going to be several hundred bucks. And well, hell, he's over eighteen. We could put him on the blotter this minute."

Out of the corner of my eye I saw Joseph nod.

"Tucker over at Mental Retardation heard about the paint this morning—believe Reed Stark called him—and called me with a proposition he wants me to put before you. That's presuming we

determine the young man here owns up to the paint job." He
turned to Brendan. "You listening, young man?"

"Yes, *sir.*" He'd been eyeing the chief admiringly. Now he
waited with an eager look. Or maybe it was a look of relief.

I felt only fear.

"Told me he'd speak to Reed Stark and Mary Silvestri, school
board head honcho, about dropping charges if we had no objection
and the young man—meaning, I guess, you, Joe—was willing to
pay for the damages."

Joseph turned to me with uncertain eyes.

I imagined Tucker on the phone with the chief, could almost
hear his silken words. "Is it common to make deals like this?" I
asked.

Walters shrugged. "Don't run into many M.R.s getting in
trouble. Usually find ways of working things out. Usually. Not just
with M.R.s, with most young first-timers. And that's where Brendan falls in. Unless we find a body over there or a safe busted
open." He paused, waiting, I think, for us to laugh. "Only one
other condition."

"What?" said Joseph anxiously.

"He's got to live in one of the community homes for a while.
Tucker says he needs a structured day program and living arrangements."

Damn Tucker! "For how long?" I asked.

"Didn't say."

"Home?" said Brendan.

"Just a minute," Joseph said, putting up his hand. "Do you
have any idea? A week? A month?"

Walters rubbed his thumb along the side of his forehead, then
shook his head. "Guess that'll be between you and them. Don't
make any difference to us. I'd say talk to Tucker over there. All I
know is we'd keep out of it. That way the young man there won't
have a record." He looked across at Joseph. "Know what I mean?"
He must have decided Joseph couldn't know, for he added, "If
Brendan were found guilty this time, he could end up with only a
fine. Second time he probably'd end up in jail too. Don't think
you'd want to see that."

Joseph nodded.

"Why do you assume 'next time'?" I asked.

"Didn't assume a damn thing, ma'am," he said, flashing a warning look. "I'm talking what-if."

Joseph turned to me. "Sounds fair to me."

"Me too," Brendan said.

"I'm not sure," I said, forcing myself to meet the unfriendly gaze of the chief. "I think we should be given time to think and talk it over."

I waited for Walters to snap at me, but, still eyeing me, he said only, "Hell, no one's in any big hurry."

They must treat him like a normal person, I thought. If we went before a judge, they'd have to do that. He'd done something wrong, yes, but Mr. Reed Stark had provoked him. And what he'd done was an act of vandalism. Eight hundred dollars. How many times a night do young men commit acts of vandalism in this country? How often are they punished? Given the provocation, there might be no more penalty than the cost of repairs.

I explained my position to Joseph. His reaction showed how badly I'd underestimated Tucker. His community home proposition was playing perfectly to a fear thick in Joseph, who fretted over the prospect of a police record, saying, "It's going to be hard enough for him to get a job as it is." He nearly panicked over the possibility—almost negligible, I assured him—of a jail sentence. No. He was embracing Tucker's offer and wanted only to know how long Brendan would have to stay at a community home.

We didn't find out.

The next day Mr. Reed Stark, blinded (I now think) by his anger over the epithet emblazoned on the wall of his office, persuaded the school board, through its superintendent, to petition for a hearing.

Good! I thought, though my reasons for pleasure were no doubt not those that had stirred Reed Stark or the board.

A day later, when I learned that the court had approved the school board petition, I began to gather evidence.

∘◒∘ TUCKER

A misty rain falls against the pendants above the courtroom windows, shaping itself into heavy drops that plop wearily to the ledge below. A lingering dankness of wool, mahogany and leather produces a stale yet somehow not unpleasant odor. There are only a handful of us here, which may be why this gloomy high-ceilinged cavern seems even larger than it is.

To my right, at the other table, sit Joseph Flynn and his representative, teacher Sarah Fuller. She says something and he nods. His yellowing eyes and sagging gray face provide argument against his cause.

That very cause, his son, Brendan, sits listless and alone on one of the benches at the back near the big leather-covered doors. Occasionally the boy makes a humming sound.

One of the courtroom doors squeaks open. A raincoat is slapped over the back of one of the pewlike benches. I wait but whoever came in has remained at the back.

A few days ago Fuller stood defiantly in the doorway of my office at Sunnyvale Special School and, optimist that she is, asked that I and, through me, Mr. Reed Stark, drop our petition to have Brendan sent to a community home rather than be tried for vandalism.

"You aren't serious," I said.

"I am," she came back firmly. "*We* are. We're sure the judge won't do anything more than fine him," she replied with the ignorant confidence of a young idealist. Perhaps I stretch the term "young"; she's twenty-seven, only twelve years younger than I. "Joseph has written a check for the work already done to get rid of the lettering. Full restitution will be made. We . . ." Here she paused as if she herself knew the depths of her ignorance. ". . . we see no reason why the school board shouldn't drop charges."

I laughed softly and shook my head.

"Joseph has been very cooperative," she went on.

"Joseph?" I said finally. "Has Joseph's presumed cooperativeness insured us all that his son won't be taken by another fit of anger and scar a building in the park or a neighbor's home or another person? The act we're dealing with wasn't committed by Joseph."

"And it wasn't an act of violence."

"Maybe," I said, pushing my chair back from my desk, nodding, "but it was . . . something." I looked up. "And it was something Brendan Flynn, not Joseph Flynn, did."

She twisted her mouth as if to speak but nothing came out. Her still eyes told me the silence wasn't strategy but confusion. When the eyes did move, they hopped from side to side as if for an exit.

"Well?" I said.

She didn't reply.

"If he's healthy enough to be on the streets, he's healthy enough to take responsibility for his acts. Am I correct?"

Her head tilted in anger. "He did nothing more than anyone might have done under the circumstances of that day."

"What circumstances?"

She hesitated, considering, then said, "Mr. Reed Stark struck him. Surely by now you know that."

I didn't know. He might have. In that mountain of a man sits a volcano. He is the sort who doesn't like himself and makes the world pay. I've heard his anger rumbling at school board meetings but have never seen it erupt. "Do you have a witness?"

"I . . . maybe." Her evasive gestures gave me a surer answer: no.

I pressed into her doubts. "Brendan did what he did unprovoked. What he did is but another example of how he's regressed." I cited his inability to communicate in simple English, especially orally, and his general erratic behavior following the death of his mother. I also mentioned his father's health. I reminded her, though I surely didn't need to, of the sheltered workshop opportunities soon to be available and the new complex; said, "I believe compassion means recognizing the limitations of a disadvantaged person and then providing an atmosphere in which he or she can effectively function. I know that's not a popular or fashionable view, but I contend it's more compassionate than, say, yours."

She stared at the edge of my desk for at least half a minute, then turned and abruptly left.

Did her silence signal a change of mind?

For two days I waited, hopeful.

Her reply was a note in which she boldly announced she'd offered to serve as Joseph's spokesperson at the hearing.

Mr. Reed Stark appears beside me. After nodding a greeting he lowers himself into a chair. His exhale is powerful enough to fan a forest fire into greater damage. He's perspiring heavily. "Damn waste of time," he says.

"You may be surprised," I whispered.

He grunts.

Judge Parker comes out of his chambers and crosses to the bench, giving Reed Stark and me, then Sarah and Flynn, his politician's smile. He's been running for office since he was twenty-six, barely moments after graduation from law school, has been councilman twice, assistant mayor, municipal judge by appointment, then municipal judge by election. He's forty-two, three years older than I, and sports enviable silver streaks below his temples. After a few preliminary remarks, he says, "I understand you wish to contest the petition of the school board, Mr. Flynn."

Joseph stands. "Yes, Your Honor."

"You may remain seated. This is a hearing, not a trial." The judge turns to Reed Stark. "I understand you and the school board have requested this hearing to determine whether to proceed with a case against young Mr. Flynn."

"That's correct, Your Honor," Mr. Reed Stark says. "If certain conditions are met, the board would consider dropping charges."

"And where is Brendan?"

Joseph turns and points.

"Right there."

Brendan waves foolishly at the judge. "Poppa?" he says.

"Shshh."

"Got to talk to *you*."

Joseph smiles an apology to Parker and ignores the boy.

"That ought to work against them," Reed Stark whispers.

"I'm sure it will," I whisper back.

"Mr. Flynn, do you or your advisor care to reply to the recommendation?"

"Poppa?"

Flynn's face reddens. He nervously points to Sarah. "She'll . . . uh, present our side of the story."

The judge nods.

"Poppa!"

"Shsshh," says Flynn, not turning.

Sarah is wearing uncharacteristic garb. Instead of faded blue jeans and a black crew-neck sweater she wears a forest green plaid skirt, white cotton blouse and pale blue coat sweater. "Brendan has lived peacefully in this community for all of his eighteen and a half years," she says in her soft dramatic way. "We admit that he couldn't have done so without the loving care and guidance of his parents, Joseph and Grace." She stands still as a stick and speaks without gestures. "Two months ago Grace Flynn died, and Brendan has since been at times disconsolate and, occasionally, a little disorganized. It's to be expected."

"You're stupid, Poppa!"

She blinks against the storm rising behind her but goes stubbornly on.

"Studies, including some I've brought to the courtroom, show that it is often more difficult for a mentally retarded person to adjust to the death of a loved one than it is for a so-called normal person. It will take time for Brendan to fully adjust to his mother's death."

"You *too, Sarah!*"

The judge blinks, irritated, and looks from Sarah to Brendan. Reed Stark twists uneasily. "Judge ought to throw him out."

I'm more interested in Sarah's thesis. "So-called normal person," she said. That's part of her pie-in-the-sky philosophy. How does it go? *What most separates people like Brendan from the others isn't their mental condition but the fact that he and his kind are in a minority.* She once showed me a quote from some study of mental retardation which said, "If those with retardation had landed at Plymouth, we'd now be living in a more loving and peaceful world." She's making a telling case for the board's position, more telling than I could have.

She tells the judge how Grace, after resigning her position as a third grade teacher was able to teach Brendan what the schools had given up on teaching him. Surely I'd insult Parker's intelligence by pointing out that without Grace's special care and attention, Brendan would long ago have been sent to the special school or an institution. If he'd had more contacts with others like himself he might not have regressed as much as he has since his mother died. He was extremely dependent on her. Now Joseph can't manage him, even with the help of his hired hand, Sarah. Brendan's vandalism is probably only the first of the difficulties he'll be in if he isn't put under the supervision of trained personnel like those in a community home.

". . . and to send him there," she now says, "would be like sentencing him to hell."

Idiotic!

The blink the judge gives Sarah's last remark is more pronounced than the one he gave Brendan. He asks Mr. Reed Stark if he wishes to speak. The principal tells him that I am the spokesperson for the other side.

After hearing Sarah I decide I can afford to be generously short-winded. I recount numerous erratic actions that led up to the vandalism at the school which, I point out, has been confessed to by Brendan, and conclude simply: "Brendan Flynn should not be subjected to a trial for this act, the seriousness of which he may be only vaguely aware. Nor should his father be burdened with his care until the young man demonstrates consistent stable behavior. The Mental Retardation and Developmental Disabilities Board, Your Honor, after consultation with school officials, including Mr. Reed Stark here, recommends assignment to County House A for a period to be determined by the court."

"Is that all?" says the judge, obviously surprised by my brevity.

"Yes, Your Honor."

"Miss Fuller, do you care to reply?"

She seems at first surprised and then, her little smile tells me, pleased by my remarks. "No, Your Honor," she says finally. "I believe that what I brought out in my presentation will refute what Dr. Tucker has just said."

"You realize," Parker tells her in a soothing tone, "if I find Brendan to be as fit as you claim he is, I'll have no choice but to order him to court. If he is found guilty, he, or rather his father, will not only be required to pay full restitution—I believe the figure is less than a thousand dollars—but Brendan might also face a brief jail sentence."

"Oh God!"

Sarah turns to Joseph, who's swung around to Brendan. "What?" Sarah looks back.

So do I.

He's gone.

∘☺∘ KEITH

I see a bag of potatoes on the side of the Interstate so I pull Dawg over. They must of dropped off a farmer's truck and will go good with the government cheese I just picked up down in Friendly. But when I'm about ten feet away, almost stopped, the bag sits up. Now I see it's not a bag but a fat dude squatting with his back to the traffic, squinting back at me and looking kind of scared. I lean out and say, "You need a ride?" He don't say a word. His jacket's got more dirt on it than Dawg, which ain't been washed since we found it at a junk yard. Now I see the jacket's also got twigs and grass and what looks like dead bugs.

"You waitin' for someone?" I say.

He stares at me like I just dropped in from the moon.

"Well, you got a ride if you want one." I reach over, take the broken Motorola off the other seat and put it underneath.

He's by now stood up and is kind of leaning toward me but not moving.

"Don't worry," I tell him, "bad as this thing looks, it won't fall apart." I say that but can never be sure. The Vet and we drove it off a junkyard late one night after taking a few parts from some nearby wrecks to get it started. It wheezes and spits but so far it ain't broke down. Now and then it even gets kind of competitive on the highway.

The fat dude finally waddles over and gets in.

I see he's a retard. They walk behind their mommas in grocery stores with their underwear sticking out over their pants. Last one I saw was picking up packages and putting them back like he was checking the prices. Maybe he was. He kept looking at me like he was worried I was going to laugh or something. I gave him a little wave so he wouldn't worry. He waved back and said, "Hi, guy."

This one don't say hello or thanks or nothing, just sits there looking at the glove box door that dangles loose under the box.

I say, "There's a radio under the seat. Pull it out and press the red button. The tuner is stuck on a country station. I had the Grateful Dead for a while coming out of Friendly."

He don't make a sound, just stares ahead. I bet I could put a rattlesnake on the seat between us and he wouldn't look.

After I go about two miles I turn and say, "Well, what else is new?"

I wait for him to smile at that but he don't.

I say, "I'm guessing by the look of you you got no place to stay. Right?"

He don't answer.

"Hey," I say in a loud voice, "you want me to talk or not? I don't have to, you know."

He says something in a whisper.

I say, "What?"

He says, "Can talk."

"Good. Now, you got a place to stay or not?"

He has to think about it but finally says, "No place."

"Okay. You can stay with us. My name is Keith Waterbury, but you can call me Slim, like everybody else. Don't really have a home but live in a shanty down by the river. My wife we call Loopey, spelled L-u-p-e. Some people say Loopay. Not us. We have three kids names of Maria, Viola and Tomas we call Tiny. Also I better mention the Vet. He's the dude lives with us. He scares people but don't mean no harm. Don't try and remember the kids 'cause you probably won't see them for a while. They got taken away last month and are staying at Loopey's mother's place over by the tracks. They was gonna put them in a home 'til they found out she has plumbing and never been in jail. I lost my job and jigged some dope but got myself clean after they took the kids. Reason they took the kids is not my dope but us not sending them to school. Only clothes they had were rags. They didn't want to go. Loopey and me were looking for clothes at the Salvation Army the day they were taken." I look over. "You gettin' all this?"

He gives me another nod.

"Good. The Vet smokes cheap grass when he can get it. He offers me hits but I don't take them. Loopey and me go over and see the kids on Sundays. You can come next Sunday. What you think?"

"I go."

Quiet as he is, he's sure a better listener than Loopey and the freaked-out Vet. Loopey talks right through what you're saying and the Vet don't pay no attention at all.

"My place ain't near as bad as it's gonna look. Made out of strong wooden crates, the ones they brought transmissions to the Jeep plant in. And I've got it backed up against the rubble of the old Mengeling warehouse. Those bricks protect us against the winds that come in off the river. The city is always threatening to shove us and the rubble into the river but Loopey thinks that's just to scare us. Anyway, our shantytown is cleaner than those big ones I hear about in Detroit and Cleveland."

Dawg adds a cough to one of its wheezes. I look down and see the gas gauge is low. Some of us found some piss-ass jobs last week to get money for the gas to go to Friendly. Looks like we didn't make enough.

The fat dude mumbles something.

"What'd you say?" I look across.

He's frowning so hard he looks like someone imitating someone frowning. "Hmmmbree."

"What?"

"Hmmmbree!"

"Say so's I understand."

"Hung-gree!"

Who isn't? "We're going to eat when we get to my place. Okay?"

"Okay."

"Got to ask you something. You got any money? We're running out of gas."

He squirms around and puts his hand in a pocket. He pulls it inside out. He then goes from pocket to pocket, doing the same danged thing. Finally they're all out, hanging like white tongues. "No money," he says.

Figures.

I don't have a license for me *or* the truck. It's gone if they stop me. I'm gone. The cheese is gone. Unless I grab all I can and head for the river. Can't leave the fat dude. Right. He can carry some.

I check the gauge and look over. "So . . . what's your name?"

He looks at the roof like he's trying to decide whether to tell me. Finally he wiggles his shoulders and does. "Evrett."

"Evrett what?"

"Ahh . . . Effernam."

I stick out my hand. He lays his in mine. It feels like cold mashed potatoes. "Okay, Evrett," I say, letting go, "with some of the kind of luck I ain't used to having, we'll be home in a few minutes. Loopey'll make you a cheese sandwich. How's that?"

"Okay."

"So, what were you doing there on the side of the highway?"

"Mmm . . . wait for ride."

"But you weren't hitchhiking. You were squatting there like someone by a campfire, not even looking at the cars."

"Cold."

Loopey and me and the Vet sit close to each other like that at night 'til it's warm enough to fall asleep. Squatting alone keeps you warm but squatting with others keeps you warmer. With fat old Evrett here we'll be warmer quicker.

"You work someplace or what?"

"Yep."

"Where?"

"Park."

"Like a city park?"

"Yep."

"Doing what?"

"Teach squirrels."

"Teach them what?"

"Ahmmm . . . tricks."

"What tricks?"

"Oh . . . go get my shoes."

"And they bring them to you?"

"Yep."

I turn.

He's nodding. "One shine *my* shoes."

"Jesus!"

He looks at me watching him, then raises his eyes. His mouth goes open, way open like someone threw a peanut from a plane and he's waiting to catch it. He sounds like he's choking the way little ones do on food, but he's not. He's starting to laugh. Pretty soon comes the rest—"BRAHHHHHHH . . . EEEEYAHHHHH . . . EEEYAHHHHH"—like a tornado. The torn ceiling cloth is flapping in the wind he's making. He finally stops— "EEEEYOOOOO"—turns and says with a final burst, "No shine *my* shoes."

"Okay, okay," I say, "the joke's on me."

"On *you*, Slim," he says, then laughs again.

The engine starts coughing when we're right at the head of the bridge. Get stuck in the middle of that and try to run, especially with cheese, and they've got you from one side or the other. Everyone who has a breakdown on the bridge gets his ass dragged into court. Reason is you make traffic stop for miles back. Don't want more trouble. They'll never let me see the kids. Got to some way get to the Washington Street exit, which is downhill. About a quarter of the way across the bridge I stomp the last bit of gas into the engine. I shove the gear stick into neutral. "Start rocking," I tell Evrett. I begin going back and forth. "Like this."

He starts doing it but not in the same rhythm as me so he's slowing us.

"No! Like this!"

"Hey," he says, "no get mad at *me*. Okay? Slim?"

He watches me and finally gets it right.

"That's it! That's it!"

We reach the Washington Street exit and start down.

He's still rocking.

"Hey, you don't need to do that anymore."

He stops.

Ahead, Loopey is coming out through the old drape we use for a door. What the hell's wrong with her? Her mouth is going and she's running faster than we're coasting. Finally I hear her say, "We've got trouble!"

What else is new?

I make it only to the Jackson hovel, two from ours.

"Trouble on trouble," she says, rushing toward my side of the cab.

I guess *that's* what's new.

°☺° LUPE

Right after Slim go out this morning, Arnold wake up with a war dream. Nothing new, okay? But this one don't go away and he soon be pissing through his eyes telling me the Cong be coming.

The Cong! Christ sake!

"Okay, Arnold," I say, "bring your brain into here and now. No fucking Cong be coming. This be nineteen-and-ninety-one."

Lot of good that do. "Thousands of 'em, Loopey!" Tell me they going to be pushing us out of our shanties and into the river.

The Vet be six foot five and always swinging his arms. Everybody in Shantytown be afraid of him but he live with us and we got no choice. Way Slim and me calm him is hold one arm on each side and baby-talk him. Now I try with just one arm but it don't do no good. He be loud-talking me and shaking his finger. "Hear the barges?" He lean down over me as I be reaching in the food basket for a oatmeal cookie to stuff in his mouth and keep it shut. "They gonna send spies in first." He whisper like they be one out there he afraid be listening, "Hey! Maybe they're already here. Maybe that little chick come here the other day." He get louder. "We got to check out that bitch!"

I grab his sleeve and say, "She ain't no Cong spy. Just a kid. Now you sit down and eat some this damn cookie and think about what you be saying."

He snag that piece of cookie way I teach my kids not to, then flop himself down on the dirt floor. He be puzzling over who know what.

One he be talking about come hitchhiking from Kentucky some

days ago and call herself Bonnie Jean. She be no more than four-
teen but got a baby started in her. We feed her, Slim and me, then
she go up in the rubble and make herself a little nest house. Come
down for food one, two time a day, 'til yesterday when she be not
feeling too good.

Now Arnold be mumbling. "They wait 'til they got us busy
fightin' more ragheads in the desert, then come sneakin' in. That's
it!" He jump up and shout through the hole in our roof, "What you
gonna do about it, huh?" Not be talking to me now but startin' his
morning word with the Lord. Don't I wish the Lord stop the war
in Nam before it be in Arnold's head! Too late now.

One Sunday morning he be with Slim and me going down
Franklin looking through the dumpsters. Black man come walking
along all dressed up with wife and a little kid look like a grand-
daughter. Arnold happen be climbing out of a dumpster and see
them. He wait and jump down like some Batman can't fly. Land
right in front of them and be all sort of crouched over. Stick his fist
up under this man's nose. The wife or whatever and kid run off the
sides afraid. "You ever in Nam?" Arnold say. Ask a lot of people
that. Be frowning and watching the black man. What the man
suppose to say when a giant crazy man with a beard look like fire
and orange hair down half his back and wild green eyes jump in
front of him on a Sunday morning? Man's mouth go "Nam?" but
nothing come out. "Speak!" Arnold say. "Was you there?" Slim
and I be working across the street but now run over and grab
Arnold by the arms. Slim tell the man, "He is sick and having an
attack," like that suppose to give the man comfort. "I ain't sick!"
Arnold shout. "You on his side or what? Ask him if he was in Nam.
Ask him!" We hold Arnold and talk him down, keep talking 'til the
whole family or whatever be out of there. Then Slim say, "Hey,
Vet, what you picking on him for? That dude was too old for
Nam!" Arnold think on that, then start crying. Soon he go soft,
way he sometime do after ranting too much. We lay him down
behind the dumpster and leave him sleeping 'til we fill our sacks.

The Vet be still carrying on when Lucinda Williams's kid,
Honey, come from rubble and tell me Bonnie Jean up there so sick
she be groaning. "You got to get up there, Loopey!" Honey say.
After they take away my kids I must suppose to be everyone's
nurse.

No choice, okay?

Leave Arnold and his garbledeegoop and go by Lucinda and Honey's UPS crate where Lucinda's lazy black head be sticking out. "Sound to me like she got some kind of colic, Loopey." Shit. "You ain't crippled, Lucinda. Why'nt you climb up there and care for the girl?" Say she can't do that cause the pus under her armpits be coming out again. When it be time to work she always got the pus. I say, "You got *nothing* but goddamn excuses under those armpits, Lucinda."

Piss me off.

Find Bonnie Jean all curled up but kind of squirming. Her dress which must some time ago been purple and was lilac pink when she got here be now dark red in the crotch. Look to me like the baby coming out. Way too soon. Her tummy don't be sticking out so much. Woman named Flower told her last week, "Go to the free clinic." She be telling Slim and me she don't want to go. Afraid someone take her back to where she don't want to be.

How she got here be, first, some traveling man knock her up and leave town. She be afraid her poppa find out what happen and kill her. She say she try and have thing be taken out but got no money and don't know where to go. Heard about Canada. Start hitchhiking. Three guys pick her up, bring her to a Motel 6 near here, hold her on a bed and take turns banging on her. Leave her out on the highway. She be afraid to stick her thumb out again. Walk into River City and find us.

Now she be twisting and turning with her face all sucked in like a old lady's. I be pulling up the dress, seeing she got no panties on. Think maybe she got none left. That ain't it. They be a little piece of panties on the bricks near her, all bloodied up. She be squirming and groaning. Look to me like the kid kicking to come out. I wait some. Nothing happen. I put my finger in and feel the little bugger's head. Something wrapped around the neck. Oh shit! Got small fingers and got to work two in 'til I got the thing loose. This baby ain't moving. *Don't be dead,* I think. Then I think, *What if it be alive?* What kind of life it be having? I know I got to be doing my best. Maybe I have to be putting it in a little bowl with clean rags. *Damn!* Why ain't she screaming and hollering like I do with mine? Look up and see why. She got her teeth in a broken brick and be grinding shit out of it. Red dust coming down her chin in spit. Not a peep. Now little thing finally be coming out but they ain't no limbs moving and nothing ticking in my fingers. Look down and see a tiny boy. Dead or not dead, I ain't sure. Got no knife. Lean down and gnaw off cord with my teeth. Bonnie Jean do nothing in all this but breathe hard. Wipe the little handful off with bottom of my shirt. "Going to get a towel and clean you up. Just stay there." Bricks under her be getting redder. Look like she spill a gallon of blood. Feel a couple twitches in my fingers but they don't be life twitches. Bonnie Jean be staring at me. She don't ask how it is. Or even what. She don't ask anything. "Put your dress tight against you down there." I pull her hands down and put them in her dress and press them against her to hold back the blood. "Don't you make no moves."

I climb down rubble with the thing in my hand. Ain't easy. Nearly lose it on one stumble but don't. Soon enough be at Lucinda's box. "Hey, Lucinda! Get your fat ass out here." Her door be a old green curtain. She pull it back just a stir. "That kid up there be dying. Look what come out of her." I hold the thing out. She puts her hands over her eyes and squeals. *Dumb bitch!* "Get back in the world," I tell her. "I got to get an ambulance. Got any juice?" She say she got some little bit of a broken carton with apple juice. "Startin' to taste like vinegar," she say. Vinegar is something. "Get it up there and in her and stay 'til I be back. Understand?" She look at me like she know I be breaking her damn leg if she don't do some helping. Soon enough she be calling, "Honey? Where you at, child?" Don't go nowhere without Honey. Got one more thing to do. Find Arnold quick and take him with me so he don't hurt no one, including himself.

They be this old man live past Lucinda in a hole under a desk he find in the warehouse rubble. Name of Charles. Only time he come out be when he got to piss or shit in the river or find food. Maybe one time each two days. Desk keep the rain off. He put what clothes he got in the drawers. Read old books we find and give him. Now I see his white messed-up hair come up and his mouse-eyes looking about. When he see me he say, "Your demented friend has gone off to find and bring back, if you care to believe it, the Ohio National Guard." He come out another inch. "Had those blasphemers of the law, our legislators, not been so eager to release the bloodthirsty riffraff, blathering boobs and rattle-brained war junkies—and I do include your boarder—the rest of us could breathe easily and . . ." I like to listen to Charles all the day but this be emergency time and I got to kick dirt on his head and shut him up. Some go in his mouth. "No time for jabber-talk," I say and stick my foot back like I be going to put more dirt in him. "Got to get an ambulance! Tell me real quick. Where'd he go?" Before he be sinking down he point to Washington Street. Soon pull his wooden lid on him.

I be running to get an ambulance when I see Dawg coming down the Washington Street ramp. I be shouting to Slim before he got the truck stopped.

"What's wrong?" he say.

"We got trouble on trouble." Get closer and say, "Who is that?" I be pointing to the stranger beside him.

"This here's Evrett," he say.

Old-looking kid come around the truck grinning. I try to keep going but he grab and hug me, nearly taking my breath out.

Slim say, "Shit, he didn't even talk to me for five minutes. That right, Evrett?"

Evrett nod.

No time for talking. "We got a dead-birth in the shanty and a sick momma in the bricks and Arnold crazy on the streets. I be looking for an ambulance. Think now I should of sent Lucinda but she so damn dumb she prob'ly be coming back with a bakery truck, or nothing. Wait! We'll take her in Dawg!"

Slim start slapping truck with both hands way he used to slap things when he lose a job. "Not your fault," I tell him. He shake his head, it ain't that. "Got no gas," he tell me. "We coasted in." He look around.

"Where's Evrett?"

He call out to him.

The boy don't answer.

"Oh, shit! Here's what, Loopey. You got up and sit by Bonnie Jean. I'm pushing the piss can down to the Seven-Eleven pump. I'll beg for gas. I'll look for an ambulance on the way." He frown, be thinking. "If we ain't got an ambulance time I get back, I'll pick her up and carry her all the way to the clinic."

Slim got no money. If he can't beg the gas, maybe he be getting caught stealing it. Then what? Shit. Don't know. Don't know where Arnold be, where Evrett be. What be going to happen to Bonnie Jean.

No answer.

Slim bring people nearly everytime he leave. Last time the Vet and now Evrett. I start toward the rubble. "Hey, Evrett!" He don't answer. Before the Vet it be a skinny black dude with a broken sax who call himself Mr. Cool. We sit up at night and listen. That sax he make whistle like a bird. Sometime Mr. Cool go play for nickels at the bus depot. One night he don't come back. Way things happen. Sometime I wonder about him and pray he put those nickels on a ticket and end up somewhere in the sun. But he prob'ly dead.

"Evrett!"

Still don't answer.

Near the top of the rubble I hear something sound like a owl. I know it ain't Bonnie Jean or Honey. Soon I see who it be. Evrett. Be kneeling on the high bricks looking down on Bonnie Jean. They be upside down to each other. He kind of cooing at her. Must be his way of singing. Can't hear what he be singing but see her hand by his cheek. His eyes be looking in hers. Hers be looking in his too. She ain't crying and don't appear sick, be just staring up at him while he sing. She marble white like a church statue. I climb up to hear his words. No words. Just some sweet humming. He hear me and look up. I stop climbing. Don't want to scare him away. He take his hand from Bonnie Jean's cheek. Bonnie Jean hand fall like Lucinda's curtain. He turn his head to me.

"*Not* come back?" he say.

I see her eyes still be looking where his face was and I know he be right.

◦◖▭◗◦ ELEANOR

Funerals I've seen. Of governors and bishops (once a cardinal), tycoons and mobsters (little difference in many cases), merchants, soldiers, teachers and, of course, beggars like myself. Superior to all others are the funerals of beggars.

Don't be deceived.

I'm not speaking about the mockeries the city provides when one of us is unlucky enough to fall in a public place. I mean those exquisite private ceremonies we create for ourselves and conduct at dusk or in early morning light at necessarily secret places. We carry on without insult of clergy, though if the departed happens to be a believer, God is invoked during the eulogy; if not, toodle-oo deity.

(Not all traditional ceremonies are forgettable. The most memorable I witnessed was the solemn High Mass said for the Marchesa de Brondoni at St. Mark's Cathedral in Venice, 1948; yet for all the variety of robes, choral music, floral arrangements and candelabra, it was, in the end, quite like many other Catholic or, for that matter, High Episcopalian rites.)

A pauper's funeral is, on the other hand, magnificent invention. The place of rest, for example, is, insofar as possible, chosen by the person departing. The old Mexican, Maria Callenda, lies beneath uncut grass a few yards from the drinking fountain at Founder's Square near the courthouse, where she begged on Sunday afternoons. And the boy Alex rests peaceful under home plate at Casey Stengel baseball diamond, where he watched his favorite sport as often as his illness permitted. I, myself, realizing I'm somewhat past my time, recently selected the soft earth near my vault at the Mid-States National Bank Building. I did not do so because my late husband, Ernest, was for eleven years a member of its parent company's, Global National Bank's, board of directors but because the bank was where I swore off, forever I trust, the only companion who ever dominated me, mind and body, Mr. John Barleycorn.

And there I sat last night, reading under my lantern from Oscar Lewis's *Five Families*, when a voice I didn't recognize called down through the grate by the sidewalk, "Hey! Lady of the Night!" I searched for and found my tin cup and clanged it against the wall of the doorless vault to let the caller know I was present. "Somebody hear the trumpets is being laid down at the morning time at River Vista!" I called back "Who? Who?" but got no answer. Was the fallen one Charles, my friend and lover? I hoped not but was too damned creaky and wound down to walk the two blocks to the river and find out.

Charles and I are the two oldest street citizens in River City, he being slightly younger than I at seventy-seven. When I find myself starving not for food or fresh air but for precise, intelligent, and, above all, informed conversation of the kind that has for some time been disappearing, I make my way to Charles's hole under his desk. "My Living Grave" he calls it. I descend by using his small removable stepladder. There is inside just room for two. We talk.

I've invited Charles to come live with me. He prefers Shantytown, which he calls Reaganville. He'd be safer here. Children kick makeshift balls made of old aluminum foil at his head. Husbands call him a fool for living in a hole and wives shout at him to keep from going mad. Rodents try to make nests in his shoes, which he keeps in a niche in the dirt. Charles, who was once a history professor at Bucknell University, values his privacy more than he does comfort, money, respect, and, it appears, me. I decided it couldn't have been Charles who passed on; they'd certainly have made sure to tell me.

I was sorry to hear it was a morning ceremony. I do my foraging in the morning because I don't attract as much attention then. Unfortunately, I get more attention than most of the local homeless. It's my ratted mink and starched eyes, the silver my wild if thinning hair gives back in sunlight. Also my pruney face (too damn many Bahamian vacations). I think, above all, it's my age. They call me Lady of the Night and Lady of the Tomb. They also, because of a previous circumstance, call me the Heiress. I married lucky, was never an heiress.

I am Eleanor Magdalena Armstrong, widow of the late Ernest

Armstrong, who was for thirty years president, and twenty chairman of the board, at P. V. Carburetor. Ernest was a lovable but unloving man. I bore him three children, all daughters. After he choked to death on chicken skin at Henry Ford II's annual Labor Day picnic in 1966, my daughters, then in their twenties, began to battle so vehemently over their inheritances that I determined their war would last throughout the remainder of their lifetimes and the rest of my own and therefore took to the streets, where I've remained ever since. My first stopping place was an abandoned store near the Greyhound bus depot in downtown Detroit, but the atmosphere became too dangerous after the Negroes began shooting at each other. I moved to River City. My daughters had me declared an alcoholic (which I am) and an incompetent (which I'm not). They're ungrateful wretches, all three of them, but I desperately miss each. The turnings of the heart abide no explanation. I'd go back in an instant if any of them wanted me.

In the morning I carried myself to the burial place and learned that the small angel I never met had passed. There was a honeysuckle sweetness in the air. It might, I fancied, be emanating from the Hefty trash bag in which she lay. A warm breeze swung to and fro and was like the faint hum of a distant choir. Fourteen or fifteen of the Shantytowners stood in their best tatters on the rarely used downy patch above the silence of the river.

(City ordinances forbid unlicensed funerals. A poor person found dead is taken to the city mortuary, stripped, examined, put into an unfinished pine box and delivered by truck to pauper's field at the back of City Cemetery #3.)

I remained at the periphery of the group, recalling artifacts of my own hopeless mortality, an early awareness of which frightened me into decades of escape and (in the word of my former psychiatrist, Immanual del Roga) denial. I decorated one or another of our three homes (Westport, Hillsborough, Ottawa Hills) as though I were preparing tombs for Pharaohs. I habitually sailed (or flew) to our winter retreat on Cat Island in the Bahamas. I took numerous other trips, like a flight to France at the end of my third pregnancy so that Ernest and I could say we had had a child born in Paris. (We did.) I, meanwhile, pasted my brain with vodka tonics ("Lime twist, please. Break the skin of the lime and rub the rim with it, if you don't mind"); in fact became the stepchild of bartenders, as dependent on them as my daughters were on me, or the government was on Ernest's tax money. My general purpose, insofar as one can say a drunk has purpose, was to eliminate thought, the earlier each day the better. Later, of course, I took shots of heroin and (warned against *that* by del Roga) tiny spoonfuls of cocaine (which del Roga had persuaded me would not become addictive). (It did.) I'd begun with booze and now went back to it. For me, Father Whiskey and Mother Gin delivered acceptable adventures. I've copulated with two senators, a monsignor, and reached coitus with the wife of the British ambassador to Mexico (who stayed with us on the Cat in 1961 or 1962). "You name it," one of my cousins, Geraldine Hunter-Parvakoulos, reportedly said, "and Eleanor has probably done it." Probably. When I had our driver, Raymond, take me from the eighteen-room house Ernest left me to the abandoned shoe store I'd found near Greektown, I had three suitcases, two filled with gin. The flights I took on Tanguery Airlines, like my rides on the Rat (heroin) or escapes on coke weren't really very different in quality from those flights taken by the wretched men who lie curled in grimy niches near the Trailways bus station, sucking muscatel or injecting themselves with the Rat disguised in quinine. Quinine is, I can attest, nearly as dangerous as the Rat, coke or gin. I know about quinine and its uses because Ernest became addicted to a certain popular tonic water, taking overdoses that caused headaches, ringing in the ears, dizziness due to high blood pressure and nearly death. Escape is escape. For me, it was the Bahamas; for the gentlemen in the doorways, the galaxies; for Ernest, whatever hideaways the quinine provided.

But I must stop my thoughts and listen to my friend, Lupe, who is doing the eulogy:

"She be going in the soft earth where we stand, the baby too, who we name Andy. No matter some people say it ain't a baby. Way I look at it is, after a certain time a baby be there. They all kick a different way. Maybe they be a baby when they start kickin'. Maybe when they start kickin' a different way. Maybe this one did or didn't kick. I ain't God. We got to take no chances and give him a burial too. Like giving him a name. He be in the bag with his momma. Anyone object?"

There are a couple of headshakes.

I hold to a radically different and, I believe, more enlightened viewpoint. At another time I may choose to share it with Lupe. I shall note here only that the object in the sack with the girl-woman is, in my view, no more her offspring than the scabs that came off her knees when she was a child. To generate more thoughts on this matter would be to produce an essay of massive proportions. I shall let it be.

"Nearly forgot to thank Lucinda for the Hefty Steel bag she foraged last week and be giving up today. It keep them dry till the small animals come through and take the soft parts back to the earth. Or maybe the river be coming in one of its rise-ups and taking them away. In case someone don't know it, her name was Bonnie Jean, and Evrett here give the baby his name."

I notice an older mongoloid boy kneeling a few feet from Lupe. He adds a nod to his rocking motion and says loudly, "Andy!"

"Right," says Lupe, "and Bonnie Jean be holding Andy on her tummy if you didn't see us put them in. We got to say thanks to Charlie and Benny and Evrett who came over here after dark to dig the hole behind me. It don't look too deep so maybe it stay dry to spring when the bag start rotting. What else? Slim suppose to be here but since yesterday he be looking for the Vet, who some of you know went off his head one more time."

"Bonnie Jean coming back," the mongoloid says. "Maybe."

Somebody groans but Lupe smiles and looks down and says, "You can believe whatever you want, Evrett."

"Coming back." He looks out past me toward the river reminding me with his curious darting eyes and fidgety movements of my cousin Gerald, whom I had to spend tedious hours attending on that trap of an island, Mackinac, every summer when we were children.

"Slim still ain't here." She shakes her head. "I got to go on without him. So we start."

The mongoloid's hand falls from the bag and he struggles to his feet.

"You know how sometime a cousin or brother or sister find out about us burying one of us and find a way to come here and be representing the rest of the family? Well, Bonnie Jean and the near-baby got no one and we got to be like their family, okay? Maybe it be better no one from her home be here. They can now think she marry some rich man or go on stage and be famous. Whatever they think be better than what happen."

"That's for sure," says Lucinda.

The mongoloid got up and moved clumsily toward the marshes. Within a few seconds he vanished. I heard sloshing noises, now nothing.

Lupe stops talking and turns around. "Evrett, where you be going?"

He doesn't answer.

"If he get in that quick-mud, we be having another funeral tomorrow. Evrett!"

No answer.

For all the dull afternoons I spent watching Gerald stumble about the island in search of turtles, odd-shaped rocks, twisted branches, dead birds, snails and the like, there were moments of great surprise. One afternoon he looked up from where he'd been digging with a stick to make a well and said, "Mother fall." He stared for a few seconds at a passing cumulus as if at a film being shown on its lower surface, then lowered his head and resumed digging. An hour later, when we returned to the family summer home on the far side of the island, we learned from the governess, Louise, that Gerald's mother, my Aunt Amanda, had fallen while balancing herself between the stepladder and the porch as she was putting up a hanging plant and had severely broken her right ankle.

"We ain't going to put up a cross or any such," Lupe is saying. "That be doing nothing but bringing people here shouldn't be. They maybe dig up our friends. Fact is, what we be having to do is put the grass back by the roots, way we took it out, so nobody know they be here."

Gerald's psychic powers, as real as the telephone, showed themselves infrequently but were each time stunning. Many had to do with birth, death and the afterlife. A few were premonitions of illnesses, accidents or injuries. Once he told me not to go to the mainland on a Saturday night with my friends. "Too hot there," he said. It was late September and the weather, day and night, had been very cool. I ignored him but, halfway across, the ferry launch caught fire and had to be towed back the rest of the way. Some passengers, including me, suffered minor burns.

"Momma?"

I turn and there, seven or eight feet behind me, stands the mongoloid, his face gathering a horrified expression as it encounters mine close up. For an instant I thought I was facing Gerald, who's been dead for forty-six years. "What do you want?" I say, almost demanding.

"*Not* Momma," he announces in words that quiver.

But, as if he isn't yet sure, he approaches and puts his soft hand up to my face, holds it against my cheek as though he's feeling for my temperature. I haven't been touched by anyone except those—police, bus station workers, librarians—who nudge me when I fall asleep in public places, for years. Ernest and I didn't even shake hands when he returned from work or business trips. He despised the human touch. Charles and I keep a distance even when we're in his hovel.

"*Not* Momma." He steps back, and stands before me, hunched and unseemly.

He reminds me now not of Gerald but of those inhabitants of my dreams. All are, one way or another, deformed. Sides of faces missing. Mangled arms welded to torsos, twisted legs dragged along like driftwood. Some of them come out of my nightmares and, taking less grotesque forms, find me on the streets. They are all needy and insufficient. I have had a crippled child to my quarters, as well as a blind man, a woman who could only crawl, another who couldn't speak. I don't seek them, they find me, as if to say, "Lead us to a better condition." I care for them only long enough to teach them how to lead themselves wherever they think they're going.

I look down and see that Evrett missed the deep places. His trousers are muddy only up to his knees. I look up and say, "Come with me when the funeral ends. I'll teach you how to forage."

We remained until the child-woman is gently lifted by four of the homeless and carried to the opening made in the earth, behind Lupe. All four kneel as they lower her, then drop her body and its residue into a grave we can't see from where we stand but which I estimate from their movements is three or four feet deep. As Lupe reaches down for a handful of dirt to throw in upon Bonnie Jean, I turn to the mongoloid and say, "Would you like to help bury her?"

He's been standing so close beside me his arm periodically touches mine and I can see out of the corner of my eye that he is scrutinizing me. "No want to see *that*," he says.

After my experiences with Gerald I've learned neither to dismiss nor discount anything falling from the mouths of the retarded, no matter how untenable it may seem. I doubt that either of the two, Evrett or Gerald, could in any sense be termed an idiot savant, which is to say one of those exceptional members of the subcategory that includes persons who can instantly and accurately tell you which day of the week any calendar date in the past 10,000 years occurred, or what the odds are against a meteor striking the earth in the next century, or the number of safety pins produced in the world during the past fifty years. Perhaps Gerald and Evrett can, after all, be counted savants. Does it matter how I categorize them? The fact is, one had a power I knew to be real and the other, against my own argument, judgment, and even near certainty, may have. "Why do you think Bonnie Jean will be back?" I can't resist asking.

"She tell Boom . . . Evrett."

Poor child, aware she was dying, might of course have wished herself to return, for a better chance next time.

But Evrett wasn't finished: "She no breathe for *long* time. And . . . um . . . don't want to say."

"Why not?"

"You laugh at Evrett."

"I will *not* laugh. To say I will just shows you don't know me very well."

He studies me again, my eyes this time and, satisfied, as he should be, says, "Okay. Say to *you*. After she die, she say by Evrett's ear. Like this." He leans close to my ear and whispers, " 'I be back.' Keep saying *that*. 'I be back. I be back.' " He pulls away and nods. "Do."

"How would she know she's coming back?"

He frowns at the question, not in an objecting way; the opposite: he's taking it in, puzzling over it. At last he says, "Okay. Bonnie Jean no know. *Maybe*. Who *do* know?"

He's retarded but, like Gerald, not stupid. I'm responding to him as I always responded to Gerald: frankly. "I'd say nobody knows."

Again he puzzles before responding. "Where voice I hear come from?"

"Have you ever heard other voices of people who died?"

"No way."

"Then . . . I don't know."

"Bonnie Jean speak to Evrett," he said, waiting for, perhaps wanting an argument. Getting none, he added, "Think so."

Lupe speaks the final words, addresses them to Bonnie Jean herself as if she too believes the girl-woman's spirit continues to exist.

"Where you're going, you got to be sure and check it out real good 'cause you know from being here things don't be turning out all the time like they suppose to. Maybe you be listening to some sweet-talking angel that turn out to be a devil. Try and tell you that the down place is up. Shit like that. Also, what you learn while you be here, you be remembering when you be there. And if you do be meeting the Lord God, you got to be sure and tell him what be going down. Lot of poor people and killings. Not only tell him be merciful with peoples that be so tired and sick they forget to pray, plus the ones be beaten up so much they don't believe He be any more real than Kermit the Frog. And even all others who don't be believing 'cause they be trying to make sense of what don't be sensible. Last thing, if you still be in a listening mood, Bonnie Jean, tell Him they have to be some emergency action in and about the hovels. The city be threatening to put us and all we own into the river. Maybe they be lying. Maybe they be not. We don't know. Living conditions not too good. He got to help. Okay, that's enough. Got to go. We all here be wishing you a happy eternity, Bonnie Jean. Amen."

Evrett and I fade away during the silence that follows and are soon making our way toward the heart of downtown where we pass people who (with the exception of children) don't notice us or, noticing, disdain us, one with spit that lands close to Evrett but doesn't quite make a connection. The passersby often spit near rather than on you, as if the germs of poverty would travel back from you along the spit's trajectory, and enter them.

The bags behind the fast food restaurants are placed in huge steel containers. I am not as supple as other foragers and must be inventive if I am to find a way into the containers. I've been assisted by crates, low window ledges and, now and then, another forager. This time I have Evrett. He gives me a cupped-hand boost. Two feet up is all I need. "You wait out there," I say as I swing my second leg over and feel the cushion of a bag. "I'll hand our breakfasts to you over the top."

"I wait," he says.

With long fingernail I slice a robust-looking bag and continue the instructions I began as we walked toward downtown. "One mistake . . . is to try to . . . carry out of one of these containers more than you can . . . eat." I dig out a breakfast carton heavy enough to let me know it's worth opening. I open it and find scrambled eggs barely nibbled at, one of two pieces of sausage untouched and toast with a very tiny bite taken out of it. Nearly mint condition, this one. "I'm going to pass your breakfast out," I tell him. "In a moment I'll have my own." I turn from my standing position among the mound of bags and raise the carton. He reaches up from outside and carefully takes it from my hand.

"I forgot to tell you," I call out. "In the mornings you always reach to the bottom to find the bags with breakfasts. They were put in first, yesterday, and are at the bottom. What's on top and in the middle is hamburgers and such, not breakfast food."

"Okay."

I soon have my own breakfast, a carton of completely untouched pancakes in a paper sack in which the customer has conveniently also left an unopened packet of syrup. Perhaps it's an order returned to the counter because it wasn't soft or warm enough. This has been a good morning. I need only find that which is most difficult, some unopened orange or grapefruit juice. If I don't, the mission will not be a failure. There are other places where liquids can be found.

"Lady?"

Poor fellow. Did I forget to tell him my name? "Just a moment. I'm trying to get to my feet to hand you my breakfast."

"Eleanor?"

Didn't forget. Why is he so suddenly impatient? With a couple of grunts and the cracking of a vertebra, I get myself up. I don't see Evrett's hand. I move to the edge of the bin and look out.

He's gazing sadly up. His left and only free hand is flapping at the side of his head, toward his right, where there stands a police officer I recognize, Henry Sanders. Tucked under Henry's right arm is Evrett's breakfast. His left wrist is handcuffed to Evrett's right one.

"A runaway, Bag Lady," he says.

Aren't we all?

"Gonna have to take you in too."

०⊜० SARAH

Clear liquid drips into Joseph's arm from a jar that hangs on a metal tree beside his bed. Though he lies very still, his breathing is labored. For a second time in the few minutes I've been there he groans. This time he doesn't remain still but pulls his head restlessly toward the side of the bed at which I stand. His eyes open slightly, reach out, not to but past me, toward the double doors. I turn but see no one. After a troubled exhale, he twists his head away.

Brendan amused himself with television or reading in the apartment while Joseph and I sat across from each other at the store counter, retracing Brendan's relationship with Mr. Reed Stark, citing numerous instances of his good behavior, finding examples of his general progress through the years. "Do we need a lawyer?" Joseph asked. No, I said, explaining that if we got one, so would they. We could handle it ourselves. There would be no subpoenas. Carlotta would therefore not appear. No matter. We could stir enough doubt as to what had happened at the school to keep Brendan from a trial or a community home. We could question Reed Stark freely. Or ask the judge to do so. And we and he and others could question Brendan too. What had really happened would rise and become visible. So I persuaded Joseph. We went into the courtroom confident.

Brendan wanted to sit in back. Joseph told him he should sit up front with us. "No," he said loudly. We were standing inside the doorway.

Tucker was already there, at one of the tables in front of the judge's bench, and turned back at the sound of Brendan's voice. He smiled at me before turning forward. How poised he seemed.

Joseph had told Brendan that this was a hearing, not a trial. He'd had no questions. But now he looked nervously about. The sight of the judge's bench, all the rest, including perhaps even Tucker must have made it seem to him like a trial. "Boombah stay here," he said. "No," said Joseph. "Come up in front with me." I spoke softly to Joseph, wanting him to give in, to let Brendan stay at the back. I wanted Brendan to be as relaxed as possible. He might, after all, be called on to speak. Joseph gave in.

Then Mr. Reed Stark appeared. Brendan tried to speak to Joseph. Had Reed Stark stopped and said something to him, something Brendan now wanted Joseph to hear? Maybe Reed Stark's imposing presence only brought back the pain he'd felt during the confrontation in the school hallway. I may never know. What I do know and must now accept is that he, Brendan, was ill-prepared for that hearing.

My mistakes, Joseph, I say silently, looking down.

His head has swung toward the nurse's station. His breathing has slowed but is more regular. "Mild coronary," Dr. Grable said. Just what did that mean? How do they know mild from severe? How do they know it won't become fatal? Often I've heard of people going to a doctor and having a so-called "perfect cardiogram," then collapsing with a heart attack as they leave the doctor's office. Might he have yet another? Of course. How likely is that?

I have no answers.

Judge Parker stopped the proceedings. "We're not continuing unless the young man is here," he said.

Joseph and I went into the hall and looked for him. We were on the third floor. We searched it and the first and second floors. No Brendan. We returned to the courtroom. Judge Parker wasn't pleased. He told us that if we did not find him in an hour he'd have an announcement to make. We looked around the courthouse area. Then I drove Joseph back to the Flynn's neighborhood, checked every street, yard, and home where he might be. There was no sign of him. "Why did he do it?" Joseph kept asking, first in anger, then with apprehension. "What the hell's going to happen?" I had no answers. After we returned to the courtroom, we learned that the city police had been alerted to his disappearance. So far he'd eluded them as well. The hearing was postponed. Parker said, "I'm ordering that Brendan, when he's found, be taken immediately to County Health Services and given a complete physical, then delivered to County House A, where he will remain until I can make a final determination as to the disposition of his case."

Joseph made puzzled sounds. I don't think he understood what the judge was saying. I asked Parker why Brendan couldn't simply be sent home. "Isn't he going to be, well, put in a situation not unlike arrest?" The judge, speaking softly, didn't address all of us, as he had been doing, only me. "In addition to the vandalism he's alleged to have committed," he replied, his penetrating dark eyes holding me with a severe look, "he's walked out of this hearing, apparently without cause. I find sufficient reason to put him temporarily under the jurisdiction of the county. Would you prefer I order him to the county jail?" I shook my head, said, "No. I wouldn't." He sat back, more satisfied with my answer than I was. He looked about. "Are there other questions?" There weren't. I forced myself not to look at Tucker because I was sure he wore a smile.

"Joseph?" I now say. I speak out of my need, not his.

There isn't a flicker of response.

At five yesterday afternoon he closed the store and began making the series of phone calls he's made at the same time on each of the three days since Brendan walked off: to the Hartsville Police Department, the County Sheriff's office, local State Police headquarters, to the homes of his friends, neighbors and acquaintances. At 7:10 he called me to report, once more, that there had been no contacts with Brendan, no sightings, not even a rumor of a sighting. A little after seven-thirty, when Joseph usually reopened the store, Anna Guerrero, Rosa's mother, called me and said Rosa and two of her friends had just come back from there. "They say Mister Flynn is fallen asleep in the counter, you know, and they can't wake him up." I hung up and called the store. No answer. I called the emergency room at the hospital and told them to send an ambulance. I knew there was a chance he didn't need emergency help. *I'll gladly suffer the embarrassment of being wrong,* I told myself.

Beyond his bed a red light blinks on the phone-set at the nurse's desk. The nurse picks up the speaker, holds it to her ear, nods once and then again. Soon she speaks back, watching me as she does so. Finally she picks up a notepad, then a pencil, writes something, nods again and hangs up. She looks at her watch, then checks the clock on the wall between Joseph's bed and the one beside it. Her movements remind me that my time is nearly up. I look down. Joseph's breathing has become quieter. Is that due to the pills he's been given? Maybe his condition is worsening. I want to say to the nurse, "Is there nothing more you can do?" I don't say anything. When I leave, she'll surely check on him. She's doing what she must.

Mistakes, Joseph, I think, looking down at him.

The nurse signals to me, then points to the phone.

I've told no one I came to the hospital.

Who can it be?

°☺° BEATRICE

Oh, dreary sky! Why don't you show your face? I'm not going to go out of my room until you do. You should be happy. I'm happy. I have a boyfriend. He doesn't know it yet. He's on this floor. I saw him come in. Then I peeked in his bedroom. He was sitting on the side of his bed. His head was down and his arms were all loose like ropes and hanging between his legs. I said, "Hi!" He didn't look at me. I know he felt like there was a big hole inside him. Everyone does when they come here. They even do after they've stayed here. Delia says he won't come out of his room. I'm going down there and peek at him.

Look. He's sitting on the side of his bed again with his hair sticking up. If I had a comb I'd comb it.

"Hi!"

I think he's deaf. "Are you deaf?"

"No!"

He's mad at me.

"Can I comb your hair?"

"No!"

When I was put here, my mother said she'd send me pictures from Florida. I screamed at her and pulled at her coat, even tore it. I wanted her to take me to Florida. Mrs. Holloway pulled me back and Mother turned away. I said, "Mother!" She walked out and didn't look at me. I kept looking out my window after that. For months and months. She didn't come back. She sends pictures but I don't look at them. The first night old Miss Goss in the other bed woke me up all night talking to someone but no one else was in the room. I was in the room but she wasn't talking to me. She said she had to go to church. "Ffumone take me!" She sometimes shouted. I couldn't sleep. I couldn't sleep anyway. I was waiting for my mother. I thought she'd start crying when she and her new husband Raymond were driving to Florida, then come back. She didn't come. After that I got mad and wouldn't go out of my room. Also, when Miss Goss talked to herself, I said, "Shut up!" Then it was Miss Goss who couldn't sleep. They took me downstairs and put me in the crafts room. It's not really a crafts room. It's a punishment room. I had to stay there all day. There is one table and one chair and one window. All I could see out of the window was a dirty brown wall. I smiled when they brought my ugly food and even ate all of it. Then Mrs. Holloway said I couldn't come out and would have to sleep there with a blanket on the floor if I didn't behave myself. Some of them here call her "Mother." I don't.

"Do you miss someone?"

Well, at least he didn't say no. I never saw anyone so sad. I just love him so much. He has big feet and dirty shoes. He didn't lace his shoes. That jacket is just a mess. I wish I could wash it. They wouldn't let me, I'm sure. You'd think we were all crippled. This boy is so sad. I like it when Delia speaks my name. I'll speak his:

"Brendan?"

His head went up but he didn't look at me. I'm going to stay right here by his door until he looks. Now his head goes down again.

"Brendan?"

It doesn't go up.

"That's the prettiest boy's name I ever heard."

"Not!"

Goodie! But I wish he would talk to me and not his shoes. "Look at me."

"No!"

"I have the prettiest name of anyone here. Beatrice. Except maybe Delia. Mine's prettier. Don't you think it's pretty?"

"No!"

"Is that all you can say?"

"No."

"Then tell me your name."

"Boombah."

I laugh inside. I hate when people laugh out loud and I don't want them to. I went to Upper Valley Day School until they figured out I was retarded. They laughed when I tried to pick up my pencil off the floor. I'm very pretty but my arms and legs don't work very well. I don't care if people laugh inside. "I never heard of such a name."

"*My* name."

"No, it's not. Your name is Brendan. Delia told me."

"Boombah!"

"Okay. Your name is Boombah. My name *is* Beatrice. I'm very beautiful. Why don't you look at me?"

He won't.

"I have gold hair and a small nose and very red lips. I am the most beautiful person in here, counting Delia. Everyone knows that. I think about it when I'm sad. It makes me happy. If you look at me you'll see. If you don't look at me I might be so sad I'll go back to my room and die. Then you'll never see me. Delia and Geezer and others will say, 'She was soooo beautiful!' But you won't know what they were talking about. I might burn the picture of myself in my drawer before I die. You'll never know what they were talking about. But you could. All you have to do is turn your head."

The top part of him is going forward and back, forward and back. A lot of people here sit and do the same moves over and over and over. Some do it with their hands and some with their heads and some with their bodies. People think it's because we're retarded. I think it's because there's hardly anything to do here. Brendan is doing it because he's trying to get himself to look at me. I think so. I'll help him. "I've seen myself with all my clothes off. Delia lets me stand on the chair in the bathroom. I look in the mirror. I can't believe how beautiful I am. I am just stunning. Do you know what 'stunning' means?"

"No."

"I didn't think you did."

"Know how *spell* it."

Triple goodie! "You *do?*"

"Ess."

"I don't believe you. Spell it."

"S-t-u-n . . . n-g."

"I don't know if it's right. Maybe it is. I think that's right. You must be smart. No, you're not. If you were smart you'd look at me before I go back in my room and kill myself."

"No kill *your*self."

"Why not? You don't even care enough about me to look at me, even though I'm very beautiful and even though I made you my boyfriend."

He almost looks but stops himself.

"When you came to this house with the policeman."

"Want Poppa."

"Poppa?" Oh, dreary, dreary. "Don't say it that way. Don't say it like you expect him to be here. He's not. Maybe he'll visit you. My mother never visits. My father never will. I don't know where *he* is. He wanted a boy. What a joke I was on him. He went away. People don't like retarded kids. They leave you here and don't come back. Sometimes. But maybe your poppa will come. If a policeman brought you, you must be in trouble. Miss Goss's sister visits her. . . . What are you doing?"

He fell down and is all curled up.

"Brendan?"

Crying. It's soft crying like someone who's afraid to cry out loud.

"Brendan?"

We're not supposed to go inside someone's room without some-one else, but I did. I don't care. I have to get him up or else they'll keep him in the dayroom. Or put him in one of the crafts rooms. Oh dreary! They let you cry as long as you sit up. I go over to him.

"Get up, Brendan!"

He feels so strong. I bet he's warm. I wish he'd lie down on top of me.

"Get up, Brendan."

"No!"

His whole body is making bubbles he's crying so hard but I can't hear him. All his crying is inside. He's like a big rain cloud with no rain coming out. He's so big. I love him more than ever. I have to stay with him. I have to live with him. I have to marry him.

"Brendan?"

He just wiggles.

"Brendan? Stop crying. You have to marry me."

He stops crying. He stops wiggling. He has a round face with stick-out eyes. My mother said I'm lucky I don't have them. No, I'm not. I'm not lucky at all. He's got a big tongue. A tear rolled right around his nose and landed on it. He pulled it into his mouth. His tongue came out again. He looks like he wants to lick me.

"What *you* say?"

"I'll tell you when you get up. Get up!"

He's so big. He has clumsy legs. He's staring at my face. He's so slow getting up. I'm no help. I'm pulling his jacket off. It comes up but he doesn't. It's just filthy. "Get up by yourself."

He has to turn around and put his hands down and push his bottom up. He pulls himself up by holding on to the side of the bed.

"You are a clumsy one, aren't you?"

He sits down on the bed. I sit down beside him as close as I can. He's warmer than Delia when she holds me when I cry. I don't even have to touch him to feel how warm he is. I want to touch him. I put my hand up on his face. I feel little tiny hairs sticking out. Not a lot. He'll have to get rid of them if he wants me to hug him. It's soft hair, not hairy hair like a man's. He won't turn and look at me.

"Don't you think I'm beautiful?"

"Ess."

I knew he would. Everyone does. "Don't say 'ess'. Say 'yes'."
"Yes."
"That's better. Kiss me."
"No."
"Kiss me right on the mouth or I'll kiss you."
He turns. His eyes are closed so tight they have wrinkles. He makes his lips tight and sticks them out. I wish he'd look at me. It will be more fun if he looks. I have such light blue eyes. "Open up!"
"Nmm." He tried to say no with his lips sticking out.
Oh well. I give him a soft kiss anyway. Hee. He's waiting for another one. "Open your eyes for number two."
He does, a tiny bit.
"Are you going to marry me?"
His lips go back. "No marry. *Kiss.*"
"No kisses unless you say you'll marry me."
"No *marry.*"
"No *kiss.*"
"One?"
"No. Can I feel you?"
"Huh?"
"Shut up." I put my hand on his chest and move it all around and then down to his stomach. He's so soft. I move it down to his dingle. It's really really hard. I feel the whole thing. Oh my! It's excellent. I never touched anyone's before. "I'm leaving unless you say you'll marry me."
He's breathing fast. "Kiss!"
"If you say you'll marry me."
"Marry . . . *you.*"
"Good! What's my name?"
"Bee-truss."
"Be-ah-triss. Say that."
"Bee-ah-trice."
". . . triss."
". . . triss."
"Good. Close your eyes and get ready."
He does.
I open my lips and put them over his. I want to make him go crazy. He starts shivering. I'm going crazy too. I don't want to stop

kissing. I want to climb inside his jacket and button it up and live there. I don't care how dirty it is. We're both going crazy. Hah. We're already crazy. I pull back. "We have to make love, Brendan. Right now!"

"What?"

"Make love. Do you know how to make love?"

"Uh uh."

"I do. I learned it on HBO. Take all your clothes off and get in bed." When I lived at home the man who came to fix the bathroom told me to take my panties off and touched me. It tickled. My mother came home and he stopped. He said, "Don't tell your mother." I said, "I won't." I said, "Do more." He said, "I can't. Maybe when I come back." I said, "Come back!" He didn't. He didn't do it right. I figured out how to do it right. Brendan has his jacket off. He's so slow. "Hurry up!" I'm going to move in this room. I have to tell Delia. Oh God! He's so slow with the buttons on his shirt. Underneath he's the whitest person I've ever seen. "You have to get out in the sun."

"No!"

"Not *now*. Some other time." I point at his pants. "Take those off."

"No."

"You can't make love with your pants on. Hurry. Hurry."

Finally he opens his snap-open belt. He takes so long. I pull his zipper partway down. His dingle jumps out. "Stand up."

He does.

I pull his pants down.

He says, "Ouch!"

I pulls his underwear down.

He says "Ouch!"

I never saw anything so big. I'm staring at it. He's trying to step out of his pants. His shoes won't let him.

"We forgot to take off your shoes. Just leave them on. We'll sit on the floor."

He sits right down. His legs are spread out. I kneel down and hold his dingle. It is the warmest thing I ever touched.

"Make love?"

"Yes. First, I have to take my clothes off."

Something hits the door. Bang! I turn around. It's Mrs. Holloway's hand. "Get up!" she says. "Both of you!"

Oh dreary! We'll be in confinement forever!

"Get up!"

"Don't be mad."

Her mouth is wide like she's got something stuck in her throat.

Brendan is standing up with his pants around his shoes and his stupid dingle still sticking straight out at Mrs. Holloway.

Mrs. Holloway is staring at it.

"Go away," he says.

"Pull your pants and underwear up," she says back.

Delia comes and stands behind Mrs. Holloway. She's not smiling.

"Take her back to her room," Mrs. Holloway says.

Delia's frowning.

"Don't worry, Delia," I say to her.

Mrs. Holloway points at me. "Get out of here!" Her mouth keeps moving like she can't spit out a bad thing that was choking her. I hear a noise like a truck. She has the biggest mouth I have ever seen. I think the noise is coming out of her mouth. But it's not. It's coming from outside. It's coming from the sky.

"And you, young man, put your clothes back on and come with me!"

I don't care where she puts me. I don't care what she does with me. I don't care how long I have to stay here. I don't care if my mother comes to visit. I don't care if I never get to go shopping. I don't care if I never get to eat. I don't care if I have to live in the crafts room. I don't care about anything as long as Brendan is here.

"Get out of here!"

"We're going to get married."

She turns to Delia. "Take her out."

Delia holds my hand. I always go when *she* wants me to. The hall is very dark. "Damn it, Beatrice," she says, "what did you do that for?" I don't even answer. I'm smiling in the dark. Isn't that stupid for someone going to confinement? Maybe. I don't care. They can't stop me from marrying Brendan. I just have to figure out how to.

°◗◖° OLD GEEZER

Old Geezer sit here seeing this seeing that. See Horse Woman pull New Boob in Hoopy Room One. Old Geezer look with one eye open. New Boob been here only seem like minutes. What he be doing so bad? Old Geezer don't know.

She turn around.

Old Geezer look down at his queen. Queen be Horse Woman but she don't know it. Sit one whole month in the craft room making queen. Now move queen all way up to middle of board. Horse Woman stop behind sniffing but don't know it be she he be fingering. She ask Muscle Max did this one eat today. He say yes ma'am but he don't know. Max hiding someplace come breakfast time. Don't know about Old Geezer. Old Geezer don't eat mush they got here. Be for horses. Old Geezer don't say that. Old Geezer don't say that or he be in Hoopy Room Two. Put no words in air, afraid he be slipping out wrong ones.

Soon later she come back with Black Tit and Pretty Chick. Say to Black Tit I hope you see she take this pill and that. Black Tit say yes, Mrs. Holloway. Horse Woman give a whinny and put Pretty Chick to Hoopy Room Two, buck up against Hoopy Room One. Hoopy rooms got little windows. Got one floor mattress, no pillow. Got one chair, one table. Itty-bitty light bulb in top. Called crafts rooms. Little wooden games on table. No one play. Old Geezer got put there for not speaking. Lie on floor bed thinking how to make his pieces. Horse Woman come in some often and stick him with needle. Nice big-size hard ass. Old Geezer look and know she be his queen. Old Geezer himself be making self king. Think up the other ones too. Next day she come in with Muscle Max and say he's never going to talk, take him out of here. Take Old Geezer and give him tiny room. In night up there and day down here he think up pieces. Take one month before they let him use whittle knife. He been spotting females he decide be his pawns. First he whittle balsa with spoon. Put chain from Geezer arm to knife. Someone always watching. Maybe Max, maybe William. Someone.

Old Geezer retire from doing clean-up in Greyhound depot and start a checkers club in his place. All kids come and play. Now and then Geezer let one or other stay when rest go home. He do some finger fussing. Some Little Pretty tell her momma how much fun it be in checkers club. Tell too damn much. Little Pretty's momma come with fists up and say get out of neighborhood or I'll see you in jail.

Old Geezer then move in with sister. She beat on him since he was a tot. She see him now making naked lady chess pieces. Say I'm going to have you put away and take your pension, crazy man. Keep saying such. One day Old Geezer up and hit her with lamp. They put him in jail. Try make him talk. He never like talking to older ones, just kids. Got an itch that don't go away. Like to touch all sort of asses. Say nothing. Hollow Head Doc say he be too crazy for prison, better put him in mental hospital. They do that. Then close down hospital and he end here with all nice-size chicks. *Now* who be crazy?

Old Geezer do fine 'til Pretty Boob sit down and say why do you always play all by yourself, silent man? She stay and watch. And who watching Old Geezer's hands? No one. Old Geezer start playing on her with one hand only. Wait 'til no one else in the room and find way up Pretty Boob's leg. Soon as he touch up high Pretty Boob say you want to come in my room. He know she liking it. Her breathing is noisy. Now he have something to speak for. Old Geezer whisper go in your room and I be up soon. She go. Old Geezer be stupid. Can't wait. Get up too soon. Horse Woman see Old Geezer going down the hall sticking out in front and give him a whack that nearly kill. She say get into your room you old devil. Never do get to Pretty Boob's room.

Only pleasure he get now is Horse Woman coming in when he taking bath. Old Geezer get hard and that make her laugh. She don't mind it being hard when no one else can see. She say you could break down doors with that thing of yours. Old Geezer think he one day break down her door and pull down his pants. What happen? Maybe she say put Geezer-stick in me. Maybe she put Geezer in Hoopy Room all his life. He don't know. Thinking about things like that keep him from going to sleep too quick.

Old Geezer hear knocking from the Hoopy Rooms, one to other. Bung bung. Bung bung. Pretty Chick. Bung bung, bung bung. Horse Woman hear Pretty Chick be in there a week. Now other one. Bwop bwop. Bwop bwop. Geezer only one here can hear? Bung bung. Bwop Bwop. They be talking with fists. Old Geezer listen in.

Bung bung . . . bung bung.

Bwop . . . bwop bwop.

Old Geezer read knocks the way his daddy read the racing sheet. Geezer Daddy lost all money in racing track. Run away and leave Geezer with Momma and sister. Momma die soon. Geezer be in hands of sister. She be fifteen, he be ten. Both got to work. Geezer find job at the Greyhound carrying bags. Doing fine 'til she run off with some dandy man. Geezer all broke up, need company. See some ones he want but they all too young. Have a few here and there ones his age of seventeen now. No good. Twelve or thirteen be just about right. Find some in park. Do nothing but finger fussing. How he got started. Be more fun than fishing. Soon he having his checkers club.

Bung *bung* bung.

Bwop . . . bwop bwop.

Best Pretty Chick cool herself else she get a nude-whip in poop room.

Bung bung bung *bung* bung . . . bung *bung bung bung*!

That girl hornier than a crayfish in April. Old Geezer got to teach her not to talk too much. He know many tricks. Can teach her to read eyes. Some eyes roll up and say I go anyplace you want me. Geezer know. Else he be caught by age sixty-one or -three, whatever he be. Don't remember.

Eye-reading do her no good in Hoopy Room! What Geezer thinking?

Somebody else hear knocking and tell Horse Woman, 'cause here she come whumping with Max and pills. Open door to Hoopy Room Two. Old Geezer hear Pretty Chick say she want to go in the Hoopy Room One with the New Boob. Horse Woman tell her she be in Hoopy Room One all alone weeks if she don't stop knocking. Horse Woman give her pills, close door and open other one. Don't give New Boob pills, just take him out. Tell Max to tell William be sure he stay in own room. Tomorrow he get first-day go-around if he behave.

Time eat itself and Pretty Chick start knocking a soft church-bell knock:

Bung . . . bung . . . bung.

Any but a fool love Pretty Chick. Geezer love Pretty Chick. Do he know that? Know he love Pretty Chick's butt. He love someone once. Sister Marlene. She run off with a dandy man. He still dream her in all his nights. No finger fussing. No tongue fussing. He dream giving her a big house on a hill. He dream saving her in a lake. He dream finding her a truck. She never do come back. Write him letters from New Orleans once in a time. Geezer save all. He been trying to dream her out of his life. Who know how to do that? Geezer don't. He like having little pretties but he love Marlene still to now. Dreaming her just last night. Make his arms a cradle and take her to mountain in flood. Old Geezer know love bite his heart. Old Geezer know love like to stay. Who tell Old Geezer about love? Old Geezer don't love little pretties. Play with them. He know that. Geezer got to tell New Boob about love. How he do that? Show him on board. Point to New Boob and point to king. Point to Pretty Chick and point to queen. Make a story.

Bung . . . bung.

That girl don't quit. New Boob going have to be careful.

Geezer put king in corner. Going to point at New Boob, then at king. Put queen on board. Point at her, then at Pretty Chick. Move queen around. Move king, show him king can't get away. Maybe he be a Fool Boob and think Old Geezer saying run away. That not what the Old Geezer saying. Old Geezer saying don't get in trap to queen.

Pretty Chick look like movie girl. Don't have brain trouble she be in movies. Maybe she break that boy's heart. Broken heart better than empty one. Geezer never did hurt little pretties. Otherwise he be in jail. Put him ten minutes in Hoopy Room with Pretty Chick and he be in jail. Horse Woman only one besides little pretties make Geezer hard. Maybe sometime he get Horse

Woman let him do some finger fussing. Then she know it not so bad. Drive Geezer crazy thinking of all females falling asleep without him finger fussing.

Bung . . . bung.

Old Geezer always be moving pieces so they don't wonder what he be thinking. Move one over here. Sit and look at board for a time. Get up, walk around table. Look at board. Move another. Get up, come back this side, move another. All day same. William think Old Geezer smart as the wind. Think Geezer know what he doing. Geezer know just a little bit what he doing. Move this one this way and that one that way. Let this one jump, don't let that one. Know enough how to make it look like he playing chess. Know enough to fool William. Know enough to keep out of the Hoopy Rooms.

Bung . . . bung.

She thinks he be still out here?

Old Geezer stand up. Everybody stop when Old Geezer get up. He go over to the door of Hoopy Room Two. He turn his back to the Hoopy Room door. Old Geezer throw his foot back:

Wack! Wack! Wack! Wack! Wack!

Old Geezer go back to his bench. They thinking Old Geezer falling off himself. Old Geezer sit down, look back at this one and that one 'til they know he ain't falling off, 'til they get eyes out of him. Then he go again to pretending to play the game.

Old Geezer go around table seven, eight more times. Don't hear bungs. Pretty Chick sleeping? Can be. Old Geezer sit and think what it be like if New Boob in there putting hand up Pretty Chick's dress.

"Bren-*dan!*"

Oh oh. Pills not working.

"Brendan! I love you!" Coming through the wall like they be no wall. "I want to marry you! They can't stop us! But you have to love me! Tell me you love me! Shout it, Brendan! Shout so I can hear! 'I love you, Beatrice!' Do it now!"

Geezer waiting. Look around. See all the rest waiting.

"Brendan!"

Old Geezer hear himself breathing.

"Answer me, Brendan! I must know! Do? You? Love? Me?"

We all been waiting for the whumping steps and here they come!

Pretty Chick be a long time getting answer.

"You're hopeless, Brendan! You're hopeless!"

In come Horse Woman with Max and handful of needle saying open up Room One. He do and pull out Pretty Chick and she see needle and say, "I'll stop! I'll stop!" but Max twists her over his knee and Horse Woman lift up her dress and in through white stocking go needle. Pretty Chick fall like a blink and Max take her back to Hoopy Room One and drop her thump on mattress.

Old Geezer don't think of hand going up her now. Be ashamed what he was thinking. He think it again tomorrow though.

∘◖◗∘ WILLIAM

Max bullies; I persuade. I make no claim to ethical superiority. I'm not sure, in fact, that his methods aren't more humane.

Consider.

A resident smashes his plate on the dayroom table, producing three or four sharp-edged weapons, and then reaches down and picks up the largest, a jagged edge, squeezing it so tightly his hand begins to bleed. He stalks about the dayroom, wielding the make-shift dagger above his head, locates a victim and lunges with a clumsy stroke, nicking the innocent's forearm. Blood greets blood. The victim cries out.

Max or I, depending who's on duty, hear the shriek and come rushing (Max) or meandering (me) out of his place of retreat. Mine is the laundry room, where I'm likely to be sitting atop the washer-dryer reading a languid fiction. Max's is Mrs. Holloway's office, where he often naps, dreaming I suspect of sadomasochistic trysts starring himself, our huge black bus driver, Weathers (also known as Octopus), and Mrs. H.

Let's pretend it's Max whom the shriek has alerted. He enters the dayroom, measures the scene, then leaps upon the poor de-mented assailant, applying a neck lock, which he holds even after he sees the attacker's blade descend to the floor, holds and tightens until the creature begins to gurgle. He then trips him to the floor, where he tears a strip of cloth from his garment and secures his hand, ordering him to stay where he is. Only when the attacker is planted does Max turn to administer to the victim.

I, physical coward that I am, shape a different scene. I pause in the dayroom doorway, then begin to circle and feint, cajoling, cooing, saying absurd things ("Now, you really don't want to go on with that, do you?"), even lying ("If you stop now, you won't get into trouble"), elocuting until, after dancing him from wall to wall, I've hypnotized the fellow and disarmed him by reaching out and simply plucking the weapon away. "Now," I say, "let's do something about that cut of yours." Dumbly he looks down and notices that he's sprung a leak. He whimpers and hops and presses his hand against his pants. I wait until he turns his helpless eyes to mine. "Come," I say, "I'll take care of it."

Let's briefly evaluate.

My method, though more risky, is less dangerous, for there is always less risk when no struggle takes place. If my gamble works, the lives of observing residents tick on with little disruption. Mine is the quieter method and would return me sooner to my washer than Max's would him to Mrs. H's office.

Max's approach, on the other hand, reminds all patients that he will deal suddenly and mercilessly with future violators of House A's code of behavior. Despite his brutal ways, he, like Fortinbras, more quickly restores order and at least the illusion of tranquillity to the kingdom.

Why, then, don't I adopt or consider Max's approach?

Because, like so many of us enclosed here, I'm subject to the tugs of my own character, including, I'm afraid, the cowardice cited earlier. I walk softly and carry no stick at all.

That's all prelude to an incident that occurred yesterday involving the new resident, Brendan, and the client Beatrice. Brendan had been given a severe warning last night after exposing himself or allowing himself to be exposed and was put into a "crafts" room for a short time. When he was released he was confined to his room until this morning, when I was assigned to escort him through the facility and introduce him to its persons and places.

Immediately I was attracted to him, not because of anything he said but because of the way he responded to my entrance. I see more in the way a person sits, moves, gestures and looks about or doesn't look about, in how he listens and turns his head, in the little involuntary sounds he makes when he's startled, than I do in anything he or anyone else might present to advertise himself.

Brendan is a gentle bear.

He sat fully dressed on the edge of his bed. When I entered his room he turned with the look of a sheepdog who, having been given the command "Stay!" waits anxiously for a signal to herd. I wasn't, his falling eyes told me, the person he'd hoped to find, but in moments he straightened his back and politely waited for me to do or say whatever I was going to.

"You don't want to sit here all day, do you, Brendan?"

He shook his head.

"Then let me show you around the home."

Again he shook his head. "Wait for Poppa."

He'd given me a significant clue. I took it seriously and pursued its invitation. "Your poppa wants you to stay here and enjoy yourself."

He didn't reply.

His father, who was supposed to have accompanied him here, couldn't, having been hospitalized for some reason.

"Don't you think your poppa wants you to be happy here?"

"No care. Boombah want to *see* Poppa."

"Let's talk about that after we see what we have to see." I waited, leaning against the doorjamb, smiling in case he looked at me. He didn't turn but, after two or three minutes, stood and shuffled to my side, from where I felt him peering at my head like an otologist. When I sensed he was satisfied, I extended my hand toward the hallway. "Shall we . . . Boombah?" He smiled on hearing me repeat the name he'd called himself, then took a tripping step ahead of me. I caught up and gently laid my hand on his shoulder. "Let's go down and start in the dayroom."

Apparently there are no staircases in his own home, for when we got to the top of House A's he stopped and excitedly surveyed it. He then quickly stepped forward, threw his leg over the railing and hung on, looking at me for approval or maybe disapproval. I knew Mrs. Holloway would bellow at me if she saw him there.

The prospect troubled me but, more urgently, I wanted his affection. I nodded, and he loosened his grip and slid. He went too fast. His bottom struck the knob at the landing with a thump. "Ow-ee!" he said. Despite his pain and without seeking permission he went to and rode the lower stair rail as well. He looked up. "Again?" "No, sir," I said, approaching. "We're going to the dayroom." He waited until I reached the bottom of the stairs, then put out his hand and took mine.

The first person we encountered when we entered the room was droopy-eyed Flora Goss, who was deposited here twenty-six years ago, two years after my birth, by a sister or cousin or someone who could or would no longer care for her. At that time, our records show, she performed many domestic tasks like baking, quilting and sewing, and was classified as mildly retarded. House A pays no rewards for sanity, and she was soon given nothing but what passed and still passes for care, and has for a long time been listed among the "severes." Brendan spotted her on the floor inside the maroon curtains. I suppose I should say smelled her, for she was rocking forward and back while defecating noisily into her nightgown. Brendan did what all sensitive newcomers do, turned and covered his nose. From behind the leather sleeve of his jacket, his eyes found and questioned mine. *C'est la vie,* I shrugged back. I mean what could I tell him? *Get used to it, kid,* or *Ah, shrug it off. She greets everyone this way,* or, *The floor is bad, but you should see when they do it on the tables.* Observation is instruction. I signaled him forward and said, "Let's meet the others." I could have added, "The ones willing to be met." We moved forward, Brendan still pressing leather to nose.

The Geezer was amenable, amenable for the Geezer, that is. He's a small lean man with white hair and a face of wrinkled leather. Indulgently he raised one eye to see who'd bent over to peer from behind at his wooden chess pieces. "Do you play chess?" I asked Brendan. I pointed to the board. He shook his head. "No way." The Geezer made the pieces himself. They're squared-off and primitive. I've noticed resemblances. The frowning king might be the Geezer himself or maybe Max. And the queen's haughty stance imitates or is being imitated by Mrs. H. How much does the imagination add in? As I watched with Brendan I found in the scattered pawns reminders of other patients. But do I see whom I think I see? Working in a place like this, one becomes a little mad, or madder. Some of my nightmares lately would probably match those of Flora or even the Geezer. Where was I? Brendan. No. The Geezer. Wherever those pieces derived they fascinated Brendan, who'd now lowered himself until his nose was nearly touching one of the kings. I've seen the Geezer thrust his hand out like a dagger when someone came within a couple of yards of his private place at the end of the table. But now he studied the spectator, as absorbed by him as the newcomer was by the chess pieces. It became a still life, the two of them and the chess pieces, and was animated only when Brendan, I think because of the strain his awkward position was putting on his back, straightened up.

Sometimes the patients climb and clamor over a new resident, especially a young one, but no one was very friendly that morning, perhaps because of the stench Flora had delivered. To make a lesson for other potential public defecators, Mrs. H. discourages quick cleanups. Eventually someone will chide Flora, remove her nightgown and use it to wipe her. Flora will not be given another garment. She will undergo "behavior modification therapy," which means having to sit around naked for a period of time. I understand that practice (naked-punishment) is not used in other homes. Well, officially it's not used here either.

"Bren-*dan?*" It comes from Crafts Room Two. Brendan strikes out toward it.

Damn! "Brendan!"

He ignores me, reaches the very place I was told to avoid with him. I rush over, say too urgently, "Let's go. There's much more to see."

"Be-ah-triss in *there!*"

"She can't talk to you."

"Just talk *to* me!" he snaps back.

Through radar, spiritual detection, who knows what, she'd realized Brendan was on the other side. These people have powers most of the rest of us don't. Within seconds after one of the staff arrives each day, they'll detect a mood. ("Did you have a fight with your girl friend, William?" I had.) You ignore messages they deliver or soon you'll be in their territory, without maps and compasses. I can't explain it.

I take his hand, but he snaps it away and turns sharply:

"Why they can put *her* in that?"

What a lovely question! How do I answer? *Hey, kid, you think this is bad? Should have seen what they could do before Walter Fialkowski vs. State of Pennsylvania twenty-some years ago.* In truth, compared to other private facilities this place is Sunday. *Friend, I can tell you about places where your honeybun wouldn't just be confined, she'd be beaten.* But that answer, were he to understand it, would mislead him. But which is worse? A three-minute beating or a three-day confinement? Besides, beatings still take place here. If legislation were introduced which prevented confinement, Mrs. H. and other superintendents like her would still use it *and* ingeniously find newer and more effective punishments. That's my perhaps-too-cynical view.

He bangs on her door.

"Stop!" I say, to save not his ass but my own. "Let's see the sun porch." I reach out, touch, just barely, his arm, which he draws to his face, and swings back, striking me on the jaw, sending me over a sofa and onto the floor, where I land legs-up upside down.

Flora, on whose level I now reside, looks across the dayroom floor and smiles.

"Hurt?" Brendan says from a place I can't see.

The legs of Mrs. H. appear in the doorway. How horribly immense they look from this angle! She's smiling. I've never seen her smile.

Wait. She's not smiling. I'm upside down.

∘◡∘ VERA

At State Hospital they called me the Sergeant. Don't tell me it wasn't a term of endearment. I know that. But you can be damned sure it was a term of respect. In those days hardly anyone ever heard of community living. I walked around with a soup spoon in my pocket and didn't hesitate to crack a nut when necessary. Inexpensive prefrontal lobotomy I called it.

Some wet-ass doing an apprenticeship from Ohio State said to me once, "Hey Sarge, why don't you try to reason with them?" Like a mental institution was the college debating society. I stuck my chin in his nose and said, "Listen, Sonny, first thing you better learn is this ain't a goddamn popularity contest. Second is, if you don't bop a nut now and then, he's gonna end up bopping you. Understand?" He started spewing out some college-type reply but I walked away. Some people you talk to all day and they never learn. He ended up teaching abnormal psychology in some little college, where I guess he's telling his students you can chitchat with a slobbering retard coming at you with a chair.

Some of the liberals working in this place now joke about me—bet your ass I know who they are—the same ones who'd be up against the wall you-know-whatted if I didn't run things the way Patton ran his army. State centers and community homes aren't textbooks. They're real places full of people whose bodies and brains don't work right. You've got to tell them what to do and most of the time stand there and see that they do it.

Another thing. You never know who they're going to drag through that front door. I've got to be ready for all sorts at all times. Thursday, late, in stop two cops with a roly-poly Mongoloid and a court order saying he's assigned to here. No one tells me shit. I'm only here that night because Max is in the mood. Max is my chief social worker and a stud. That's that. I can't have him permanently because he's got a girlfriend. That ain't saying he'd go for me if he didn't. She must be a real ball-buster because he can't put out for me more than once a week. Anyway, we're in the storage room upstairs on a rolled-out mattress surrounded by all the crap the families bring in along with their loons and dump on us. Delia, who's in charge downstairs, knocks and says, "We've got a new one, Mrs. H." I say, "Take care of it, Delia. Max and I are trying to straighten something out in here." Max grunts a laugh and whispers, "Yeah. Me." Some other time I might of thought that was funny. Not then. Anyway, Delia tells me the cops have papers and want me to sign them. My luck. If I wasn't here, Max would have to do it. "Okay, okay," I say. "I'll be there in a minute." I don't have to comb out my hair because it's short like a man's. Or put on new lipstick because I never wear any. I just whip up my panties and go.

A mongoloid, seventeen maybe eighteen, is standing over in the corner near the front door with his back to me but I can tell at first look he needs a cleanup. He's shaking too, cold or maybe going to crack up or something. You ever deal with a mongoloid having a nervous breakdown, you remember. Bad stuff. "You okay?" I ask him. He doesn't answer but has a kind of fuck-you look on his face. He is, I find out from the cops, the one who ran away from the courthouse and was to be brought here as soon as they picked him up. While I'm looking over the papers, Max finally swagger-asses down the stairs. I go over to the new one and take a closer look. He's got quiver-mouth and smells like a garbage can but will make it through the night. I tell Max to get him some warm milk. "We'll clean him up in the morning."

Delia's still hovering around. I call her P.D. for Public Defender. She's always talking about residents' rights. She's got a face black as coal, but I swear it turns pink when I try to get her pissed by saying things like, "What rights, Delia? The ones over thirty-five can run for President. Which one you want to nominate?" Sometimes I get pissed. Last night I said, "Ain't you got enough trouble with your own people? Half of them never make it out of the eighth grade. They're gonna need education if they're gonna take over Africa." She just smiles that misty smile of hers. She hardly ever lets me or anyone else think we're ruffling her feathers.

"So what do you want?" I ask her.

"Before you came downstairs, he was calling for his father. Shouldn't I give the father a call?"

I'm still holding the court order and the transfer papers. I check them, then push them at Delia. "Where does it say we're supposed to call anyone?"

"I don't know if it says we should. But I thought . . ."

I stick my hand on her shoulder and say, "Someday, honey, you might be running a place like this. Not that I'm wishing it on you. One of the first things you're gonna learn, if I don't get it into your head right now, is do what you're supposed to do, do it well, but do *only* what you're supposed to do. Understand?"

"But . . ."

"But me no buts. You may think you're doing the retards or their families a favor when you do something you're not required to do but you'd be wrong. Listen."

I tell her about this old fog at the state school name of Morton Sanderson who couldn't, like a lot of them, maneuver very well and had to be carried up stairs. A social worker name of Jessup decided to build a steep ramp and fit it onto the three steps leading from the main part of the ward up to the dayroom where Sanderson often came and went. Jessup left a wheelchair beside the stairs so someone, usually Jessup himself, could push Sanderson up and down. He'd often leave Sanderson to do other things. On his way out he'd say, "Morton, you enjoy the TV. I'll check back every so often." Well, Sanderson had to piss and Jessup wasn't in the dayroom. He decided to take it down the ramp by himself. He got the brake off and wheeled himself over to the ramp. His hands were too weak to control the wheels and the chair went whizzing down and hopped across the room, throwing him into the wall. His face was all broken and splattered. Now, his two brothers, who never came to visit him, found out about the accident. They had some specialists look at their brother's face, then sued the state. The state lost and had to fork over $400,000.00, not to Morton but those brothers, who were also his guardians.

"How many times afterward you think they came to visit?" I say. She didn't know.

"None. Jessup, of course, was canned and is still paying his part of the damages."

Her pink is up. She's in an arguing mood but can tell I am too. She lets it drop.

Tucker came to Hartsville a few months after me, and one of the first things he talked about was the soupspoon, which I was then still carrying and even using now and then. "Vera," he said, "the approaches have changed." We were having lunch in his office. One thing he did which everyone appreciated was invite home managers, one by one, to have a brown-bag lunch in his office. "The state institutions permit a good deal of authority to be exercised by mental health professionals like you and, as you know even better than I, they often need such authority." He gave me some stats I never *did* know, about the number of nurses, social workers and clients, even a few doctors, who'd been attacked by clients. "The main reason for the change of emphasis to community-based services is the prospect of improved care for the developmentally disabled, and that includes not exactly less authority for supervisory professionals like yourself but, let us say, a different kind of authority." I worried about what he might be getting at and said, "I doubt you can run a home without a supervisor being like a general." He smiled one of those nodding reassuring smiles of his and said, "I completely agree. Authority is authority. I'm only hoping we can all start thinking about it in a different way." I told him I didn't know what he meant. He nodded again and said, "You're under the direct scrutiny of politicians, relatives and people who live in neighborhoods around the homes—nearly everyone. You're—we're all—going to have to be careful." I told him that the first thing I do with a new patient (which he later suggested I refer to as "resident" or "client") was let them know who's boss. "As far as I'm concerned," I said, "that's just as necessary here as at the state centers." He clapped his hands like a seal and said, "You bet it is. Your role *must* be established. I'll support you in that at all times. I'm merely suggesting that our methods be, how shall I say it, a little less direct." I told him I wasn't the subtle type. He laughed and said, "Ah, but you can be." I shook my head. "I'm forty-two years old, Mr. Tucker. Been in the system twenty-three years, mostly at big institutions. I think you're trying to get a tiger to change her stripes." His head was going forward and back like a rocking toy. "Not at all, not at all," he said. Then, with a puff of excitement, he asked, "Do you mind if I tell you a story?" He was the boss and didn't need my permission. "Shoot," I said.

"I've got a lap spaniel. I call it Thrombus. When I bought it as a pup, the breeder taught me how to use a newspaper to slap it when it did something wrong. I used the newspaper for a while, but soon the dog would see me going for the paper and run upstairs or out into the yard through its exit hole. I wasted time getting the paper, then chasing Thrombus and finding her. Once I twisted my ankle coming down the stairs after her. After that I decided not to go for the newspaper. I just pointed, aiming my finger right at the dog's nose. Watch." He brought his hand slowly up, set it between his eyes, then popped the forefinger at me and stared over it. He didn't say anything. I started to feel real uncomfortable and looked away. "You see," he said. "Now, if I kept doing that every time you did something I didn't approve of, you'd soon stop doing it, wouldn't you?" I nodded but said, "I can't go around House A all day sticking my finger out at patients." I quickly corrected myself. "I mean clients." He leaned back. "Correct, Vera, but—" he crossed his arms—"think about what you *can* do, short of physical punishment." "You mean stuff like withholding privileges?" "Exactly!" he said. I named other punishments, including withdrawal of reading, picnic, and TV privileges, confinement to room, even isolation. He nodded to each and, when I finished, he said, "As long as you can get the treatment team to agree and show a constructive reason for what you do and apply your methods judiciously and document, document, document, you won't have problems. We call it behavior modification." Like I told him, I'm not the subtle type, but out of that conversation came my idea for the crafts rooms. After a while I got rid of the soupspoon. For a while it was like not having a hand.

When my first time came to hire an assistant, three applied. One was this mannerly divorced woman with two kids, both in high school, and some nurse's training, and another was a Baptist guy with a limp and a green birthmark on his cheek who was studying to be a preacher and had experience as a nurse's helper in the county hospital, and one was Max. He had been a bodyguard but never had been near a hospital or community home or even a loon. When I took a look at him, I said to myself, *I want this big hunk around here.* Call him my bimbo if you want. I don't care. I told Tucker the patients were getting bigger and tougher to bathe and such and said we needed someone here with muscle on him. He went along. I told my sister, Maggie, who's in the National Organization for Women, why I hired the guy. She said, "You act just like a man. Doing to men what they did to us isn't what the liberation movement is all about."

Her opinion.

She may be my sister but she don't know me from Mother Goose. How could she? She was the pretty one whose problem growing up was keeping guys' hands off her. I inherited our old man's ugly big chin and our mother's bulbous nose and a big appetite. In school they called me Hairy Hilda after some woman in a story we had to read. I learned quick and early my problem was the opposite of Marla's and by the time I was eleven or twelve had worked up some methods for getting guys that no pretty chick ever has to learn. You learn to kiss a guy the right way behind his ear, and he soon forgets what you look like. Hey, with the lights out we all look the same. Every guy in Chillicothe soon learned I was a great lay. What they never figured out—I used to wish just one, any one, had—is that I'd have been an even greater wife. They call me Mrs. but I've never been married.

The breaks.

Anyway, Max turned out to be an easy hit. In a way he's like my sister, only with females. "You want me? Stand in line and take a ticket." People make the mistake of thinking guys who look like sexy movie stars make love the way sexy movie stars do in the movies. They usually don't. The expectation is too much. The so-called sexy guy can't take the pressure. Someone like me comes along and says, "Relax. Around your girlfriend, you got to perform. Around me you can relax." The method worked on Max, especially at first.

"What kept you so long?" I ask him when he finally gets back to the storage room.

"The new one started mumblin' about what someone named Eleanor told him. It sounded all screwed up. I didn't get a word of it." He opened his belt and added, "This dude really has problems."

"Think about where we work and what you just said," I tell him as he slides his jeans down.

It isn't until he gets his bikini underwear down that he gruffs out a laugh and says, "Oh, yeah. I see what you mean."

I doubt it. I fondle him. Nothing happens.

He trys to make an excuse. "Sometimes when I get interrupted . . ."

"Bullshit!" My panties are off but not my dress. "Wait here." I go down the hallway to the bathroom.

Flora Goss is on the crapper. "Oh oh oh oh," she says, all panicky, as though a mugger had just walked in on her.

"Ignore me, Flora," I say. "This has nothing to do with you."

As I unlock and search the medicine chest, I think we should get a picture of her going by herself and send it to people who criticize community home care. She couldn't be trusted to relieve herself by herself when she came into the system years ago. Now you can leave her alone on the toilet. The only time she goes on the floor is when she's excited. Finally I find what I want and go back to the storage room.

"What's that?" says Max, who's standing there wearing his shirt like he's waiting for an Army physical. I take the lid off the jar of medicated petroleum jelly and grab his limp device and start to rub.

Nothing happens.

"That feels good," he says.

"Not to me." I keep rubbing but the damned thing gets smaller and limper. "What in hell's wrong with you?"

"I'm nervous all of a sudden."

"Nervous? Would you be this way if that slut of yours were doing this?" I'm losing my cool and know it. That's the worst thing I can do. But I go on doing it. "Next thing you'll be telling me is you have a headache."

"As a matter of fact, Vera . . ."

"You're worthless!"

From somewhere comes a screeching voice: "Miffuff Holloway!" A voice I soon recognize as that of Flora. Now what? "Miffuff Holloway!" Closer. "Miffuff Holloway!"

"What?" I shout.

Her voice is at the door now. "Beatriff is . . . in a room wiff . . . a fat boy and . . . whrrrppp . . . whrrppp . . . whrrppp . . ."

Her and her speech impediment! "Spit it out!"

". . . and their book . . . whrrppp . . . their book . . . whrrpp . . ."

Their book? "What book?"

". . . whrrppp . . . naked."

Buck naked. Oh, Jesus! "Let's go!" I say to Max.

He kicked his shorts under something and must go to his knees to search for them.

Worthless.

I fling open the door and go.

∘👄∘ DELIA

No one pushed us around in prison any worse than Max and Mrs. Holloway manhandle the so-called residents here. The two of them just bullied little Beatrice through the hall and down the front stairs. I wondered why Mrs. H. about ten minutes ago told me to pull back the red curtains to the dayroom. Now I know she wanted the ones in there to catch the action with Beatrice and feel chills. Prisoners protest. Retarded people hide under tables, suck their thumbs, or piss on the floor. No one's sucking or pissing yet. They're on their way to the front porch to watch Max and Mrs. H. put Beatrice into the house sedan.

One resident who didn't see the action is the new one, Brendan. He's in Crafts Room Two, has been banging his fist against the wall in there all morning. Beatrice called to him as they were dragging her down the stairs, and he started shouting and trying to kick the door off. I can still hear him all the way out here on the porch:

"No take *her* away!" Fwampp! Fwampp!

All that's going to do is get him an extended sentence.

Just after I started working here, a state law was passed that forbade the locking of a resident in a room unless there is a doctor, nurse, social worker, or some other authorized person in there with the resident. Mrs. H. removed the locks from the confinement rooms but had a meeting and warned residents not to try to open the door when they were confined. She told Brendan not to try to leave. "Or you'll suffer the consequences," she said. Despite the banging, he's complied just like the others. What he's being put through is what she calls First Stage Behavior Modification. It gets worse.

They're holding Beatrice down on the middle seat, but she's fighting back with elbows and feet.

Wait until she sees her quarters at House B. Octopus drove her personals over this morning. He said Norman Thorn, the supervisor there, had him put them in "the mouse hole." Each Victorian house in this part of the country has one, a small room once used by the house servant. The "mouse hole" at House C has one tiny window so high up you can't see out of it. Two people can't be in there without bumping each other but, believe it or not, it meets the minimum required size. It figures that's where they'd put Sweet B. The main game around here is harassment. Beatrice is being taken from the second biggest room in A to the smallest in B. Thinking and acting for yourself is a big offense. Anyone shows independence and we're supposed to knock it out of them. I try to knock it into them. Otherwise they become vegetables, the ones who weren't already vegetables when they got here.

Last time I worked four to midnight the residents were given little lumps of creamed beef slush on toast. I tasted it. Terrible stuff. Most of them didn't finish their meals. Around eight o'clock many were complaining that they were hungry. I'd just gotten paid and decided to order pizzas. Flora Goss right away reminded me that there was a no-eating-between-meals rule. Several others nodded like chickens bobbing for seed. I leaned toward them all and whispered, "Sometimes you have to break rules. This is one of those times." They all popped backwards together like they'd been practicing the move, then made gasping sounds. I could read their thoughts: *That nigger woman sure does say some strange things!* and, *If we don't follow rules, what do we follow?* and, *I can't do anything without rules.* Maybe they were just my thoughts. Anyway, I leaned closer and said, "For some people in the world, rule-breaking is no good. For you folks it's as important as . . . your goddamned lives." I got a few stupid looks and a couple of nods. You never know what gets through. We ended up having sausage pizzas with green peppers and mushrooms and free orange drinks and colas. Following that there was a lot of contented burping and a few of the usual squabbles and after that everyone went peacefully to bed. A few even thanked me. The supervisor that night was Max, who found out about the pizzas too late to stop anything. He gave me a stern warning; then, to cover his ass, told me to get rid of the three pizza boxes and all other evidence like napkins and such. I did. Later I found the hypocrite eating a piece of leftover pizza. We talked for a few minutes about something unmomentous like baseball or the weather and then, for some reason, I said, "One of these days there's going to be a rumble in this place."

He gave me one lazy eye over the top of his pizza slice. If the subject isn't sex, Max has little interest. "That right?" he said.

"A first-class revolt."

He bit hard into the crust and the eye closed.

"They're going to pull out our hairs and stick broom handles up our asses and hang Mrs. H. from the flagpole."

"Guess you'd like that, huh, Delia?"

A serious discussion would not take place. I got out of there before either slow eye made another move.

They've managed to still Beatrice, Max by wrapping her arms together behind her, then cuffing her wrists in one of his meaty fists, Mrs. H. by reaching to the floor and using both hands to lock the ankles.

Do any of the leering residents on the porch see more than subjugation?

Are any of them inspired by the battle Beatrice has put up?

Why do I myself care?

I don't know.

When I saw them manhandling her down the stairs, I was angry. Now I wonder why I didn't protest or offer to talk her down.

Shit. The scene was clear until I put myself in it.

Octopus follows an instruction from Mrs. H. and drives off.

In come the residents, their shoulders fallen, eyes passing over the purple hall carpet with its medieval scene of knights and ladies and squires and shepherds. They shuffle back to the dayroom, where Brendan still persistently thumps at the walls of his cell, though less frequently now, less loudly. In one of those always surprising outbursts you come to expect in this place, Little Willie, the last one off the porch, gaily sings a few lines from the old song, "My Heart Belongs to Daddy," ending it by falling to one knee and throwing out his hands, and bellowing to me, "Da-aa-aaa-aa-aaaaady!" None of the others turn or clap or give any recognition. I'm a few feet from the window.

He grins at me. "That good, Delia? That good?"

"Yes," I say. "It put some joy into the afternoon."

"Hee!" He turns and dances into the dayroom.

William stands by the banister scratching his crotch. He went off duty half an hour ago but has hung around. Why? Don't know. He witnessed the Beatrice adventure and acted as if he were watching water run out of a faucet.

"Hey, William," I say, "you been bit by the numb bug?"

"What are you talking about?"

"Never mind. What did you think of Beatrice and the bullies?"

He turns away and shrugs. "They had to do it, but . . . it wasn't nice." He never comes down on one side or another. Because of that I gibe him.

Now I say, not gibing, "One of these days they're going to take their lives into their own hands."

"Who?"

"The residents. Who else?"

He shakes his head. "No way."

Behind us Brendan still thumps.

"I'm going back there and talk to the new one. Keep thinking about what I said. When it happens, it'll be like popcorn in a hot pan with no lid."

He gives me one of his lazy smiles. "About the time it starts snowing on my parents' house in St. Petersburg."

"Wait and see." I throw a wink that's meant to tell him I know shit he doesn't. "When the time comes you're going to have to quit sitting around rubbing your nuts. You're going to have to make a choice."

"Fuck choices," he says, turning away.

I stop, disappointed. "That's the glummest comeback you ever gave me. Where's that more or less quick wit of yours? Your brain go off when you punched out?"

"Uh uh. It's . . ." He looks toward the front door, which hangs half-open. ". . . Queen Bitch. She wants to talk to me about what happened yesterday in the dayroom. I hear from Max she's going to get Tucker to have me transferred to House C."

The profoundly retarded are in House C. They need a lot more help than the "milds" or the "severes" who are here and in B.

If I'd been a tourist dropping in from Mars or Des Moines, I might ask, "Why would you take someone you think showed incompetence and put them in the house that demands the most skills?" But I came from prison, not Mars or Des Moines. I have no need to ask. "I'll bite my fingernails for you."

"Thanks."

About all you need to work in a place like this is a nose and a high school diploma. I'm not even sure about the diploma. I had one, or so they think, because of Judy Barg, night warden at the prison.

Judy had three kids and what looked like a happy life. It wasn't. Her husband had given her the kids but no affection. She told me that after we got to be friendly and she hired me as her office assistant. Turns out I was soon the husband's substitute. We exchanged troubles on the warden's sofa every night. One night she said, "In all the ways that matter most, you're a better companion than Bernie, even at his best." She was filling a big need for me too. We began to kiss and caress each other. We became lovers. One night she said, "I'm going to do something for you." The next day she did. She created a new record for me. It showed me not as a prisoner but as Administrative Clerk II. Because of a procedure called Periodic File Review, she kept my official prisoner's record intact both in the prison computer and her office file drawer. "But when you write for a reference, put 'Attention: Judith Barg,' and I'll be sure to send the records that show you as a prison employee only." I asked her if she was worried about the risk she was taking. She said, "When you love someone you take risks."

Because of her I may never have to explain that I'd been sent to prison for using a frying pan to cause brain damage to an ex-boyfriend who was trying to rape me.

The residents are milling around the dayroom, imagining what Max and Mrs. H. might be doing to Beatrice now. I've got time for the little task I decided to perform when I saw Beatrice being pulled down the stairs. I press my face against the door to Crafts Room One.

"Hey! Brendan?"

His thumping has let up in the past couple of minutes. His foot must be tired. "What?"

"I'm Delia. Beatrice's friend. I work here. I've got a few things to tell you."

"Where they put *her?*"

"I'll get to that. First . . ."

"Want Beatrice. No want *you*."

"Don't be impatient. Listen. I'm going to find you a way to communicate with her. Understand?"

"See Beatrice?"

"I didn't say see her. Understand? Communicate. Bring her messages. Take messages back to you."

"Where *she* is?"

"Another house. Like this one. Not far away. Now listen. The more noise you make, the more you fuss, the worse it's going to be. I mean they might keep you in there for a week. Who knows? Stop banging your fists and feet."

"Want to go out of here. Too hot."

"If you want to get out, pay attention. Are you listening?"

He doesn't answer.

"Brendan?"

"Listening!"

"Tomorrow. I'll bring you back a message tomorrow. You should be out by then. If you stay quiet in there, they'll worry that you're sick or died. Stay quiet and they'll let you out. Now, you want me to tell Beatrice that you love her?"

"No *love* her. Want her talk to me and sit on me."

"Okay. I'll tell her that."

"Where's Poppa?"

He might be dying. Why else would he be in intensive care? I can't say this to Brendan. I say, "He's sick and doesn't want you to get sick."

"Want to go home."

"You can't go home. You ran out of a courtroom or something. They're keeping you here for a while." Forever, if Tucker has his way. He wants healthy people for his little operation. There are a lot of truly needy people out there waiting to get into homes, needing to, but they can't put boxes together and therefore didn't fit neatly into his plan. Tucker wants them, too. But not now. Now he wants people like Brendan who not only can put boxes together but, once trained, can do a lot of enforcing too.

"Sarah come see *me*?"

"I told her you're here. I'm sure she'll come by at visiting time." Maybe she'll come when it's not visiting time. Few relatives or friends visit anyone here. Those who do rarely drop in by surprise, though they can. They see little.

"See Eleanor?"

"Who's Eleanor?"

"Friend."

"Listen. You stop thinking about those people and, I don't know, count fire engines or something. Just keep still 'til they let you out of there. I'll be back tomorrow. But I hope by then you'll be in your room."

"What *your* name?"

"Didn't I tell you? Delia."

"Deer-ya."

"It'll do. Talk to you tomorrow."

William, I now notice, has been sitting on the captain's bench in the outer hall, peering into the dayroom, watching me. I approach him, hoping not to have to explain or lie.

"What were you doing, Delia, getting your revolution started?"

"He's quieted down, hasn't he?"

He rolls his eyes. "You didn't answer my question."

"Can't unless you tell me which side you're going to be on when it starts."

He smiles. "Don't know yet."

I let out a laugh, a long rolling laugh, the kind William calls my big nigger-momma laugh. "I think you'd be a good spy, William."

He nods, letting me know he's proud of putting himself wherever his own ass is best protected.

A tall woman comes walking through the front doorway without even knocking. She's about thirty with a long determined stride. Comes right over to William and me.

"I'm here to see Brendan Flynn," she says. "I'm his teacher, Sarah Fuller."

·◯· SARAH

She hesitated after I asked to see Brendan, then turned her head slightly back, toward the open door to the dayroom, where several residents were milling back and forth and chatting nervously. She then turned further, to a young man in blue jeans and weathered flannel shirt seated on the captain's bench against the wall behind her.

He'd just said something to her I couldn't hear.

"Why not?" she said.

"Policy." As he raised his head and nervously fingered back the long hair over his ears, he caught my curious gaze. "Sorry," he said, giving me a little bow. "I'm William. I guess, for the time being, I'm stuck with being the person in charge, until Mrs. Holloway . . ."

"Wait a second," said the woman, cutting him off. "You're off duty now."

The young man's eyes flashed toward her. "The house regulation says that the senior person present should assume supervisory duties in the absence of the supervisor." He spoke tensely. "I don't *want* to be in charge. I . . . just am." He shrugged toward me with apologizing eyes. "It just may not, at this time, be in Brendan's best interests, for you to, you know, see him."

The woman mumbled something and turned away.

"I hate to pull this on you, Delia, but, under the circumstances, I can't afford . . ." He turned from her. "Never mind. I've made the decision."

The woman's voice had seemed familiar, but until William spoke her name I didn't match it to the one I'd heard a half hour earlier in the hospital phone booth:

"Mr. Flynn can't come to the phone?" she'd said.

"No, he can't. Who's this?"

"Delia, a worker at Community Home A for the mentally retarded. You a friend of the family?"

"Yes. I'm Brendan's teacher."

"I called the Flynn number. Woman from their church who was there said he was in the hospital."

"Why are you calling him?"

She hesitated, then said, "Brendan was brought in here last night. Picked up in River City. I thought his father should know."

"My God!"

Why hadn't the police called Joseph? Maybe they'd tried to. Maybe no one was in the store or at the apartment. But someone from the church was there when the social worker had called. Before I could ask the caller another question, she hung up.

"Where," I now wanted to know, "is Mrs. Holloway?"

"At another home, transferring a resident," said William.

Delia turned to him. "Look. It's time for me to take a break. If you *are* in charge, you watch the place for a few minutes. Okay?"

"Sure," he said, sounding grateful. "I don't care." He gave me a quick smile and her a lingering fretful one. "Go ahead."

"There's a coffee shop on the corner," she said, nodding toward the front door. "Mrs. Holloway should be back in fifteen minutes."

"I'd say . . . a half hour," William inserted.

"All right, all right," she replied, pointing me toward the front door. "Will you come along?"

I knew I should. "Yes," I said.

After removing a gray windbreaker from a hook near the door, she moved ahead of me with a long stride, leading me across the tottery porch, down the wooden steps and across the badly cracked walkway to the sidewalk. "William's sometimes a nervous kitten," she said, closing the black iron gate behind us. She was tall, nearly my height, five-eight, wore pale green slacks and low-heeled shoes. Her movements were fluid and confident, the movements, I thought, of an athlete.

After calling her, I'd called Chief Walters. Yes, he told me, Brendan had been picked up in River City. "Found him digging through trash containers with some bag lady," he said, his tone puffing with amusement. He paused as if giving me time to puff too, then said, "Guess he'll be better off eating what they serve in the home. Looks like he'll be there a while." He waited as if he expected me to react. When I didn't, he went on, "Anyway, that's where we delivered him, per the judge's order." Again he waited. This time I asked if I could stop in and see Brendan. "Hell if I know," he said. "Why'n't you just go over and talk to the woman who operates the home?"

Before leaving the booth I'd called the cardiologist Doctor Grable had called in after Joseph was taken to the hospital. His name is Carl Stone. I'd heard he was the oldest doctor in the Hartsville area. I fed the phone an extra quarter before he finally came on. "So you're that teacher Joe mentioned," he said in a voice that reminded me of dry branches crackling. "Hope your day isn't as busy as mine. What can I do you for?" Sensing impatience, I reduced a number of general questions to a few specific ones.

"Did he have a heart attack?"

"That's what the blood tests show."

"How much heart damage is there?"

"Too early to know anything about that. I'll know more tomorrow."

"Is he going to be in intensive care for . . . well, for how long?"

"Couple of days, I'd say. No need to keep him there if the EKG test doesn't say we need to. We'll probably put him in a regular hospital room tomorrow or the next day."

He was reciting. These were the sort of questions he'd answered a thousand times. "Maybe he can go home in a week or so."

"That soon?"

"Why not?"

I'd noticed one youthful onlooker fidgeting in a lounge chair near the single phone booth. I then saw another pacing about, making abrupt movements, glancing into the booth with annoyed looks. I fought off the impulse to step out, say sarcastically, "Go ahead. Your calls are surely more important than mine." Anger had been rising, maybe because of the news about Brendan, maybe over Doctor Stone's impatience. I now took my time lifting the phone book from the shelf beneath the phone and looking up the number at Community House A. Only after finding it did I realize it might be best not to announce my visit. I watched the two little boys posing as men for a few seconds, then dropped the phone book, letting it twist on its chain. "All yours, kids," I said stepping out.

If Joseph was sent home, who would take care of him? Ought I begin lining up helpers? His sister-in-law? People from his church? Others? Would he have to hire a private nurse? If so, could he afford one? Was he insured at all?

Delia opened the squeaky door to an old diner that stood on the corner of Maple and Western, a block from the community home. I'd seen the place many times but had never been inside. On a sign that angled out from above the door was the word HAMBURGS painted in white against a faded red background. Delia led us to the counter, from which several flies politely removed themselves as we sat down. A thin wrinkled woman—seventy, I guessed—sat at the farthest of four small tables along the windows. She lowered the newspaper she'd been reading and stood with a groan.

"Mud, Julia?"

"That's right."

" 'Bout your friend?"

"How do you want your coffee?" Delia said.

"Oh, cream and a little sugar."

"Sweet dishwater," the woman corrected as she moved with stiff steps to the coffee machine where the container showed about a quarter of a pot.

Delia pressed her large weathered hands together and, looking at them, said, "Better start by telling you Brendan's in a confinement room back there."

"What?" I said, startled. "Why?"

Eyes still on her hands, she reported what had happened since Brendan was brought in the night before, beginning with the scene she encountered when she arrived at Brendan's room and ending with Brendan's placement in confinement after he'd tried to speak to his new friend following her confinement. "There are always bizarre happenings at the house," she said, turning to me for the first time since we'd arrived at HAMBURGS, "but I think we've now got something more: a situation that amounts to the unstoppable force meeting the immovable object." She nodded. "In fact, I think there are two unstoppable forces."

"Brendan and Beatrice?"

"Right." She took a sip of the coffee the old woman had set before her, then closed her eyes tightly. It smelled burnt and looked like the name the woman had given it. Mine was only slightly lightened by the cream she'd put in for me.

The woman pressed her elbows onto the counter and leaned into the conversation. Across the top of her plain white apron the name Opal was sewn in pale green. "Things get worse before they get better," she said.

"Get worse for sure," said Delia, turning her troubled eyes to me. "Mrs. H. has overreacted. There was no need for either confinement. And having Beatrice transferred to House B was a radical move, even for her."

"How long will she keep Brendan confined?"

"Probably just overnight. She knows someone will be dropping by to see him."

"Joseph or me."

"Wish some of those lunch regulars of mine behaved half as nice as those ones come in here with you sometime, Julia," Opal said. "Don't mean you," she went on, turning to me. "The ones from the home."

Delia delivered a nod that seemed intended to cap both my remark and Opal's. She was resting her eyes on the blackboard menu behind Opal. "No reason the two of them shouldn't have been in the same room." She now drew her gaze inward to me. "Is there?"

It seemed to be a question she could answer better than I, yet her tone told me she didn't know or wasn't sure. None of her remarks had been frivolous or academic. I knew this was a serious question and I gave her the only answer I could. "I can't think of any."

But *she* could. "Beatrice might have forced herself on him. She's capable." She drank cautiously from her white mug. "If she did, putting her in confinement won't change her. That's for sure." She shook her head. "And sending her to House A is even worse. It's run by a flophead named Norman Thorn. He's forgetful, erratic and says some of the most amazing things. Wouldn't be surprised to find out he has Alzheimer's disease. How else can anyone explain the way he acts?" She looked at Opal. "The later in the day I come in here," she said, "the worse this stuff is."

Opal twisted her mouth into a smile and winked at me.

I asked about Beatrice and learned that she'd been in the home for several years. "Abandoned there by her mother," Delia said. "She doesn't need to be confined. Just doesn't."

At a countable few times I've met someone whose very presence from the beginning inspired such trust that I quickly dropped my guard. A boy from a different high school happened to sit next to me at a basketball game, and by half-time we were trading feelings, about parents, teachers, sports and even sex, as though we'd been friends since infancy. This Delia—was it her unblinking eyes? her confident stride? her frankness?—had from the moment I stood before her drawn out of me a desire to share my uncertain emotions about Joseph, Brendan, even, I confess, myself. The desire was two-edged. I wanted to know how she felt, especially about the situation at the home.

"If Beatrice could find her way out of the system," she went on, "I'd get out, too. I don't stay because I can't get a better job. And I don't stay because I'm a Mother Theresa. I'm not."

"Except to her?"

She shook her head. "It's some kind of protective feeling. Got to see that little wonder out into the world. It's like I'm carrying a baby."

"I feel something similar, about Brendan."

She pushed the coffee cup aside. "Let's try to get you back for some visiting time. William will have let Mrs. H. know you came by. I'll bet Brendan's back in his room."

I'd been on tours of each of the homes but wasn't familiar with the visiting times. "I can't visit during the day whenever I want?"

"There are no hard rules. They prefer afternoon hours, two to four, and evening hours, seven to nine. The rule of thumb is 'resident's best interests.' "

"Who decides that?"

She closed her eyes. "Who do you think?"

"What about nonparents, nonguardians?"

"She screens them. Being his teacher will help."

Opal's eyes had been sliding from one of us to the other. "I got to admit one thing, Delia," she said.

Delia grunted.

"That coffee machine has seen better days."

Delia nodded as if the observation were as pertinent as anything that had been said. She then reached out and put her large hand on mine. "I've got a good feeling about you."

I nodded, not to verify her feeling but to let her know she'd produced the same in me.

"You two want to stay for supper? I got in some real good ground round back there."

"No, thanks," said Delia.

Within a few seconds we were gone.

ᵒ◉ᵒ NORMAN

These old houses were converted for the use of something like a dozen residents and now we have—how many is it here in House B? Twenty. Twenty-one if I count the one-eyed man from Pakistan who may have to be moved to Cleveland to be nearer his family. Wait. Twenty-two. I forgot that young lady from House A who's been sobbing like a hyena in the servant's room—former servant's room I should say—since, let's see, Thursday? No. Friday. Actually, she's gotten better. At first the sounds were so irritating I had to ask my housekeeper, Mrs. Tottabunda, to go into the kitchen and make my coffee. She, by the way, wouldn't do it. Which is another story.

Quite honestly, though I am owner and proprietor here, I don't like being around the mentally retarded or even social workers. Myra, my wife—former wife, she's been dead for eight years—and I took over this place some eighteen-was-it years ago? No. Seventeen. We thought it might not be a half-bad investment. She was then a substitute nurse at Cleaver County Hospital and I'd been marked for selective early retirement at Third Northwest Bank. We wanted a business of our own. But . . . oh, my Lord! We didn't know we'd have to take care of people urinating in bed or on the floor in the middle of the night or . . . or someone dropping all his food on someone else's lap. Or another wandering off and getting onto a bus for where was it? Lubbock, Texas? Good Lord! We wanted to run a simple Mom-and-Pop community home. We soon found you don't always get the kind of residents you'd like. Yes. Mom and Pop soon weren't enough, I can tell you. I think all that running around brought on Myra's gynecological condition. It affected my eyes. And after we came under the jurisdiction of the new county board, there were so many bills! So many letters! So much paperwork! We needed help. We got social workers! Sometimes I wonder what trees they fall out of. They come in drugged or drunk or just plain sleepy. Some don't come in at all. One failed his dope test last week, leaving me with . . . let's see. One, two, three, four. Four. (But no. She quit.) Three then. I'm not good with numbers. Three. Three of us, no, no, back to four counting me, having to cover twenty-one, no, twenty-two patients. Day and night.

Tucker came to the system. Tucker began consolidation. One day Tucker said to me, "A computer would ease your work, Norman." He tried to get me to use my operating budget to purchase one. I thought . . . actually said I didn't need a computer. I needed another social worker, inefficient though most of them are. I hate computers. They're one reason I did so poorly in my last years at the bank. "I wish you wouldn't do that to me," I said to Tucker. "Just try one out," he said.

I tried one out over at his office one day when I was waiting for him and his secretary—can't remember her name, Lois, or Louise—to come back from lunch. There it was, the little monster. I sat down and turned it on and started playing with the keys. Some had strange symbols. I confess becoming fascinated with the keys. I paid no attention to that other thing . . . the screen. When Tucker and Louise or Lois came back, Tucker led me into his office for a chat. In a few minutes the woman screamed. She said someone had deleted her files and removed the directory. I'd been the only one in the office. I'd taken nothing. She explained to Tucker that she'd been updating current caseloads in her computer, and now they were gone. "Gone!" she shouted. Tucker said, "Lord, no! Don't we have back-ups?" "No!" she said. Lois or Louise burst into tears. "Damn!" said Tucker. I told them I hadn't taken any files or directories. Tucker said, "You don't understand computers." *I* could have told *him* that. It was a terrible moment.

There was one good result. He hasn't said a word to me since about getting a computer. That's just fine with me.

I admit I'm a dodo when it comes to technology. ("Life too," Myra used to joke.) I once made this entire house go dark while trying to rewire a switch. Another time I was fixing a toaster and it exploded. I accidentally sucked a resident's slippers into the vacuum cleaner. "Don't you get near any of my equipment," Mrs. Tottabunda, the housekeeper, says. She's not only afraid I'll break something, she's afraid of my electricity. Once I walked by her and she popped like a balloon. I apparently carry a lot of static electricity. She says, "Don't come near me, Mr. Thorn." On the wall in my office, right behind my chair, is a block of wood I found at an antique sale I went to with Myra. It's from World War II and has carved on it, or had:

Situation
Normal
All
Fouled
Up

Some terrible person used a knife to change the *l* in "normal" to an *n*. I'm sure it was a social worker. No resident would have the what is it? Dexterity? Yes. Manual dexterity. I tried to take down the sign because of the insulting alteration, but I had used huge . . . what are they? Molly screws. Yes. To put it on. It would have ruined the wall to take it down.

Oh, I'll be so happy when the county takes full control of this home and I can retire! When will that be? Two years? More like two-and-a-half, I think. I've wanted to look it up but I have, it seems, misplaced the contract.

Delia from House A was in the kitchen when I got here this morning. She's here often, so often that I wonder if I missed a memo in the mail saying Tucker had her transferred to this house. I said, "You don't work here now, do you?" She said, "No, Mr. Thorn, I came to visit Beatrice and bring some clothes she left." I said, "I thought maybe you might have been transferred but you're telling me you haven't been." "Right," she said. "Who's Beatrice?" I asked. "The young woman in that room over there." "What's this?" I said when I saw milk heating on the stove. She said, "I'm giving some to Beatrice. I rub her back and she stops crying but she also needs nourishment." Delia may be black but she always has an answer, which is more than I can say about my workers. "You go ahead," I said. My mind was elsewhere.

On the refrigerator to be exact. I stick all my important messages on the refrigerator with a magnet because my office desk is so piled up with paperwork that if I put something important down there I'll never find it again. I started to explain this to Delia but she'd already poured Beatrice her milk and was back in the room where this Beatrice keeps herself confined.

I must say she visits frequently. I'm not comfortable with that. It might appear to Tucker that my people aren't doing their job. I don't like to order my workers around, but I did say to Mrs. Tottabunda when she was carrying sheets upstairs, would she mind looking in on the newest one now and then? I picked Mrs. Tottabunda because she's the oldest and most cooperative person here, which is not to say that she *is,* very. She constantly says the same thing: "I do what I'm paid to do." She doesn't like to talk to anyone. She's about fifty-seven and the residents call her Tottabutt because her bottom sticks out and bounces when she moves. Jake the Announcer sometimes reports her movements. What *does* he say? Oh, yes. "Tottabutt rounding the far turn, lays and gents, and coming down the stretch, buppety-hupp, buppety-hupp, buppety-hupp." Mrs. Tottabunda hears Jake's remarks, but they don't seem to bother her. Neither do anyone else's. The only time I ever saw her mad was when old Thaddeus Carter, whom some call Carter the Farter, because hypergastric acidity has caused chronic . . . oh, what is it? . . . means farting . . . tried to sing to her. The song was "Genevieve, Sweet Genevieve." Genevieve is her first name. Oh, wait. Her name is Grenadine. No, not Grenadine. Geraldine. That's it. Anyway, he used the name Mescaline, instead. Good Lord! She struck him on the head with a plastic bottle of ammonia which broke and spilled all down his head and onto his shoes. Everyone in the dayroom gasped for air. Some liquid got into Thaddeus's eyes and I had to call the doctor for community homes. His name is Fuhrum. Dr. Rahib Fuhrum. He told me to have someone flush his eyes out with water. We ducked his head several times in a full sink, but still he was blind for nearly three days. Flatulence is what I was trying to think of.

In any case, I said, "Mrs. Tottabunda, would you mind going in there, say three times a day, and see that she's not choking on something or hanging herself?" She asked me if that would be part of her normal duties or a personal favor. I remembered her motto and quickly replied, "I consider it a special task, yet still part of your regular duties." "Then," she said, "I'll consider doing it." An hour later she said, "I will look in when my other duties permit. I do what I'm paid to do." This time she added a little kicker: "And nothing more."

Delia visits Beatrice frequently. When I go in for my coffee I hear Beatrice's excited chatter. Delia speaks in a way that comes through the door in a low hum. For minutes at a time Beatrice shuts up and the humming goes on. I know I shouldn't do this, but I twice went over to the door and put my ear against it so that I could find out what they were talking about. Beatrice jabbers so fast I couldn't tell what she was saying, and all I heard of Delia was the hum. Mrs. Tottabunda came into the kitchen when I was at the door listening. "What are you doing, Mr. Thorn?" she said. I was caught eavesdropping when I worked at the bank. I decided then I must always be at the ready in case I was caught again. I was ready for Mrs. Tottabunda. "Oh," I said, "I was rubbing the side of my ear against the door because I have an itch." She showed no surprise but went to the stove and made herself a cup of tea. While she was doing so, I said, "Mrs. Tottabunda, would you mind, when you check on Beatrice, finding out . . . ahm, trying to, I should say, find out, what she and Delia talk about in there?" Mrs. Tottabunda blew on the top of her tea and looked at it and not me and said, "Snooping is not one of my regular duties." I told her that in my opinion what I'd asked her to do wasn't snooping but—I used a phrase Tucker uses in his memos—*informational reporting.* "I need your report in order to manage this home." "Reporting is not my job. And management is your job. I do only what I'm paid to do." I made an attempt to redefine "reporting" and "management" but she was regarding me with a cynical eye. Apparently I'd gotten nowhere.

Back to where I was. Oh, yes, the refrigerator. I found a note reminding me about a game in preparation for the Special Olympic Games Tournament. I must arrange for the game. Why did Tucker pick me? I don't know. Do the other supervisors have more to do than I? One does. Mrs. Kindy over at House C with the "profounds." But why didn't he choose Vera Holloway, or her helper, Max, who, I'm told, is going to be the coach. I mean, after all, I'm taking a resident off her hands who was reported to have had an affair with their new person. Why couldn't Vera have put this Beatrice on Thorazine? Or else taken over the Special Olympics? Oh well, what's what is . . . whatever.

I've got to find three more players for the team the county is fielding for its first game. I've already got three and someone to work the loudspeaker, Jake the Announcer. Jake has had plenty of practice. He sits at the window by the feeder every morning calling the action of the birds, which keeps whoever is in the dayroom quiet except the ones who are helping him. "That no finch fly down from the pin oak, Jake. Was a lady card'nal." Jake corrects himself: "Okay, okay, don't get yourself in a tizzy. Listen up, layboobs and gentiles, Jake's making a correction on that last call. . . ." He'll babble away at the game and keep the spectators from wandering off. Oh, he irritates me at times. Yet I'll tell him to do a play-by-play. But I wasn't thinking about Jake, I was thinking about . . . what?

I forget.

Oh-oh.

The door to the little room just opened. Just minutes after I pulled away my ear. Whew! Close. Out steps Delia.

She doesn't look at me.

What does that mean?

She slow-waltzes over to the sink and folds her arms and looks out the window, keeps looking, finally says, "Mr. Thorn?"

"Yes?"

"I think I may have found a way to get Beatrice to come out of her room."

"Really?"

"Yes. And she'd like to participate in your Special Olympics games."

"Oh. Well, that may be a problem. Our teams, these teams we're putting together now, as presently constituted, will have only men on them and . . ."

"Mr. Thorn?"

"Yes?"

"She wants to be the cheerleader."

"She . . . does?"

Delia turns but doesn't unfold her arms. She's not saying anything, but I feel threatened. Must be the stress of this job. I tell myself not to feel threatened. It doesn't work. I must consider the proposition fairly.

"But isn't it strange," I say, "that someone would stay confined like a spider in a hole and then . . . then suddenly want to come out and dance like a butterfly?"

"Not to me, Mr. Thorn," says Delia, as though she'd been expecting the question. "In moving here Beatrice had to make a very difficult adjustment. She's still trying to adjust."

"And so . . . you, then, think, are recommending she be a . . . the cheerleader."

"Yes, I am."

"Then," I say, moving toward the doorway, "I'll, well, consider doing just that."

∘👄∘ JAKE

'Kay, babes, Jake the Announcer gonna be your man here. Doin' it right, babes, doin' it the way Big Jake would of no doubt done it for the Bulls of his home Chicago town if he hadn't of missed a turn or two along the way. Hey, what happens happens, as the Jaker likes to say. Maybe they would of fired me after half a season. You don't know. I don't know. More about the trials and troubles of the Jaker later. Let's take a look at the lineups.

The Jaker is eyeballing the Maddox County Marauders sheet and sees he ain't gonna be able to pronounce a few of these names.

Ho boy!

You know, folks, if they'd of let the old Jaker out for an afternoon, he could of taken ye old public transportation over to a practice in Maddox County and interviewed those boys on the other team. First thing he'd ask is, "How do you pronounce this name of yours?" That's fundamental sports broadcasting, ladles and geritols. Fun-da-mental! Maybe next year. Meantime the Jaker will do what he can with what he's got.

First name's as long as the old Jaker's sleeve. W-o-j-c-i-e-c-h-o-w-s-k-i. Wodge? Woje? Wudge? Can't tell. And the c-i-e. What's that? Key? Sigh-ee? Man, oh man. Next part must be chow. But is the s-k-i skee or sky? Wodge or Woje, key or sighee, chow, skee or sky or maybe skih. Woj-sighee-chow-skih. Or Wodge-sigh-chow-sky. Woj-see . . .

Hell with it.

Next one's shorter but . . . damn! Vrktn. No vowels in that family. Psss the bttr. Opn th drr. Cln yr rm. Ver-rec-ton?

Looks like there's a Japanese here too. M-a-r-i-s-o-c-k-i. Could be Italian. What do I care, as long as I can pronounce it? Mary-socki. A guess.

Get them wrong and their coach complains.

Too many complaints and I lose my job.

Nowhere to go from here but down.

Hey! Who am I kidding? From here, brother . . . there is no down. Am *at* bottom.

Don't know your situation, lays and gentitals, but my parents keep having me declared incompetent. Started when I was four-teen. That's twenty-four years. But, let's suppose. Right? Let's suppose they have a religious conversion and repent and sign my walking papers.

Where would I work? Where could I?

I go to a small radio station and the manager says, what was your last job?

Announcing games of a county mentally retarded team.

Over the radio?

No. To the other dips—sorry Mr. Thorn—um, community home residents in the stands.

How many?

Oh, sixteen or seventeen.

Not very impressive. Anything else?

Yes. I was fired.

Fans, I better prevent the latter from happening and do something about that Marauder lineup. Let's go back.

That first one I'll call Wodgy, like stodgy. And that second one, Verkton. Marisocki is Marisocki. The next two are blessings: Jones, John Paul. And Carlson, Joel. But this very last one—B-o-d-e-k-k-e-r could be Bow-decker, Bod-decker, Boe-decker, or some strange hometown pronunciation like Boo-docker or Bee-ducker.

I knew a resident spelled his name D-o-s-t-e-r but pronounced it Duster. Also a D-o-u-g-h-e-r-t-y who was a Doe—like bread dough—Dough-erty, but another who was a Doc—like Doc Grable—Doc-erty. The Jaker could go on with this interesting game but has got to keep in mind the attention span of his audience.

So let's call that last one Bow—as in bow down—decker.

Apt?

I'd say so.

The boys'll be comin' out on the court soon, so I'd better get to the Cleaver County line. . . .

Hold it. The Jaker ain't perfect. Forgot to make a couple of announcements. First is, this year the Slicers will have a cheerleader. Little Beatrice Dove, who was in House A but has been moved to none other than the residential facility of yours truly, House B, has volunteered to lead a couple of cheers. She's gonna first teach you what they are, which will be no insignificant feat. F-e-a-t, not things you put socks on. Look it up. You folks in House B have no excuse. We've got a two-book library, and one of the books is a dictionary.

I see Mr. Thorn nodding. He remembers, same as me, when we cut the coupon out of *Family Circle* magazine seven, eight years ago and got that Noah Webster abridged at a special price. It's been like a friend to the Jaker ever since. Anyway, back to where I was, which will be good news for you Marauder fans who haven't yet showed up. Pretty Beatrice has agreed to do a guest cheer for them, reason being they don't have a cheerleader of their own. Fair is fair, as Mr. Thorn always says.

Right, Mr. Thorn?

Always good to see Mr. Thorn nodding.

Let's try to keep Mr. Thorn nodding. Cheer for your team. Behave like ladies and gents, not looney tuners. Remember what

Mr. Thorn can do. One, put you in confinement for behavior modification. Two, cut off your effin' food. Three, take away private bathroom rights. Or, four, your pass to the city swimming. . . .

Okay, Mr. Thorn. Didn't mean to emphasize the negatives.

Listen. Let's all give the old Cleaver County cheer for Mr. Thorn. Here we go.

Hip, hip, hooray!

Way to go.

Again.

Hip, hip, hooray!

Way! To! Go!

Good to see Mr. Thorn smiling.

The Marauder team was supposed to be here by now in their little yellow bus. Comin' right here to the Hartsville Junior High any minute. The Slicer team and their fans got here a little early. No problem. *No* problem. Team's down in the locker room sittin' on their thumbs. Too bad. They could be out here list'nin' to old Jake.

Oh-oh. The second announcement. Forget what it was.

Mr. Thorn, do you . . .

He's already shaking his head.

Something about . . .

Damn!

Okay, okay, Mr. Thorn. Darn!

You're not gonna dock my pay for forgetting. Are you?

He's shaking his head.

My pay is a Milky Way candy bar. I wanted my favorite, a Snickers, but Mr. Thorn said they didn't have any left at the carry-out. Don't mind a bit. No, sir. The two are like cousins. In fact, when you have a Milky Way, if you don't run your tongue around your mouth too much, you think you're having a Snickers. You folks try it sometime.

Where was I?

Can't remember.

Oh, well. It'll come wigglin' back sooner or later.

Now, let's get to the Slicer lineup.

Startin' at point guard is none other than Little Willie Chambers from Lime City, Tennessee, by way of one of the Volunteer

State's better mental hospitals. Willie ain't but five foot six, folks, dribbles like he's got the dance they named after that spastic man, Saint Vitus, and can make his way among opponents like a wildcat in a jackrabbit pen.

At the other guard slot, we'll see Slow Poke Billy Burris, whose age is hard to tell. Looks to the Jaker to be the second oldest player on the court today, putting him near forty. But Billy says . . .

Wait a sec'. I remember the other announcement: Don Atkins, who teaches and coaches at Hartsville Junior High is the Special Olympics coach for this area and will be here today, looking over the Slicers to see if he can find a player or two to add to his team. Good luck to Don—ain't here yet, I see—and those erstwhile recruits of yours. His.

Who was I talkin' about? Slow Poke Billy Burris. Billy tells me he's thirty-four but he's more like forty, if you take a close look. Slow Poke Billy ain't all in one spot at a time. I guess you could say that about any or us. But Billy's pretty bad. When you ask him what country we live in he says, Israel. He pronounces it like newsreel: Is-reel. When you ask him what town this is, he says, Big Fork, Montana. And if you say, No, it's not, he says, May as well be. When you ask him who the President is, he says, Mrs. Reagan. Someone told him she doesn't even live in the White House anymore, Mrs. Bush does. He says he still thinks it's Mrs. Reagan. If we ever get on Quiz Bowl we better not have Billy on the panel. He thinks Miss Goss is his sister and takes her walking downtown on Saturdays. On the other hand, I'll tell you something Max, the Humper, who's coaching the . . .

Okay, okay, Mr. Thorn.

Start over. Max Rummell, coach of the Cleavers, told the Jaker in a pregame interview that in practice yesterday Billy scored five of five push shots from fifteen feet or more. But—tune in to this—three were in the wrong basket. So here's the deal. If he starts dribbling the wrong way, we got to yell at him to go the other way, Cleaver fans. Okay?

Good.

Anyway, Billy is thirty-six if he's a day. When the players come out, take a gander. I asked Max how old he was. Max wouldn't let me see the players' records. Well, the Jaker don't need to see that confidential crap. Sorry, Mr. Thorn. They won't even let him see his file. What could there be in the file that I shouldn't see? Hey, wait a minute. I haven't seen my own file. What's in there that I can't see? Maybe my parents wrote another god-do-dangled—didn't say it, Mr. Thorn—letter.

Okay, okay.

Point is, was.

What?

Oh, that Billy is a lot older than Billy looks.

Now we go to Homer Spreitzer who come to us through the special schools right here in Cleaver County and has been known for years as Homer the Large, being one of the tallest men in this part of the world at six foot six and one quarter. That's without his shoes on. And he sleeps with his legs danglin' off the end of his bed. I know. I sleep right down the hall. And, since the Marauders ain't here yet, I'll fill in for you loyal onlookers and drop-ins and tell you that Homer's got bad varicose veins and sometimes moves even slower than old Billy. But I'll also tell you this, folks: You get Homer under the basket and he surely will go up with the best of 'em. He don't have to get off those achin' feet of his, just reaches up and taps it in.

I forgot to mention for you newcomers to Slicer basketball that Slow Poke's got a deadly no-look hook shot no one can figure out. Which is why last year he was the Slicer's highest scorer with eight points in five games, all in the opponents' baskets.

Chili Mendoza plays the other forward. Chili is a new resident of House B. He don't talk to anyone except himself, and all he says is, "I wouldn't be here if I wasn't Mexican." I think he's right. If the homes meet minority quotas, they get more state funds.

Am I right, Mr. Thorn?

He shakes his head.

No one's always right.

Anyway, I don't have other good info on him except he looks to be about twenty-six and used to be in some kind of migrant re-tarded home in El Paso 'til his pop stopped bein' a migrant and settled in this area permanent. Nice guy, Chili. What else can I say?

Don't know the last one either except he's new in House A and is in the lineup as Brendan Flynn but wants to be called Boomer. Also I heard he wanted to be the ref but they wouldn't let him.

Hell's bells, Boomer, we need you in the lineup. He weighs in at about two hundred pounds but is not all blubber, according to Coach Max. Max sees him as a strong forward. Got no word on his shooting.

It's still no show for the teams, but, what the hey, old Jake can entertain you with andydotes and diddleys he picked up on his way to nowhere. Hey, if mental institutions are the world, the Jaker's been around it.

Started when I was, let me see, nine. The Jaker's Momma and Poppa moved to a creepy part of Big Chi and put him in Sam Gompers School. Looking back now he thinks it was the odd sort of boxlike shape of his head that gave the prickeroos his age an excuse to make fun of him. He's also got, if you who are strangers to the scene will see if you look up, kind of frowny eyes. They all started calling me Frankenstein. Okay, I know, kids everywhere get called names because of their noses and ears and feet and all that. But those parts can be corrected. What you gonna do with a head that won't go away? Hammer it into a new shape? The Jaker was, still is, slug-ugly. He's got no friends, even in his own family. He remembers Momma saying, "Get your ass out of here by eight and don't come back 'til five." She and that old dog, Father, worked all day and worried Little Jake was going to come in and burn the house down. He often thought about it, I can tell you. Anyway, he was, had to be, on the street all day.

Trouble?

Hoy! He ran from one alley to the next to escape tormentors. Someone having a bad day with girlfriend or parents? Go out on the streets and throw rocks at Frankenstein. How it was. So he started doing looney tune things like kickin' and bitin', which only brought more trouble.

Thanks for lettin' the Jaker fill in, Mr. Thorn.

Whoops. I think Mr. Thorn has fallen asleep.

The Jaker can therefore get into material he wouldn't of otherwise.

One day he caught a neighborhood rat and put it in a box and fed it and trained it 'til finally he could put a leash on it and walk it down the street. The little sucker went after everyone's ankles on Wabash except Jake's and was a fine protection against the bullies until the cops made him get rid of it which he pretended to but didn't. He hid it in his closet. But still it worked for him when he went out. It worked as well as it had before. If the nasties stopped him and said, "You ain't got your rat with you, do you?" he said, "He's right over there under that garbage can. Alls I got to do is whistle." They'd leave him alone. He had the protection of his rat without having to lead it around.

If you don't have friends, you talk to yourself. Jake didn't enjoy himself very much and decided to talk to others he couldn't see. He became a broadcaster. Rebroadcast neighborhood softball games and cars in traffic and people walking down the street. He became known as That Boy Who Talks to Himself. At home matters got worse. At home he was hearing, "What in the hell are we going to do with the jerk?" Which parent said that? They both did. One never gave the other the same answer. One time it was, "Leave him on the street when he's old enough so they won't bring him back." Another it was, "Get him a job in an effin' factory and make him pay a hefty rent." They never talked to him. At least they talked to each other. They enjoyed each other very much. He watched through a crack in his wall and silently broadcast them makin' love. *Poppa unzips his pants and points his finger and Momma goes down on the grimy kitchen floor and flings her legs out and unhooks her stockings and pulls 'em down along with her pinky-pink panties. And now, ladies and gentlemen, Raymond himself goes down, drops to his knees and falls into Phyllis.* They you-know-whatted each other everywhere, including in their closet, on the kitchen sink, against the radiator, against the wall, in the doorway. Jake broadcast even the exchanges he couldn't see. Funny life.

One day a new cop in the neighborhood brought Jake home after he'd been broadcastin' women's legs on a windy Chicago day, rating them good, bad, and awful. Cop picked him up after a woman he rated awful complained. Cop said to Jake's parents he believed the boy here was a little short of all-present and it just might be a good idea to have him examined by the county psychologist. They just might have to have him put in a home. Jake's mother said, "How much does that cost," and the cop said, "Well, I think it depends on your income, it just might be free." Jaker's parents' eyes lit up like they had just won the Irish Sweepstakes. This bigger older Jaker doesn't want to go through the painful details of their phony announcement to little Jaker that night, that what they were going to do they were doing in his best interests, or into the anger that followed later, after they filled out the petition for his incarceration. Eternal, it seems. All he will say is that the morning he was sent away he managed to put his rat into their bedroom closet. Without feeding it. By the time they got home it would be looking for ankles. That wasn't the worst thing the Jaker ever did.

While the Jaker has been mutterin' and meanderin', there's been some action courtside. Mrs. Holloway came rushin' onto the court and woke up Mr. Thorn, with whom she is now consultin'. Hey, gang. This thing's gonna start pretty soon. Players'll be comin' onto the court any . . .

Whoops.

Mr. Thorn is comin' up to the broadcast box and . . . wavin' his hand at me and sayin' . . . what?

Sayin', "Something's happened. I have to make an announcement."

What's happened?

"Give me that mike!"

It's only a fake mike, made out of cardboard. He's forgotten that. The Jaker has been so good he's made Mr. Thorn think it's real. What a compliment!

Here you are, Mr. Thorn.

○◯○ BEATRICE

I'm not even going to say what happened. It's so embarrassing. I'll say it later.

Oh, horrors!

Delia visited me. Every day. She's the only one I wanted to talk to. The only one I did talk to. She brought me news about Brendan. They wanted him to be on the county basketball team. She said he just sat in chairs and wouldn't speak. She said his teacher had brought him books and he was reading them with his finger. That melted me to my toes. I could just see his fat finger going along the words. I could see his big lips moving at the same time. I told Delia I had to have a picture of him.

"I'll borrow William's camera," she said.

I wrote a message to Brendan. On a tiny piece of paper it would be hard for Mrs. Holloway to find. Or her bully helper Max. It said:

> Dearest Brendan,
>
> I won't eat a bite until they let me be with you.
>
>> Your Only Love,
>> Beatrice

I thought he'd send a message just as beautiful. I tried to guess what he'd say. One was:

> I will love you till the sun turns to ice.

That was the best. They were all pretty good.

> I will love you till there's no more time.

I made up eighty-two altogether.

Delia came back and said she had delivered my message.

"And what did he say?"

"He wants to kiss you again."

"But what about my message?"

"That's important, Beatrice."

"But what did he say about my message, Delia?"

"You have to know, don't you?"

We have a promise. I will never lie to her. She will never lie to me. I reminded her and said, "And that means not keeping things from each other. Tell me."

I wish she hadn't. "He said, 'Tell her, "Don't be stupid." ' "

"That rat!" I said. "I hate him!"

"Be patient," she said. "I think I talked him into playing for the basketball team."

I know why she did that. All the residents get to go to the games. That meant me. "You can see him once a week at least."

"See him!" I said. I hated him but I'd love him again in a few minutes. "I'd turn into a doorknob if I can only see him. I have to touch him. Oh, Delia! I changed my mind about the picture. I don't want one. It will only make me want to touch him more. And I don't care if he said, 'Don't be stupid.' He's young. He'll change. If I can't touch him, I'm going to stay in this room. I promise!"

Delia got mad. She said they were going to give me Behavior Modification if I didn't come out of the room and mingle with the other residents.

I've seen people who were in Behavior Modification. They start with training and some are taken away and given pills and some other kind of training. Before they left they were chatty and cheerful and maybe angry. When they came back they stared past your ears.

"If you want the truth," Delia said, "I believe moving you to House B was a start. I think they might do more." Maybe she was trying to scare me.

Well, she did.

Dreary!

When you're retarded, you don't belong to yourself. That's the worst part, even worse than living with other retarded persons and all their smells and screams. When I got here we were called mentally retarded. Not anymore. Now we're something else. The name is so long it took me three months to say it: developmentally disabled. I thought things would get better. We'd be given new sofas or be let out more often. No, sir. It was just a name. I hate the new name. Uck and yuck! Once we were called idiots. I told Delia I wish we were still called idiots. "At least it's closer to how they treat us."

After Delia scared me, I remembered something. My best friend was a cheerleader at Upper Valley Country Day School. She taught me every move and every cheer. If my legs worked right, I would have been a cheerleader too. I certainly had the looks. Here my moves don't have to be perfect. I could ask to be the team's cheerleader. It was such a brilliant idea I jumped off my bed and hit my head on the slanty ceiling. Ooo, ouch!

"What's wrong with you?" Delia said.

Oh, I am such a schemer!

I told Delia my plan. She hugged me and laughed so hard she cried in my hair. She said she'd talk to Mr. Thorn and Max, the coach, about me being cheerleader. Then she said, "I'll find some way, before or after the game, for you two to be together."

"Oh, Delia," I said, "you have made me the happiest person from here to Florida!" That's what I always say when I'm happy. I've said it since my mother left me here to go to St. Petersburg with her lover. She said, "Beatrice, I'm going to Florida to find my happiness." She never came back. Her lover is Harry. He's very handsome. He's ten years younger than her. I keep seeing them driving off. The car had no top. I saw their heads 'til they turned on Main Street, her blonde hair flowing back like a flag in a wind. She's a little bit prettier than me but only when she fixes herself up. That takes her an hour. It used to. It probably takes more now. I want to get Revlon for my face and mousse for my hair. There's money of mine somewhere. Some is being used to pay for me here. I don't know. I once asked Mrs. Holloway if I could have some of my money for makeup. She said, "No!" One thing about Mrs. Holloway. She doesn't waste your time.

Delia talked to Mr. Thorn and then told me I'd have to agree to come out of my room for good or Mr. Thorn wouldn't let me be the cheerleader.

Around here you always have to agree to something. "What about Brendan? I won't come out unless he's going to play. For sure."

"I think he will, if you come out."

"Okay. Then I'll come out." I'd be cheerleader and hug him every time he got near me.

"For good, then?"

"Yes yes yes yes yes."

After Brendan found out I'd be a cheerleader he said for sure he'd play for the Cleaver County basketball team. Delia got a key so I could have this storage-kind-of-room all to myself. It was between the rooms where the teams would be. She said that was part of the agreement she had with Mr. Thorn. I should have a dressing room. The players had a dressing room. Why not the cheerleader? It was just a trick so I could see Brendan. Mr. Thorn would do anything to get me to come out of my room. Anyway, Delia said Brendan and I could be with each other for a short time before and after the game.

"How long?" I said.

"A few minutes, I'd guess."

A stupid few minutes! Oh, well. Something was better than nothing. My mother used to say, "Get *what* you can *when* you can." Maybe she still does.

I practiced in my room as much as the space would allow. Lucky for me I didn't do cartwheels. I also practiced in my brain before I went to sleep. I also did leg exercises. I only had three days. That's when Cleaver County was playing Maddox County in the first game. I would be so good the Maddox players would stare at me and lose the ball. I just knew it. I told Delia I was ready.

Game day came. Delia took me to the little room, then went to check on the residents in the gym. I could hear the players in the dressing room next to me. The room was a storage room with a little rug on the floor. I stood on the rug and took off my blue jeans. I wore them because the weather was cold. I started to put on the maroon shorty skirt Delia had gotten for me.

The door popped open. There was Brendan. He wore a maroon basketball top and old basketball shoes. They smelled like garbage. I didn't care. He was as beautiful as ever.

"Oh, Brendan!" He had made me so breathless it came out like a whisper.

He just stood there panting. He reminded me of the gorillas in a movie I saw, I think on HBO. It was *Gorillas in the Mist.* You had to love those animals. Mrs. Goss watched with me and said, "Majeftic." They were. So was he!

"Oh, Brendan!" I tried to say but nothing came out.

He had been staring at my legs but now his eyes came up to mine. "Kiss," he said in a growly voice. That's just how the gorillas would have sounded if they talked.

"Oh . . . oh . . ." It was all I could say. My knees wouldn't hold me up. I fell to the carpet on my knees.

He closed the door and plopped down beside me. "Be-ah-triss," he said.

"Yes, Brendan?"

He slid closer. His soft face touched mine. Then I felt his hard lump against my leg.

"How we *do* this?" he said.

Oh, dear!

On TV they never show what goes on down below. "We'll figure it out," I whispered. "Kiss me."

He did. His mouth was open so wide he swallowed nearly half my face.

We kissed and kissed.

He started biting my cheek.

"Ow! Ow!" I said.

He stopped.

"No," I said. "Keep doing it."

Something tore.

We both looked down.

His pants had unzipped in front and his dingle was sticking straight out. It was big as a giant banana. "Oh no," he said.

"Don't worry," I told him. I put my finger to where I was tingling and then pulled back the crotch-part of my little red panties. "We have to finish. I think I know what to do."

He was lying on his side. I rolled on mine and reached down. His dingle was on fire. He was breathing in coughs like the House A lawnmower does when Octopus tries to start it on a cold morning. I touched his dingle to the part of me that wanted it most. He reached down and put his hand next to mine. His dingle was so big and I was so little. We started to work it into me. It didn't do any good. He rolled me over until he was on top. My legs were stretched as wide as they would go. I saw a burning meteor breaking into the earth. The earth was spilling hot liquids up its sides to make room. My legs and tummy, then my chest and knees, then my head and feet were suddenly filled with Brendan's heat. "Oh, Brendan!" I said. He was panting and panting but finally said, "We . . . get . . . married?" "Oh, yes!" I said. "Yes!" We were breathing in and out exactly the same.

"Yes!" he said.

"Yes!" I said.

Up and down.

"Yes!"

"Yes!"

Up and down.

"Yes!"

"Yes!"

Up and down.

"Yes!"

"Yes!"

Way up and *way* down.

"Oh boy!" he said.

"Yes!" I said.

Our breathing slowed down.

I was pulling him closer when he did a push-up and popped out. "Put on underwear, Be-ah-triss."

"What?"

"We go."

"Go where?"

He smiled a strange smile that made his bottom teeth show. Then he kind of laughed through the smile. *Like the gorillas,* I thought. But he didn't answer. That was the gorillas too.

"Where?" I said.

"*You* see." His dingle was hanging out. It looked ridiculous.

I got on my knees and put it back in his pants. Then I started pulling up on the zipper that had popped open.

"Care-*ful*," he said.

I was careful. I pulled and pulled. Finally the zipper came up. "Tell me where we're going," I said. "We have a basketball game, you know. In a few minutes."

"No way. Uver team not here."

"But it will be."

"No care. We go. C'mon." He reached down and pulled me hard to my feet. "Put on pants."

"Brendan? Where—?"

"Can't say *that*." He looked at me, frowning big wrinkles the way he did the first night when he was thinking hard. All he said now was, "Surprise!" real loud.

I didn't want a surprise. I've had too many. Most are bad. The best was Brendan coming to House A. And now coming into the dressing place. We had made love. It was so simple! It was so beautiful! What a wonderful surprise! But I was also remembering the bad ones. Like Mrs. Holloway coming into Brendan's room. And me being taken away. And Delia telling me Brendan had been in confinement. I looked at the storage room door. Maybe Mrs. Holloway would push it open. "You have to go back to your team," I said.

"Bull."

"Max will come and get you."

"No way. Go to call uver team."

"Okay, okay. But he'll be back. Or Mrs. Holloway will come."

"Right. Have to hurry."

"No." I was mad. "I'm not moving . . . until you tell me where we're going. Then I still might not."

"Pwooofff," he said, closing his eyes. He stood there swaying like a weeping willow tree. When he opened his eyes, he said, "Okay. Go see Poppa first . . ." His father was in the hospital, Delia said, waiting to have surgery. ". . . then go see Eleanor . . ." Who was that? ". . . then go get married."

"Married?"

"Yep." He put his arms around me and smacked his lips against my hair. "We *can.*"

"Who said?"

"Sarah."

She had probably told him we could apply for permission because that's what Delia told me. I had heard of retarded people getting married. A few. They had to fight to do it. The social workers talked about retarded people wanting to get married and laughed. Max and Mrs. Holloway laughed. The Retardation Board sometimes lets us get married. I had been talking to Delia about how to get married. Because of Brendan and me. Now he had been talking to Sarah too. That's good but he's not used to living in a community home for the mentally retarded and—hah hah—developmentally disabled. You don't even go down the street for an ice cream cone without permission.

I had made love to him so well he was going crazy. "Brendan, sit down with me. I have to explain something to you."

"No! We go! Is a free country. Right?"

"Not for us it isn't."

"Okay! Have to try and *be* free. Says in book."

"We don't live in *your* book. Goodness sake! Look what happened the first time we tried to make love to each other!"

"Right. Why we got to go."

He's such a dreamer! But all the time I was feeling happy in the strength of his words. I really didn't care if he was wrong. I wanted him to keep thinking the way he was. Also I didn't want to part from him any more than he wanted to part from me. But I was trying to be sensible. We'd be in such trouble if we didn't be sensible. But with him holding me . . . "How would we keep from being caught, I mean before we had a chance to be married?"

"Hurry. That *how*."

"To where?"

"First hospital. See Poppa."

"To the hospital? By the time we walked over there Max or someone would be waiting."

He made a fist and hit his forehead with the thumb side. I thought something sensible had finally gotten into his thick head. It hadn't. He said, "We find a way."

"I doubt it. And we can't get married either. Not right away. You have to petition to get married."

"Petition?"

I remembered two who had married had to wait three years before the board said okay. And before that they hadn't been in trouble like Brendan and me. It might take us ten years! Maybe more! Maybe they'd *never* let us get married! "Oh, Brendan, I don't know if we should bother with a petition."

"Good! We get married. See Poppa after."

"Who would marry us? Where?"

"Eleanor tell *us* that."

"Eleanor?"

"Friend. C'mon, Beatrice."

"Where are we going?"

"See Poppa, then go on highway and sit down."

"Sit down? For what?"

"How you get ride."

Now it was my turn to slap my head. Not because I said something stupid. Because he did. I should have slapped his. "That's *not* how to get a ride."

"Is too!" He sounded insulted.

"You get a ride by sticking your thumb out."

"Not me."

Oh, heavens! This marriage is not going to be all hearts and roses.

He was fidgeting to go.

"Wait. I have to get back in my jeans. You have to get your clothes. Go get them. Then come back here and change quickly. Wait! Maybe Max came back. No. We would have heard him calling you. I hear the other players in there. Don't tell them what we're going to do. Hurry."

He went.

I hurried.

When I peeked out the door of the storage room he was already next to it, waiting. He was holding his jacket and pants. No one else was around but someone in the Cleaver County dressing room called out, "Hey, Brendan. Come back!"

We ran.

◦◓◦ BERNARD

I'm sleeping on the top shelf. Big wooden shelf you get to by use of a sliding ladder. Goes back so's you can pack two rows of sheets stacked three high. I have myself a nest in the back row. Even the FBI couldn't find me here. When the others go home, I rise on the sliding ladder and have me a snooze. Never more than a couple of hours.

Well, this very afternoon I'm wakened by a commotion down below. This is strange since after two o'clock there's usually no one in the linen room except myself, Bernard Schmidbauer, linen and laundry assistant and native of Cleaver County here all my life. I remain to do cleanups and be ready in case there comes the un-expected and they need sheets or scrubs in a real hurry. Mrs. Nell

Fanning does the same in the night. We got just about everything you wear in a hospital. Not much happens here after, like I say, two o'clock. Back to where I was. I pop my head up, see first the clock above the door. It says 3:05. Now, along with the bumping and kicking I hear some mumbling. I scoot my head over the first row of sheets and look down.

Just below me is what looks like a couple of kids. It also looks like they're opening the uniform packages. I pull back. First thing I think of doing is what I would have done if I, say, come walking in on 'em from the hallway. Say, "All right, you two, what do you think you're doing?" Give 'em a scare and call for the security guard. Because of where I am and what I'm doing I can't make a peep. If Mr. Turner, the administrator, finds out about me napping, I can kiss this job good-by. And then I think, well, maybe these two were told by a nurse or doctor to come in and get something. If I speak they will be able to say, "This man who was snoozing up there on the sheets tried to stop us." Or, even if it turns out they are thieves, it will come out in the investigation where I was. After considering all the angles I can think of, I decide to do nothing more than a little eavesdropping. I work my head over to the edge again.

I see a chubby male and a blonde-headed female. The female has put on a green scrub. Why she did this I don't know. It looks too big on her. The frock part only, not the pants. On the shelf next to her it looks like three packages are open. He makes some kind of odd sound and his head raises up like someone who's about to sneeze.

"I told you not to . . ." She runs across the room to the shelf where we stack spare pillows, snatches one up and starts back.

I duck my head out of the way.

A second later I hear a soft thump. I don't dare to peek over. They might be looking up.

After five seconds after that I hear a chugga chugga noise.

Well, now I'm just like that cat curiosity killed. I've got to peek down.

Which I do.

The male's on the floor with his legs out and the female's kneeling beside him holding the pillow against his face with all her weight. It looks like he's having some kind of convulsion.

Oh, Lord!

I think of yelling down. It is the strangest danged sight I ever saw. I think, Bernard, you could be witnessing a murder.

Lordee Lord!

Before I say what happened next I want to explain a few things about myself and situation which may clear up any doubts anyone might have about me performing my duty as a citizen.

Great-Grandfather was just about to leave a poker game over there on Frog Prairie Road late one evening in the year of Nineteen and Eleven when he was still a young man. A troubled player named Ephrom Cheeks, who was from Pennsylvania, took out a Colt pistol and put a bullet right through the third and fourth ribs of Lester Forrest, whose farmhouse they was playing at. Course I was very little the only time Great-Grandfather told that story to me and don't recall from then. But, after Great-Grandfather was gone, Grandfather repeated it many times, as did Father. Same as I'm doing now.

Seems it turns out that Ephrom there had been building himself on the notion that Lester was deliberately scheming amongst his friends so's Ephrom would lose every Friday night. Which he did. It wasn't that way at all, as was brought out by Grandfather and in the trial. Seems like Ephrom just wasn't much of a poker player. In testimony after testimony, the other players recalled for the judge times when Ephrom broke up flushes to draw to three of a kind, or beckon a straight when alls he had was three in the same suit. Lester's cousin, Thurstin Forrest, said under oath he had once seen Ephrom bet all of what was in his pants against Thurstin when Thurstin hadn't discarded a single card. All Ephrom had was two pair. At that point the judge, B. K. Gamble, slapped his desk and said, "Any damn fool knows you don't bet two pair against a no-hit hand, 'less you got a hot full house or four of a kind." Great-Grandfather was one of the testifiers. Great-Grandfather was at the door of Lester's when he saw Ephrom reach under his coat and bring out a pistol. On seeing what he did see he didn't step out and close the door but stepped in and closed it, giving himself the chance to see the shot fired. I'd like to have bravery of Great-Grandfather and what he done. I don't pretend to be as brave or bright as him, or, for that matter, Grandfather or Father either.

It ain't just a matter of bravery.

In my forty-two-year life, I have lost twenty jobs. I ain't about to lose another, if I can any way help it. My motto has become what it says in my parlor under my three stuffed monkeys, one holding his ears, one holding his eyes and one holding his mouth: "See no evil. Hear no evil. Speak no evil."

So here I sit on my perch with a murder in progress, helpless as a fly on a wall.

To the best of my recollection none but Father lost a job before me. Every single one of them ran the farm 'til the bank come along back in 1983 and took it from Father. He was shamed, though it wasn't his fault, and went to work in the implement store north of town. There have come rocky times for all of us in the years since. I, for one thing, began losing jobs about the time Father lost the farm. He himself passed on two years later. Defeat kind of chews away a man's confidence the way the blight can chew away a whole crop of beans or corn. Therefore I have promised wife and mother and the three little ones, the fourth being too young to understand, that I will not lose my job here at the laundry by failing to carry out my functions in a suitable way. I *will* say that, when I left my last job, pumping gas down at Cliff Maxner's Sohio, Cliff gave me a nice compliment before he let me go. He said, "Bernard, you do a fine job of gettin' the gas into the cars and cleanin' the regulars' windows." He went on to say, "The trouble is, you ain't so good with the parley voo. What I suggest is you find some work that don't involve a lot of contact with people."

Which I did.

I believe I hear laughter.

Danged if I don't.

I lean over and, sure as nails, the fella lying flat on the floor is not dying but at the chuckle-end of a long laugh.

He ain't the only one laughing.

The female is sprawled out beside him and giggling like a fool.

This is sure good news in one way, meaning no one got choked to death. It sure ain't in another, meaning they're still here.

I see now the male is a mongoloid like my cousin Lewis, in fact if he wasn't as plump as he is, could be a brother of Lewis. Lewis must now be twenty-two or -three. Trouble with mongoloids is you just can't tell their ages. Lewis is a harmless one. But that ain't a way of saying this one is. This one appears to be a thief. Criminals come in all shapes and forms.

They are helping themselves up now.

I slide back but keep peeking.

He puts on the top of a scrub while she opens one of the packages with the pants in them. He has trouble with the top and she helps him. When it's on he bends over in a bow and says, "Nurse Butter ready to help you, Doctor, hee hee hee, Marigold."

She giggles and says, "We have to stop being silly or Max and the police will be here." But she giggles again.

He chuckle-laughs as he goes over by the door where the masks are in see-through bags. Danged if he doesn't start opening one.

What is this pair up to?

I lie back to do some thinking. All I think is I better not lose this job. If they make too much of a mess, I could be blamed. Well, I shouldn't worry too much about that since nobody usually comes in here in the afternoon, giving me time to clean up after they go. If they go. And suppose they break something. I can just hear the administrator: "Where were you when that happened?" I'd never be able to tell him. This is quite a pickle. Jo Ellen said, "Bernard, if you lose one more job, I'm going to have to take the children and go back to Fort Wayne." She just can hardly put up with my bad luck. Course I might have done better if I didn't have the need to sleep in the afternoon. Been that way since I was a kid. You'd figure a person would grow out of that.

"Hello, Operator, I would like some information."

What in the world! I ease up to the edge.

The female is talking in the wall phone.

"The number of Mr. Flynn's room." She puts her hand over the phone and turns and grins at her friend.

They both are dressed in scrubs now. They have the masks that were hanging loose around their necks.

"Forty-six? Thank . . . Oh, *one*-forty-six . . . Thank you, very much." She hangs up.

The fella raises his hand out to his shoulder and she slaps it. "Way to go, Doc Marigold," he says.

"Way to be, Nurse Butters," she says back. "We'll just walk straight down past that restaurantlike place we passed after sneaking in, and go up the stairs there. You kind of follow a little behind me. I'll try to walk straight."

"Oh, boy!"

She pulls him by the hand to the door. "We can't stay long."

The one she called Nurse Butters is quivering excited. "Go," he says.

They go.

What in heck are they up to?

I twist around and get my feet on the ladder and start down.

I saw a movie once where a couple of killer-types went in and put on doctor outfits and took a patient on his way to the operating room out the back of the hospital and sliced him up. Put all the pieces in a garbage bag and walked off.

Could be they're going to kill the one in Room 146.

And if they do, who gets asked about where they got the scrubs?

Gosh dang it!

Seems like my life is kind of destined. Even me being here in this room when the strangers come in. All I know is this job has got to be my last. Ain't nothin' for me to do but clean up after these folks and figure out an alibi.

Dang!

⚬◉⚬ JOSEPH

I know, even before I'm fully awake, that the warm hand on my forehead is his. I reach up and place my own hand over it. He leans down and hugs me tightly.

"Poppa," he whispers.

"Brendan," I say, hearing the hoarseness that, since my illness, has been as much a part of me as my thumbprint. I twist around, having to blink a couple of times to clear my eyes. Finally

I see his beautiful smile. I also notice that his face has thinned and carries an expression I've never seen, a stark look that frightens me because it's so unfamiliar. One thing that is familiar is that unsightly jacket of his. It's filthier than ever and hangs loosely the way I've seen it when he's put it on hastily. "Sarah told me they found you in the city."

"Wiss poor people, Poppa. *New* friends."

"Well, you've survived pretty well, haven't you?"

"Yep." His hand slides away and his eyes take a troubled trip around my face. "Too white, Poppa." He nods at his own remark. "Got to go in sun."

"I will, soon enough."

"How you feel?"

"Okay. Just sleepy all the time. Sarah told you what happened to me?"

"Heart attack."

"Yes, but it's not too serious. That's why I'm now in this room, not in intensive care, where they keep the very sick patients."

"This like Momma's room."

"Right. She was just down the hall."

His eyes travel busily over the walls.

"I'll be going home in a few days," I say. "Some people from the parish are running the store. I'll be back on my stool in no time."

"Good, Poppa."

"Where is Sarah?"

"Don't know."

I assumed she'd brought him. "How did you get here?"

"Walk."

"Alone?"

"No. Talk 'bout you, Poppa. Not Boombah."

Sarah said she'd asked him why he left the hearing and ran off. He told her he was angry at me and her because he'd been trying to tell us about something Mr. Reed Stark had said to him when Reed Stark entered the courtroom. "But he wouldn't tell me what he said. He said, 'Tell Poppa *some*time.'"

"I'd rather talk about you . . . Boombah."

He smiles at my use of the name he likes. It's not the one Grace and I gave him, but I now believe accepting it is part of accepting him in whatever changes he's undergoing. I myself find it foolish.

"Why, Poppa?"

"Because I need to know some things. That's why. I'd like to start with what Mr. Reed Stark said to you in the courtroom."

His mouth tightens. "Want to tell you *that* day. You not listen. Sarah either."

"But we were, or Sarah was, talking to the judge."

"Right, Poppa! Why Boombah want to tell you."

"It couldn't have waited?"

"No way!"

"So what did he say?"

He slaps both hands against his forehead and pretends he's knocked himself back. "Now you say *this*. Oh, Poppa!"

"I guess in the courtroom I wasn't a good mind reader. I'm still not."

His eyes move slowly back and forth. "Right, Poppa! *Not*."

"So what did he say?"

"Okay. Lean down at me, Mr. Ugly Face. Look like this." He makes a widemouthed face and does begin to look a little like Reed Stark. Then he bends toward me until his eyes are only an inch or so away from mine. "Say, 'You step in shit now, Mister.' Spit when he talk." He manages to spit as he speaks, the way Reed Stark must have. I'm about to ask if that was why he'd run off, but he goes on. " 'Going sue that father of yours for everything he got.' Sue, Poppa!"

"But . . ."

"Say *that*, Poppa!"

"Wait. Do you know what 'sue' means?"

"Take everything you got. *He* say that."

Brendan had sat there, I'm sure, imagining me, and, I suppose, him too, being pushed out of the apartment, the store too, losing the car. Maybe more. "What people say doesn't always mean what they're going to do, or even can do."

"What Boombah say he do he *do* do."

"Okay. But not everybody is Boombah."

"Boombah want you hear what Mr. Ugly Mouth say. Judge too."

In the courtroom I thought his interrupting words might make the judge think he should be confined. I cut him off. Now I think he might have defended himself more effectively than I or even Sarah. Mr. Reed Stark had twice behaved impulsively, irrationally, and cruelly. Brendan was smart enough to know how important it was to share that knowledge. But I'd heard only his disrupting sounds, had ignored him, left him in back, apart and useless. Yes, the judge just might have favored the testimony of a senior principal in the school system over Brendan, who was, after all, retarded. But he *might not* have.

"No want him sue *you*," he says. "Go outside and cry. Then think Boombah go away. Then he not sue *you*."

"So you took off for River City."

"Yep. Policeman catch me. Was wiss . . . *with* Eleanor."

"Eleanor? Who's that?"

"Friend. Hey, Poppa? What that stuff is?" He's pointing to several bottles on the table between me and my roommate, Mr. Katzenbach, who's sleeping.

"My drugs," I tell him.

"Drugs!" He marches around the bed, stops at the table, looks them over, then picks up the telephone that sits beside the pills and dials.

"What are you doing?"

"Police station? Okay, send policeman to hospital. Man here take drugs. In room . . . ahm . . . ahm . . ."

"I don't think this is funny, Brendan."

"One-forty-six," says a female voice from somewhere behind him. "One-forty-six! Come quick!" As he puts the phone down I see his finger coming off the receiver button. "Bwahhhhh!" He swings his arms wide and slaps the curtain between Mr. Katzenbach's bed and mine. He staggers backward, laughing as he goes. "Bwahhhh, hahhhh hahhhh hahhhh . . ."

If his volcanic laughter didn't wake Herman, nothing will. In fact, nothing seems to. He slept through a thunderstorm early this morning. Yesterday he slept through his enema.

He comes staggering back. "Man your age," he says finally. "Tsk tsk tsk. Should be ashamed of *yourself*."

"Be careful," says the mysterious voice.

"Who's that woman?"

He frowns. "What woman, Poppa?"

"There's a woman back there somewhere."

"Oh, boy!" He moves to the phone, picks it up. "Better bring a . . . um, kysologist, too." He means psychologist.

I try not to smile but do.

"Radio man *you* like. What he say?"

"Radio man?"

"On tapes."

"Oh." I have played for him my Jack Benny tape. I've repeated lines afterwards. He has a favorite. I repeat it: "Now *cut* that out!"

"Bwahhhh, hahhhhh hahhhhh hahhhhh . . ."

He leans down and kisses my forehead. "Miss you, Poppa."

"Missed you too, Bren . . . Boombah."

"Boombah." He nods.

I'm newly aware that this isn't, after all, visiting time. If it were, Mrs. Katzenbach would be here, sitting beside her husband, who's remained asleep in the bed beyond the curtain. He has a bowel obstruction and she visits every day, staying from start to finish during both afternoon and evening hours.

"Boombah?"

"Got news, Poppa," he says as if he's sensed I'm going to ask him a troublesome question.

"Good, but . . ."

"Boombah get married."

I nod. "Someday. Now . . ."

"Tomorrow, Poppa. Maybe today." He turns. "Be-ah-triss?" He goes to the bathroom door, tiptoeing. He pulls it open and there, in blue jeans and a maroon sweater, stands a slender woman as pretty as the prettiest nurses in this hospital. Her searching blue eyes explore me. She's wearing lipstick identical to that of Ruth Katzenbach, who keeps a few cosmetics, a hairbrush, and small dryer in the medicine cabinet. Boombah takes the young woman's hand and they approach the bed. I notice she moves with a kind of pigeon-toed movement that makes the walking look difficult.

"My Poppa," Boombah says as they reach the bed. "Beatrice, Poppa."

She leans closer and peers down as if there's an important message written on my face somewhere. Finally she rises and says, "You have a square head. Don't you think I'm very pretty?"

"Yes." I nod. Sarah told me that Brendan had a friend. She said nothing about marriage. I have many questions. They melt in the presence of this woman looking down, making some kind of communion with me. My hand rests on top of the blanket. I raise it toward her.

She comes a step closer, takes my hand in both of hers and bends down and kisses the top of my fingers. "You be *my* poppa too?"

Oh! Doesn't she have a father? Maybe not. Such are the times. Look at those hopeful eyes! This is not someone asking for a second helping of potatoes. This is somebody who wants to marry Brendan and also wants me to be her father. Is that so strange? An excitement that yesterday, an hour ago, would have triggered palpitations and the need for a tranquilizing pill, now sends heat flooding through my veins. So it feels. My heart pounds. There is no pain. It pounds hard and confident. Will I be her poppa? He stands beside her, waiting too.

"Of course I'll be your father."

Together they come down on me softly and soon we are all three holding each other.

"We be free, Poppa," he says in a calm assured tone. "Why Boombah not afraid. Or Beatrice either."

"I am," she corrects. "A little."

There are questions, questions on questions. As we all hold each other, they flood in upon me. Why don't you wait? Won't you have to get permission from . . . someone? And when you marry, where will you live? Our apartment? Her family's house? Separately? Is separate living possible for disadvantaged people? Where? How? I don't have the answers to any of these questions. Do *they?*

"Brendan?"

He hugs me tighter.

She does too.

My heart throbs against my ribs. Isn't mine the heart of a man whose sickness is of the heart? The throbs are relentless, those of an athlete, a runner going top speed. Is that good? I feel no chest pain. I feel strong. It must be good. Heat surges through my back, up into my neck and chin, across my skull. Warm and strong. Maybe the heat is only the heat our bodies are making. Boombah's perspiring in my face. Maybe the heat is coming down, from him and Beatrice.

Boombah is the first to pull back. "Have to go, Poppa."

ₒ⊜ₒ MARIA

Here's what Sal told me:

"Don't drive the car back on the Interstate, take it on the little roads. Don't pick up nobody. When you get back, take it straight to Ferraro's Garage. If Ferraro's is closed, bring it to Eddie's house. Don't bring it home. Last place you want to bring it is home, Maria. Leave it. Let Ferraro or Eddie take you home."

I asked my friend, Angelina, on the phone, "Whose life am I livin'?"

"Not yours, Maria."

"You didn't need to say," I tell her. "Listen. Theresa don't even want me to visit. She's got tests comin' up and is gonna be home in three weeks anyway. He tells me he has to have her car back. He's gonna get her a new one. 'She don't want a new car,' I tell him. He don't listen."

"Tony's the same," she says.

"I have to go down on a bus. I don't like goin' on buses. And I'm afraid drivin' on little roads. You never know who's gonna jump out from behind a bush. He even tells me when to go. 'Thursday,' he says. So whose life?"

"Not yours, Maria."

"He'll thank me by buyin' me a coat made out of one of those animals that aren't supposed to be killed. I'll wear it once. To church Christmas Eve. The only time we go, right? And church for him ain't really church. It's Business. Everyone in what's left of the Family goes to Immaculate Conception on Christmas. Sal writes a big check for the monsignor. The monsignor has been a character witness for Sal and the boys six or seven times. Remember. He's the one said nice things about Carlo the Plug last year after the beer wagon blew up comin' out of the Stroh's brewery in Detroit. I read in the paper Carlo didn't go to jail. Sal didn't tell me. Sal tells me nothin'. If I ask the wrong question he don't like, he says, "Business, Maria." That means don't talk about it. Is Theresa's car Business? I don't even bother to ask."

"What good?" she says.

"You wanna come along, Angelina?"

"Naw. I get my nails done Thursday."

So here I am on a lonely back road with no companion and can't find good music on the radio.

Theresa and I had hamburgers with two of her friends at a greasy spoon named Wimpy's. I told her, "Your father said, 'Go to a nice Italian place and put it on the plastic.' " No one listens. She takes me to Wimpy's with her friends. Their hangout. I feel funny all dressed up in the place. She tells me they got the best hamburgers in the Midwest. The meat is hangin' out of the bun and drippin' fat all over the plate. I tell her, "There's enough cholesterol here to kill your father and two of his friends." My little joke. I expect her to laugh. Her friends too. They don't. She says, "Don't say things like that, Ma." The others stare at me like I'm shoes on the table. I smile. For the rest of the meal I listen. After the hamburgers I take her keys and say, "How you gonna get home?"

Her hair is hangin' over one eye in that new frizzy style. I was there an hour and didn't see that eye. It could have been poked out. "I'll get a ride," she says.

"If he wants to send a new car?"

"He don't need to send a car."

Was that an answer? I don't ask.

She kisses me good-by in front of Wimpy's. They're gonna walk back to their apartment. Last thing she says is, "Ma, you're putting too much purple under your eyes."

If I die between now and next time, that's all she'll remember. Ma had too much purple under her eyes.

So here I am. Maria Anna Pasquale Mangione. Known to her friends as Maria the Tush. A happy woman, you would say if you saw her parkin' her Coupe de Ville outside Petrini's Gourmet Market Saturday morning. Always smilin'. A summer place on

Lake Tahoe. A winter place on St. Thomas. A happy rich woman.
Her only daughter on the way to bein' a lawyer. Most of the time
treated by her husband like a queen. "You want a new dinin' room?
We get a new dinin' room. Go pick one out." But what you see ain't
the real Maria Anna Pasquale Mangione.

Who is?

I don't know.

I'm forty-two years old. You'd think by now I'd know.

All my life I believed in God but last time I went to confession
for Christmas I told the priest, "I been doubting God. I been
doubting for months." He said, "We all do that," then mumbled
something and told me to go in peace. Hah! I went in more doubt.
Right now, drivin' Theresa's car back, I'm still doubtin'. If there's
a God, why am I on this lonely road? If there's a God, why can't I
get one good music station? If he's up there, why didn't he find
company for me? No sooner is the last question fallen out of my
brain than I come around a turn by some woods and see people
waitin' by the side of the road.

One is this round guy in a filthy jacket squattin' with his back
to me, and the other is this pretty girl or woman who's restin' her
butt against his shoulder. Her thumb is stickin' up in the air, not
like a regular hitchhiker's but over the top of her head. I must be
the only car that's come by in a long time. What are they doin'
here? If I don't stop they might be here for a week. Sal said, "Don't
pick up no one." Him and his don'ts. Still, they could be dangerous. I am a little scared. But I am more lonely than scared. And a
good judge of character most of the time. Better than Sal. That's
right. These do not look like bad people. Sal's friends not only look
like bad people but are. I'm so mad I answer him out loud right
there in the car. "You know what you can do with your don'ts,
Sal."

This could be a delivery from God. I pull over.

The girl-woman starts hoppin' up and down all excited and
then the guy gets up and starts dancin' with her. In a second they
are dancin' together and pretty soon they kind of stumble-dance
over to the car.

I bring down the passenger window.

"Oh, we are so grateful!" says the girl-woman. "We've been
here for years."

He's one of those mongol guys. She looks regular except she kind of limp-walks like she might be crippled. But she had no trouble hoppin'. She hops up and down a couple more times and says, real excited, "Getting married!"

He leans in and grins at me and says, "Me, too," then laughs so loud the car shakes.

What a couple of darlings! "Get in," I say.

They fumble and struggle, pullin' the front seat forward, him helpin' her the way Sal never does me, then him gettin' in himself.

"One of you can sit up in front," I say.

"Oh, no," says the girl-woman as he wiggles to get back with her. "We haven't been able to see or touch each other for days, until today. We *have* to sit close. We're *so* much in love!"

My heart is meltin'. I been lately asking Angelina, "What happened to love?" Here's the answer. No one talks like that anymore. Thank you, God! "Where are you goin'? I'll take you wherever you're goin'." They could say Alaska. I'd buy a road map and find the way.

"River City," says the young man. I notice in the mirror he isn't handsome the way she is pretty but is nice-lookin', despite his bulgy eyes.

"What part?"

I hear mumblin' and look back. They're conferrin' with each other. How cute!

"Downtown," says the girl-woman finally. "We have to go to the courthouse and get marriage licenses."

"More than one?"

"One for him and one for me."

"You only need one. One covers both of you."

"Oh, goodie!" she says to him.

Then we find some food. My heart is poundin' out of my ribs. "How much money do you have? Altogether."

"Have *no* money," he says.

"And you have to get a license and supper and a bus ticket back?"

"No *come* back," he says, like if I don't shut up I'm gonna make him mad pretty soon.

"Goodness! And you have nothing?"

"I have some somewhere," Beatrice says. "I don't know where.

Mrs. Holloway keeps it. We'll have to beg. Should I tell you why I didn't have time to get some?" She turns to her friend. "Should I tell her?"

"Tell what?"

"That we're running away."

"Be-ah-*triss!*"

"Oh-oh. Oh, well, don't worry. She won't tell anyone." She leans forward. "Will you?"

Livin' with Sal means tellin' nobody nothin'. I may as well not have a tongue. "You don't need to worry," I say.

"We're in a community home. No. We were. But it was terrible. We couldn't see each other. Well, Brendan was . . ."

"*Not* Brendan."

"Oh, that's right. Boombah—he likes that name—was there only a few hours really, and . . . Well, first I have to tell you I fell in love with him as soon as he was brought in. I mean the very first second I saw him. What's your name?" She pulls herself forward.

"Maria," I say, turning. "Maria Mangione. They call me Maria the Tush. You don't have to call me that. In fact, I wish you wouldn't."

"We won't. Anyway I was just heels up in love with him. I still am. He didn't fall for me right away." She turns. "Did you?"

"Don't know."

"I embarrass him. But he loves me. We're going to fight a terribly lot when we're married. It's going to be one of those kinds of marriages. I've seen plenty on HBO. People really love each other but, you know, they fight."

"Believe me. I know."

"I hope we don't."

"You have to have money to get a license," I tell her. "You have to have money to eat. You have to have money for a place to stay."

"*Some*body help us," he says.

"Who?"

"People live by river. Friends."

She eases closer to me. "Do you think we're criminals?"

"You're not criminals. Take my word."

"You think it's okay if we run away?"

They wouldn't have done this if they weren't driven to it.

That's what I think. They couldn't touch each other. That's terrible! Things must have been very bad. It wouldn't surprise me if they are also doubtin' God. I know what I'd need someone to say at a time like this. I say it. "I think runnin' away was the best thing you could do."

"Oh, you're *so* nice!" She kisses me on the neck.

I hear him gruntin' and in a moment I feel arms around my neck. He pulls hard and my head goes back. I can't see the road. I think he's gonna choke me to death the way Sal said a couple of the Gombino gang tried to choke him in the Napoli Restaurant one night. An off-duty cop happened to walk in or he might be dead. Tony had finger-scars on his neck for days. I lose sight of the road and the car wiggles. Boombah's head clamps itself to mine. "Thanks," he says as the car goes bumpin' off asphalt and onto dirt. Finally he lets go, my head snaps back and I steer us back onto the road. "You're welcome," I say. I've never loved two people at the same time so much. "So where are you going, after you get your license?"

"Bank," he says.

"Oh."

"Hold-up," he goes on. "Got to get money. Boombah put stick in pocket. Go in, say, 'Everything you got in bag, okay.' "

Is he serious?

"Tens and twenties only, please."

Sal's kind of people. At least this Brendan/Boombah is.

"We'll go together, Beatrice and me."

Am I just attracted to criminal types? I don't want to be. Anyway, they'd better consult with Sal if . . .

"Boooowahhhhh!" He's laughing a tornado laugh! What a breeze on my neck!

She starts laughing too.

They're holding onto each other laughing.

I suddenly understand, and laughter comes falling out of me for the first time in days.

"It's just a bank *building*," Beatrice explains. "There's no bank there. Eleanor lives down below. Boombah told me when we were waiting for you."

In the mirror I see her rising and kissing him on the ear.

What cuddlebugs. I just *have* to help them. The license. I'll buy it for them. "When are you gettin' married?"

"Can't know *that* yet," he says "Have to see Eleanor first. She know who can marry us."

"Are you going to have a reception?"

"Re . . . what?"

Beatrice explains. "It's like a party. You're supposed to have one after a wedding. You don't have to. My mother told me her reception after she married my father was in the Brown Palace Hotel in Denver and had three hundred people and lasted two days."

"Oh boy!" he says.

She turns to me and says, "But we're just getting married."

"No," I say.

"What?"

"You're goin' to have a reception and a big weddin'. Both as big as your mother's. Or as big as you want. And you can have anyone you want there."

"Oh, my goodness!"

"Yes. You *are!*" These kids are gonna have a weddin' they'll talk about the rest of their lives!

"Boombah?" she says. "Isn't it beautiful! Isn't it wonderful?"

He doesn't answer.

I look in the mirror.

He's gone.

I glance at the road, glance back.

She's gone too.

I turn around.

She's holdin' him on the seat, where he's collapsed and is crying.

She starts crying too.

Me, too.

Sal, do I have a surprise for you!

०᠗० TUCKER

The pessimists are telling me the Sunnyvale Project has been endangered, first by the recent flight of Brendan Flynn and now by the disappearance of both Flynn and resident Beatrice Dove. The pessimists—Vera Holloway, Chief Walters, and a few others—are unnecessarily alarmed. The project, the system itself, is being challenged but is in no great danger. In fact, the Beatrice/Brendan escapade has presented me with an unusual opportunity.

During the past twenty-four hours I've accumulated statistics regarding community home runaways, residents lost in crowds, accidents among the developmentally disabled, evidence for a rather plump addendum to my annual budget, soon to be submitted to the MRDD board.

The pressing question, the only one that ought to concern us now, is the whereabouts of our daring friends. Until they are located and brought back to Hartsville, the pessimists will appear to be credible. For that reason I formed a Recovery and Corrective Task Force, including me, Chief Walters, and MRDD board member Linda West French, who's been a consistent supporter and mover for the Sunnyvale Plan.

The three of us met yesterday for the first time and agreed that, after the pair are apprehended, we will petition the court to have them returned to the community home system. "There might be a problem with Brendan, since he's twice defied the court, but we should do our best to have him put under the guardianship and probated to MRDD. If he's brought to court, there will be some very bad publicity." I said further that I'd instructed Vera Holloway, operator of Home A, to perform an investigation of the part played by social worker Delia Fall in the flight of Flynn and Dove and to recommend dismissal if Fall is found to have been an accomplice. After a brief discussion the others expressed support for both of my positions.

We met again this morning, when I theorized that, based on young Flynn's actions the first time he ran off, the two had probably fled to River City, where police have been alerted. Naturally my hope is that they will be apprehended before we stir the lions of the media or politicians in search of an issue. I've projected three days and believe there's little chance anyone outside the system will find out about the escape before the fugitives are in hand.

The chief seems always to be drinking a beverage or eating or chewing on or biting something. This morning he was gnawing on the eraser of his long yellow pencil. After spitting a bit of rubber onto the floor, he pointed the lead-end of the pencil toward me and said, "Meanwhile, I suggest you find some way to cork up that black one."

"I wouldn't worry," I replied calmly. "If she's an accomplice, the last thing she'll want is publicity."

"People don't always act rational." He used the lead-end of his pencil to poke for a bit of rubber that had gotten caught between his teeth. "Hell, I once had my best detective go to the john and leave the charge sheets and other evidence on a little table in a room with nobody in it but the suspect and his lawyer."

"Christ sake," said Linda.

"What the hell. Everybody slips up."

"I just hope you haven't put that absentminded detective of yours on this case," Linda told him.

"Had to. He's the best I got."

"You ain't got much," she replied in her raw whiskey-fed voice.

"Only thing I could do."

Linda shrugged.

She grew up with a profoundly retarded older brother, whose care cost her family a good part of the income it made farming soybeans and corn south of Hartsville. She married a farmer and took a job in a small farm implement store. Most of her earnings went into her own bank account and eventually she bought out her employer. Over a ten-year period she built the company into the biggest of its kind in this part of the state. At some point she dismissed that husband of hers who's still, I believe, plowing the same 114 acres he had when he and Linda married. When I learned about the retarded brother, I sought her out, had a few long conversations with her, and persuaded her to seek appointment to the board.

She waited until the chief got his mind off the piece of rubber in his teeth and his eyes on her, then said, "Fact is, if either of you can't keep a lid on your subordinates for three days, it seems like you ought to do some replacing or get yourself into something safe and simple like window washing."

"Nobody here's gonna leak," the chief snapped.

"You sure, with that detective of yours on the job?"

"I ain't runnin' an implement store," he said testily. "This is a police department and, like I told you, he's the best one I got."

"I'd hate to see the second-best one." She turned on me. "Now, even though I agree we ought to keep quiet about all this, we'd better have a good story cooked up in case there is a leak."

"It won't be a problem."

"You gonna have to lie or what?"

"I prefer to call what I have in mind an explanation, not a lie."

"Whatever. Shoot."

"Well, we say news was withheld so as not to frighten our residents into doing something drastic, like fleeing to another state."

She plucked a thread off her bright green slacks, twisted it between her fingers, leaned forward in her chair and let it float into the wastebasket next to the chief's desk. "What do you think?" she said, looking across at Walters.

"Sounds fine to me," he said indifferently.

"Wouldn't hurt either of you to put a no-leaks-or-else message in a confidential memo. Send it to the people you need to. Like that detective of yours."

Walters said nothing.

"Anything else?" she asked.

There wasn't. Linda and I had earlier scheduled a lunch to discuss my budget before I presented it at the next board meeting. She drove us from the police station to Frisch's Big Boy restaurant. Over the soup portion of our soup-and-salads, we discussed the draft proposal I'd sent her, plus the addendum that resulted from the Flynn/Dove escape. It included an additional $17,452.00 for the installation of a security system, including door alarms, locks, cyclone fences, outdoor lighting, and fence alarms at each of the county homes.

"They didn't run away from a home," she pointed out.

I nodded but said, "I'm going to do more to keep residents within county home property. I'll let the board know that and tell them about new security measures I intend to introduce for games away and such. What do you think?"

"A big add-on," she said. "You're going to get some tough bread-and-butter questions because of the breakout."

"What I've told you about is only a first step. I'll also be using other means, including one that, in my view, has been minimized in this area: drugs. I'll use them in conjunction with a complete review of our behavior modification programs. And I don't intend to leave out the human factor."

"What the hell you mean by that?"

"Flynn's and Dove's self-perceived goals. We may eventually be able to lift the personal restrictions and actually allow Flynn and Dove to see each other, maybe as much as twice a month. *That's* how effective a good behavior modification program can be."

"Why don't you just have the female transferred out of the system? Why not have her sent to Florida where her mother lives?"

"For two reasons," I said. "This is Beatrice Dove's community, the one she knows and, thus far, has adapted herself to."

"Go on."

"The second is that our success with her and Flynn will strengthen support for the Sunnyvale Project." I paused, waiting for her to comment.

She didn't.

"I'd like to tell you more. Shall we get our salads?"

"Why not?"

As we picked and plucked at the colorful variety on the salad bar, I spoke about new phases I might propose for the Sunnyvale Project, such as apartment living under the guidance of a guardian for a group of selected residents, expansion of the small industry, continuation of the county's special school.

"Ambitious," she said.

"And more, I hope."

She nodded and then listened as I outlined the schedule for the phases that newly interested me. Finally she said over a forkful of avocado, "Mind if I tell you something you don't know about me?"

It seemed an odd time for autobiography, but with Linda, nothing surprises. "I'm always interested in what you say." And the truth is, I usually was.

"I've never gotten over having to live with that younger brother of mine. Never. I mean what he did to my parents and, in a roundabout way, me. He sucked time, attention, and money out of that family in such a way we ended up being pretty much slaves to him. In high school my parents came to very few of my parent-student events and never did see me play for the volleyball team, of which I was captain in my senior year. They didn't have money for extras for me because he sucked it up with doctor visits, medicine, surgery, therapeutic equipment, psychological treatment, you name it. I watched those two, my parents I mean, grow old in the few years it took Davey to reach adolescence. He's thirty now and he still chews up all their time. They don't have any life except the one centered around him." She'd parked her fork and was sitting there facing me with arms crossed. "Maybe I'm not your typical mental retardation board member. When you talked to me a couple of years ago about trying to get on your board, I became interested not out of any great love for the retarded but because I knew a system like yours would end up taking a burden off people like my parents and help free people like me." She shook her head, remembering. "Believe me," she said, "I spent many weekends when my friends were going skiing or to somewhere else sitting home and keeping his head from dropping into the cereal while I was trying to spoon the stuff into his mouth." She uncrossed her arms and took a sip from the coffee cup a waitress had just refilled. "I never came right out and said so, but for me the promise of your plan, the attraction of it, was the idea of a continuum of care, keeping these people within the system in the hands of paid professionals. Your social workers can't be paid enough, as far as I'm concerned."

I hoped my nods had let her know how sympathetic I was to her story and the attitudes it had shaped. "Your views are central to the system," I assured her.

"Maybe not central enough," she said. "And I'd feel just the same if my brother had been only mildly retarded. A nice pleasant manageable person. Someone I could take with me here or there. Less of a burden on my parents. Why? Because he'd still have controlled their lives and, to a degree, mine. Normally an eight-year-old grows up and leaves and frees the parents. With the retarded, it's different. The child stays. I know a lot of parents willingly devote much of their lives to such offspring. That's their business. But, like women and abortion, the rest of us ought to have a choice. Anything that gets away from long-term care and supervision is risky."

"As I said, nothing is in concrete."

"You continue with liberal moves and these people or clients, as you call them, will soon be back in the community, living side by side with regular citizens and you'll have to open a complaint office."

"I've planned always to have firm control."

She shook her head. "Are you going to have control, Tucker, when at three o'clock some morning, some horny client of yours decides to go next door and climb into bed with some widow lady? You see stories in the paper all the time from places where they've tried community living. Neighbors complain, don't want the retarded living among them. Neither would I. Would you?"

"As I said . . ."

"Yes, yes, it's not in concrete. Well, bottom line is, if you'll get that apartment living idea—in fact, all ideas that would take residents out of the direct control and supervision of community home operators, the ones *we* can hold responsible—I'll bring the board around on the rest."

"I'm very grateful." I asked if she wanted more coffee—I myself needed a refill—and she did. I signaled the waitress, then said, "About a more immediate issue, the runaways."

"What about it?"

"Well . . . what do you think I ought to do when the two fugitives are brought back?"

She stared at me, thinking I guess. She kept thinking until the coffees were poured. As the waitress moved away, she said, "I suggest you put the torch to your sweet-treatment approach."

I didn't like her description of my plan. "Which part?" I said.

She blew steam from the top of the coffee cup toward me, then said, "I guess all of it." She nodded and lowered the cup. "That's right. I think you ought to ship her off to Florida, like I said."

"I can't just decide . . ."

"That's one of your handicaps, Tucker," She leaned toward me, eyeing my forehead. "I don't want a couple of overheated residents embarrassing the system. Neither do you. Makes us all look like fools. You've been damned lucky so far."

"So I should . . ."

". . . get the paperwork started." Her eyes fell to mine. "Work on it. If you keep those two within a day's distance from each other, you're gonna have problems up the ying-yang, friend. And not from me. They're gonna want to get married." Again she nodded. "Florida or someplace far."

Linda had, fortunately, given me room in which I could operate. "Moving Dove is, I think, a possibility."

"Good."

"As for Brendan, I still think, don't you, that a carefully supervised behavior modification program will eventually bring him around to behaving as a community home resident is expected to."

"I'd sure keep a close eye on him. That kid's erratic as hell. And I think he has some criminal tendencies. He hasn't been in residentive programs long enough. Maybe he'll come around." She nodded, finished her coffee and reached for the check.

"Here," I said, putting out my hand, "let me take care of that."

"No," she said. "Today I'm the one who's buying."

⚬◡⚬ ROSA

I get on the little bus and right away I'm scared 'cause the only one I know there is Andy. He's sitting in a sideways-seat behind the driver's seat next to a pretty lady. Everyone is staring at me like they never saw a nine-year-old before. Andy is no help 'cause he's staring too. He's not doing it in a nosy way like the others but like someone who's looking at you but doesn't see you. I stop on the step and try to say "Andy" but nothing comes out.

"Come all the way in and have a seat," says the lady. I make myself take a step up and make myself look past all the strange faces I saw from the step and all the ones I now see behind them. I search around but don't see any seat.

Then an old-lady's voice comes from the back. "Therff room neff to me," it says.

"That's Miss Goss," says the driver. He's a very round black man and he's smiling a huge smile at me.

"My name is Delia," says the lady next to Andy. I think Delia is the name of the person who invited me. She's black but not as black as the driver and not very old. She has friendly eyes.

Now I see popping up from the back seat an old-fashioned kind of straw hat with a pin sticking through it that looks like it's also going through the head that comes up with it. It's a real old head with gray hair poking out under the hat every such way. When the lady grins I see only three teeth. She looks like the Wicked Witch of the West. *Get me out of here,* I think. "Huh . . . hey, Andy," I finally get myself to say. "Let's not go."

That must have sounded real stupid to him 'cause it was my idea for us to get our parents' permission in the first place. The one who must have been Delia called him and asked if he wanted to come with a few people from the community homes on a field trip to the zoo. He didn't know why she asked him but he wanted to go. He wouldn't have to get permission from school because it was going to be on a Saturday. He asked if he could bring a friend and Delia said yes. And then he called me. I wanted to go 'cause I'd be around people like Brendan. I really miss him. Nobody has seen or heard about him since he painted the school building. Andy heard he had run away. Poor Brendan. Last week I got permission to take home the drawing I made of him after Mrs. Dill took all our pictures down and put up horrible Easter bunny cutouts. Anyway I told Andy, "I want to go." Only now I didn't.

I can see he's too scared to speak. He's visited old people's homes but the only retarded person he's ever really been around is Brendan. He just smiles. No help from Andy.

Okay. I decide not to get off the bus 'cause I'll feel stupid. I go to the back and try not to look. But I do. Every time I do I see a weird face. I get to the back and sit in the only seat that's not taken.

When you see a bunch of retarded people all at once it scares you. You think they're making faces at you but they aren't. Their expressions are just, you know, their expressions. And after you figure that out, which I did after the bus was going for a while, you figure out they're staring 'cause they don't know you. After a while they stop making me nervous, and I start watching them.

They look out the windows. At cows. A flat trailer with a tractor on it. People's faces in cars going by. They rock forward and back or lean way over. They make odd sounds. Sometimes they say something to themselves.

Suddenly this Miss Goss I'm sitting by climbs over me to see a train that's under the overpass we're on. When she stops looking and climbs back, she says "I come from Finfinnati." It sounds like her nose is talking.

A man on my other side turned his back completely away from me when I sat down. He also blew his nose in a real loud way that made me uncomfortable. He wears an old dark blue jacket, the kind I don't think people have worn for years. The flap on one shoulder is torn and hangs down. There's a finger-sized hole right below the shoulder in back. Now he turns back, comes all the way around, snorting and snuffing as he comes. I see his skin is real white and has a lot of zits. His black hair has some kind of greasy stuff on it and hangs down messy on both sides. He leans down to me. "Says that *alla* time!" he says real loud. He hammers the bottom part of his hand on the steel part of the seat in front of us and says it again, "Alla time!" Then he turns back, wiggling and twisting and snorting. It takes him about eleven moves to get himself back to where he started. When he is completely back around he says the same thing again. "*Alla* time!" Says it over and over. "*Alla* time! *Alla* time!"

Miss Goss just ignores him. "Whaff your name?" she asks me.

"Rosa Guerrero."

"Pwinfeff name."

"What?"

"Pwinfeff! Pwinfeff!"

"Princess?" I say.

She nods and looks out the window again.

She did a funny thing after I sat down. She put her hand over mine and held it. I thought it was to make me feel at home but the way she squeezes when a loud truck goes by or we hit a big bump makes me think she's holding on to me to make herself feel at home.

I remember my grandmother Antonia telling us how she came to the U.S. from Mexico on a bus. She tells the story just about every time she talks to me and my sister. She says her mama and papa who were with her were afraid the Immigration would send them back at the border. When they didn't, her mama and papa cried. She didn't know what they were crying about but she cried too. That's the end of the story. I'm tired of hearing it but now, on this bus, I'm thinking I know now why she always tells it. It must be easy to remember a bus ride. The same people are there for a long time and you keep seeing them do all sorts of things and it all stays in your brain.

"Kind of animaff you like?" Miss Goss says.

"Hippopotamuses," I tell her.

"Yippee!" She stands up and claps her hands. She's not much taller than me. She claps her hands several times and plops right back down again.

No one else seems to notice except Andy, who's looking back and smiling.

The man with the greasy hair works himself around again and says in my ear loud as the first time, "Lions!" He must think I'm deaf!

I lean away and nod but he doesn't see me 'cause he's working his way around again.

"Delia fay, 'Who wantff to go to foo?' " says Miss Goss. "I fay, 'Me!' " Up she stands again. "Yippee!"

She's wearing a blue dress with white and purple flowers on it. She's the only one in any way dressed up. I think it's strange to dress up to go to a zoo. I don't like dressing up even for church.

An old man with sneaky eyes in the row in front of me has been watching me ever since I got in, turning back and looking at me up and down. I'm trying not to look at him.

I hear animal noises. First I think it's the man with the sneaky eyes. I look over. He's still staring but his mouth isn't moving.

They're grunting noises. Others are looking around now. Then I see the man next to Sneaky Eyes kind of roll off his seat and land in the aisle on his feet but all hunched over. His arms are real loose and he starts screeching.

Everyone starts laughing.

A man with white hair combed real neat turns around and is holding a hard sandwich bun to his mouth. "Good afternoon, ladybugs and chitlins, and welcome to the Cleaver County Community Homes Special Bus, where Slow Poke Billy Burris has just begun his animal imitation act. Appears right now to be . . . a baboon? That right, Slow Poke?"

Slow Poke turns but makes only grunting sounds.

"Hey, hobos and tramps, the man looks like a baboon and hops like a baboon and answers like a baboon. When Slow Poke gets into his act, he gets into his act! Slow Poke Billy Burris is being one big baboon-type monkey! Let's give a hand to Slow Poke!"

No one claps.

Some people are in the aisle now and some are standing or kneeling on their seats.

Billy hops up on to the seat he was in and leaps off backwards into the aisle. Just like a monkey. Then he rushes to the back and almost touches me and turns around and rushes to the front.

We're all laughing and cheering, even Andy, who's kneeling on his side seat to see better.

"More!" someone says. "More!"

Billy does more jumping around until he gets tired and holds onto the steel bar on his seat. He's breathing real hard.

At first Delia was looking like she was enjoying Slow Poke but now she says in a soft voice, "Time to sit down, Billy." She's not at all like the supervising teachers when we're in buses on field trips. They only give orders. "Keep it down!" "Don't stand up!" "Stop talking!" "Do you want me to report you?"

Billy climbs back in his seat and turns into a man again.

Sneaky Eyes pats him on the back.

I think Billy was ready to stop anyway. He looks tired.

Someone says, "Yeah, Billy!"

Now a lot of us clap.

When everyone is back in a seat, Delia says into the mirror, "I have a question."

"What?" the man next to me says. He has turned and is facing the front now.

Others who were talking to each other turn to the front too.

"Who does your life belong to?"

What a weird question! I think.

"Wife?" says someone.

Several people laugh.

"Life," Delia says loudly.

"*I* know, *I* know," says Miss Goss.

"Who, Helen?"

"Miffuff Holloway!"

"No!" says the man on my other side. "Not right."

"So what is the right answer?" asks Delia.

"Ohio," he says.

"Ohio?" says someone.

About three people groan and the one who was staring at me snaps his eyes closed.

"Muff be Miffuff Holloway," Miss Goss says.

"What about you yourselves? Each of you."

"That's crazy," says the man next to me.

"Why, Melvin?"

"Want to live in China. See those round bears. Can't go there."

"Pandas."

"Right, *Deel*-ya. China. Can't go."

"Any reason you can't start finding out how you might be able to, someday?"

"Don't know."

"There isn't. Someone can help you look into how to get to China. The way Mrs. Oliver at the county library helps you find books. In fact, when we get back, I'll help you find out how."

"O-*kay!*" Melvin turns and looks down at me like the teacher just said he got the highest grade.

Miss Goss starts crying.

"What's the matter?" I say.

"Want to go to Kanfaf and fee my niefe."

"She'll help you," I tell her.

"Yes, Helen, I will," says Delia. "I'll help you. Now, all of you, I have to tell you something."

"Tell us!" says someone.

"You're going to get a chance today to decide something for yourselves."

"What?" says the one who said, "Tell us!"

"When we have snack time, you're going to have a chance to see a wedding."

"Yippee!" says Miss Goss. She leaps up again. "Yippee!"

"Beatrice Dove, whom you all know, and Brendan Flynn, who was the newest person in House A, are getting married at the zoo."

"Andy!" I shout.

He's jumped up on his seat and is squatting there and grinning at me with his fist up high in victory. He's worse than Miss Goss.

"Wow!" I say.

Others are shouting too. "Yeah!" "Yippee!" "Way to go!"

"Delia?" says Melvin over the noise.

She doesn't hear him.

"Hey, Delia!" he yells.

"What, Melvin?" she says when the noise dies down.

"Can't go. They ran away. We can't go."

"No one *has* to go," Delia says. "You can have your snack time at the snack bar. Or watch some animals."

"They have to come back with us," Melvin tells her.

"They *are* coming back."

"Are?" Miss Goss says like she can't understand why they would.

"That's right. Sarah Fuller, Brendan's teacher, and I are help-ing them file a petition—that's a request—that will permit them to live by themselves."

"Wherever they want?" says Slow Poke. It's the first time he's talked since I've been on the bus.

"Wherever they want."

"Damn good," he says.

The one next to him is nodding, looking at Delia and nodding.

"I ain't doing to the wedding," Melvin says, and he folds his arms, making himself wider and kind of pushing me into Miss Goss.

"*I* am!" Miss Goss says.

"You're a bubblehead, Melvin!" someone says.

"That's not true," Delia corrects. "In fact, Melvin is doing just what he should be doing, making a choice for himself. Sarah and

I will take turns staying with him, and anyone else who doesn't care to watch the wedding."

"Not me!" says Miss Goss.

"Before you decide, you'd better realize a couple of things. First, Beatrice and Brendan made a choice too. They decided to have their wedding at the zoo. They want you to be there only if you choose to be. Beatrice called me and told me this. She said she and Brendan didn't want anyone to come to the wedding if they didn't want to. She said she didn't want anyone to be in trouble."

"They be in trouble," someone says.

"You might be in trouble too, Delia," Melvin warns.

She nods. "I'm making a choice too. It wasn't an easy thing to do. I made it for myself. And I know it might affect yours. But *it's* not your choice. You have to make your own. Like Melvin."

"I made mine," says someone.

"Me too," says Slow Poke.

"Me me me too too too," says Miss Goss.

"What about you, Andy?" Delia says. "And you too, Rosa? You didn't know why you were invited. Do you feel tricked?"

"Yes," says Andy. "But I don't care."

"Me either," I say.

I see Delia's eyes smiling.

Andy can hardly sit still.

I can. I have to pee. If I move around at all, I'm going to pee on this bus. It will be very embarrassing if I do. If I have to, though, I'll try and get some on Melvin's shoe. I do know he should be able to do what he wants. I just don't like him.

"Rosa?" Delia says.

"Yes!" I say so loudly I make some of the others laugh.

I hear a kind of a growl.

Everyone's been chatting, but now they all shut up and turn. First I get scared 'cause I think they're turning toward me. But they're not. They're turning toward the old man with the sneaky eyes who was watching me when I first got on the bus.

He's not looking at any of them. Just staring at the back of the seat in front of him.

There's another growl.

"Was that Geezer?" says Delia in a surprised voice.

The growl was so low, like a giant frog in the bottom of a well, and scratchy too, like a snow shovel when it starts scraping the street.

"I think he's gonna talk," says someone.

"He ain't never talked," says someone else.

"Shh," says Melvin.

Everyone's watching his head. It has silver-black hair kind of thick like a young person's, but cut short. I can't see his eyes. He does speak, real slow, in the strangest voice I ever heard. "Best. God damn." Like it's coming out of the ground. "Day." Like one of those voices the devil makes when it talks through other people's mouths in scary movies. "In. My. Whole." Even deeper, way deeper than his voice when he growled. "Fucking. Life." That's all it says. There's a kind of sound at the end. "Bpp." Like that. But then it doesn't go on. He just sits there, the one Delia called Geezer, just sits there and stares at the seat in front of him.

I have the feeling he won't speak again for years.

"Wafn't that ffomething?" says Miss Goss.

I think Delia forgot what she was going to ask or tell me.

∘◉∘ SALVATORE

What am I doin' at the weddin' of a coupla boobies in a big fuckin' birdcage at the River City Zoo? I'm doin' what my precious Maria told me I'd better be doin', pretendin' to enjoy myself. She was just about gonna have a crack-up if I didn't say I'd come.

Hey, the truth of it is, so far this ain't half-bad.

The boobies remind me of clowns. With them and the animals it's like bein' at a circus when I was a kid. That's not all. For the first time in a long time I'm at a place where no one is sizin' me up for a hit. That I know of.

I wouldn't of been here if I hadn't of needed someone to go get my girl Theresa's car. Eddie the Pipe—supposed to be one of my right-hands, right?—got his ass on a jury. "Hey, boss," he says when he finds out, "get me off."

I have to explain. The bird-turd las' month was suppose to go down the courthouse and see who of us was on the jury rolls, and then pay the county clerk as usual to take any of us off. Kind of job almost a kid could do. So he goes down with a list with all the guys' names on it and comes back and says, "Didn't see any of the guys there." Dick-brain didn't bother to check for his own fuckin' name! Beat that? Now it comes up and he's cryin' in my office, "Get me off the list." Jesus! My old man, Mario the Snake, would of put his cigar out in this ball-sack's eyes! Not Salvatore the Truck! I'm so fuckin' softhearted I think I should of been a priest like my cousin Dominic. Truth is, I want to watch his teeth come out his ass but know how hard it is to get even bad help these days. I want his garbage-face out of my sight for a while so I say, "Look, mush-brain, I'm gonna let 'em call you on the jury. I'm not only gonna let 'em call you, I'm gonna pay off the clerk to put you on some miserable hairball of a case like two ugly tits suin' each other for everything they got, somethin' that will drag on for fuckin' weeks." What I should do is what I did to Alberto Erkalino in Miami in '71. What I might of done if I had in my hand when Eddie came to me cryin' the fuckin' pitchfork I used on Alberto! "Now get the fuck out of here!" He hopped away. I paid off the clerk and the dickhead was put out of my sight for days.

I don't miss him personally but I got no one to do my pickups and deliveries. When it was time to get Theresa's car I said to Maria, "Why don't you take a bus down and pick up Theresa's Celica so's I can trade it in." I didn't tell her I'm tradin' it in 'cause I heard the fuckin' Gombino Family might be comin' lookin' for it and the other eleven my guys stole out of their warehouse in Detroit last month. Others are in use around the city, but I gave a nice red one to Theresa. I figure why not send Maria. She ain't seen Theresa in quite a while.

Truth is, I hardly ever get Maria mixed up in Business. There's a lotta things she don't know about. One is Legs Diamond, my girlfriend. Her real name is Barbara Fuselli, Mike the Skunk's sister. Reason I call her Legs Diamond is I bought her a garter belt with three three-carat beauties right on it. Only way Maria is ever gonna find out about Legs is over my dead body. Which is just what my body will be if she does find out. A no-win situation. Hey! Way I got it figured, in this life nobody wins. It's who gets the most fun out of losin'.

So Maria anyway comes back from Theresa and is waitin' in the kitchen with a story I can hardly fuckin' believe. About pickin' up two boobs who run away from a looney house and are gonna get married.

"What the hell you pickin' up boobs for?" I'm thinkin' they could of been Gombino tomahawks in disguise from Detroit. I'm thinkin' I should of sent one of Eddie's brothers or someone other than my precious Maria.

"I ain't as dumb as I look, Sal. You see these people, you *know* they ain't trouble."

"Awright, awright," I say. "So what do you care if a pair of boobs gets married?"

"They've become my friends, Sal. I even went with 'em to get the marriage license. And we're both goin' to the weddin'."

"Weddin'? I ain't goin' to no fuckin' boobies' weddin'."

"You're goin', Sal. You're goin' for me. And you're gonna at least pretend you're enjoyin' yourself."

"Hey!" I put my fingers together and wiggle my hand upside down at her. "What the hell you gettin' so uppity with me about?"

"My time has come to be uppity."

She says she found out from one of the boob's friends there's people livin' in rubble down by the river and the city is gonna scrape the people and the rubble in the water.

"Who's pushin' the rubble in the water?"

"I told you. The city."

"No, Maria. The city don't do that kind of work no more." It don't because of me. I had my lawyers get an ordinance pushed through that says they got to contract out for work like that. And they're supposed to contract with us. "Who did the city *hire* to do the job?"

She's standin' at the stove. She turns around with her face in a fist. "They're gonna shove poor people in the river and you want to know who owns the bulldozer?"

"That's right, Maria. I need to know."

She turns away. "On my mother's forehead, I swear I made a mistake marryin' into the Family."

"Don't say that, Maria!" I got my finger pointed at her. "Don't fuckin' say that!"

"I said it." She ain't lookin' at my finger. She bubbles on about the Family. She remembers how my old man and his guys treated her like a lady. She remembers him slippin' a grand into her bra on the porch of the yacht club the night we was married. She remembers a lot of nice things about my mother and my brothers and sisters and about my guys and their wives. "*You're* the problem, Sal," she says. "I live with a man who's got Business all over the place and don't tell me nothin'. I come in after makin' a couple of new friends, and you give me the third degree." She turns with her spatula and puts a line of tomato sauce across the table. "I need people to talk to. Everybody does. You got the guys. Maybe you also got a girlfriend. You got a girlfriend?"

"Hey! You think I'm crazy?"

"Don't ask."

On she goes about the boob friends.

I got to know who the fuck's got the contract for the rubble. I decide I'll later call Louie, my warning guy, and send him down to Public Works to find out.

Maria is now tellin' me the weddin' is tomorrow. Says the boobs are right now in a bank downtown making their weddin' invitations on cardboard with fuckin' crayons.

"It's eight o'clock at night." I wonder if she's gone fuckin' crazy. "What bank?"

"A closed-down bank."

I only now notice she's got a ton of pasta cookin' and is also simmerin' eight hundred gallons of sauce. The kitchen's been gettin' like the steam bath down at Ballestrere's Gym. Whew! I open my collar.

"What the hell they goin' to a closed-down bank for?"

"Their friend lives there." She turns with the spatula and it makes a splash on the wall that looks like modern art. "Why would they be sittin' in a regular bank at eight o'clock at night doin' invitations?"

I swear to God, it's like listenin' to Gracie Allen. Bring up

Gracie Allen and my kids don't fuckin' know who I'm talkin' about. They got no history, the kids these days.

Before Maria turns back I see the sauce spilled on her apron. Looks like the bullet holes we left in Beans Rafetto the night we found him messin' with Dondero the Prick's girlfriend. Everything I notice has somethin' to do with Business. I'm prob'ly goin' nuts.

More important than which is, I'm burnin' to know who's gonna be puttin' the fuckin' rubble in the water. Who could it be when I just got done makin' a deal with the city's Public Works director that says our guys will get all the rubbish and landfill?

I'll get Louie to find out.

"Maria?"

"What you want?"

"Why you cookin' all that stuff?"

"For the reception," she says, turnin' an' lookin' at me like I should of figured it out.

"When is this weddin'?"

"Tomorrow mornin' at ten."

"Tomorrow! Where?"

"In the birdcage at the zoo."

The zoo! Fuckin' crazy! "Maria?"

"You heard me right, Sal. They want to get married at the zoo. I know why. The animals don't tell 'em where to stand. The animals don't tell 'em when to eat. The animals don't tell 'em when they can go to the john. The animals don't tell 'em when to pick up somebody's car. They feel comfortable around the animals. They feel safe. They want to get married at the zoo and that's where they're gonna get married."

"The reception. Where's that?"

"At the zoo."

"You're makin' a joke with me, Maria."

"I ain't makin' a joke, Sal. Not only that." She turns again with the fuckin' spatula. This time the sauce comes my way. I duck but a lot of it goes across my shoulder and cheek. "You got to call the guy who runs the place and make sure we can use the cage from ten to noon."

"I don't have Business at the zoo. Tell 'em to have it in a church. I know a lotta churches I can fix 'em up in."

"The zoo, Sal," she says like my old Army sergeant. "Are you deaf?"

Fuckin' boobs!

"You hear me?"

"Yeah, yeah, I hear you."

So, like I started out to say, this is where we are. At the fuckin' zoo. Boobs and strange birds and other things all around me. After I got the clearance by callin' Louie who called the mayor who called the zoo director, I myself personally got the Armando Balducci Trio, two violins and a flute. A surprise for Maria. They're her favorites after Sinatra. She kissed me when we got here and she saw 'em over in the corner under the palm fronds. "You prob'ly ain't as bad as you act," she tells me.

It ain't all hearts and music here, though.

They got these fuckin' big lizards in the pools around where we're standin'. Look like fuckin' alligators but Maria tells me they're iguanas. One little hop up and they got you by the leg. I got Pistolino ready in case they open their mouths. I'm watchin' one of the monsters watchin' me when Maria brings over the two that's gettin' married.

The chick walks funny but is a real cutie. Blonde too. I like blondes, the exception bein' Maria, who's got black hair. Legs is a blonde but her blonde comes out of a bottle. This one's looks real. I give her the royal treatment the way my old man used to do with the babes. I bend down and kiss her hand.

"You phony!" Maria whispers as I come up.

"Are you a count or something?" Blondie says.

I laugh. "Naw, just a bill collector, you might say."

"Oh." She's impressed. I can tell.

I don't look at Maria 'cause I know she's rollin' her eyes.

This Brendan who she says I got to call him Boombug or somethin' looks like a regular-type boob but he ain't. I know from what Maria said and I been likin' him ever since. Ran away from a fuckin' courtroom in the middle of his own trial for tryin' to demolish a school. That's big league! Then is picked up and escapes, bringin' the babe with him. These two are the Bonnie and Clyde of boobs! I stick out my hand and shake the shit out of his. "I'm pleased to know you, Mr. Boombug."

"Boombug?" says Blondie.

He starts laughin' and don't stop. Roombly roombly boom! He laughs in a way that makes the parrots on branches all around us start squawkin'. The other boobies look up and around the way people look up when a storm is comin'. He keeps laughin'. He laughs so hard he falls down on the asphalt path where we're standin' and starts kickin' his legs in the nice tuxedo he got on.

What the hell's so funny?

When he finally gets up with the help of Maria and me and his woman, he says, "Mr., heh, heh, heh, Boombug." He starts laughin' again.

"His name is Boom*bah*," says Maria.

I screwed up his name. He don't get mad. He laughs. He's laughin' again. I see one of the alligators openin' his mouth. But he ain't goin' after anyone. He must be laughin'. One of the parrots says somethin'. It sounds like, "Don't forget to feed the fish."

That gets everyone laughin', me included.

"Hey, Boombug," I say. "The wife and me are gonna take care of you and the missus. No question. C'mere." I not only like this kid. I love him. I stick my arm around him. "Where you guys want to go on your honeymoon?"

"On island," he says.

"That's terrific! Which one! I got travel connections that can put you on any island you want. Virgin. Hawaiian. Bahamas. Whatever."

He turns and points. It looks like he's pointin' at the monkey cage.

What the fuck?

"He means the river," says Blondie. "We want to have our honeymoon on the little island out there. We might even want to live there."

"What island?"

"We saw it when Maria drove over the bridge."

"Pilgrim's Island?"

"I don't know what it's called," she says. "We were going to make it our country."

The little lump of land she means is right across from Marcello's Restaurant. Marcello was going to buy it from the state and put his restaurant on it. Marcello ain't smart. Someone had to tell him bad weather and ice in the river would cut down on business. The place is about fifty-yards long and thirty-yards wide when the river's low, and full of trees except for a little landing place at the north end.

"You pullin' my leg? There's nobody on the place."

They both smile. "Why we go there," Boombug says.

"Okay. You like privacy. But there ain't even tents. And that wind off the river is cold at night."

"Eleanor gave us old blanket *she* find."

"We may bring water," says Blondie. "That's all."

This ain't no joke!

"Got to go soon. Police come."

"Listen," I say. "You don't want to go to that dump. Just lay low for a while. I'll find a way to get you outta the state."

"No," says Blondie.

"What you mean, 'no'?"

"We're going to start our new country. Fresh. With as little help as possible."

A coupla boobs are gonna start a new country. I gotta put my hand over my mouth to keep from laughin'. I look at Maria. She ain't laughin'. She's lookin' at Beatrice and waitin' for her to say more. Now I know *she's* gone fuckin' over the end. I say to Blondie, "You can't go live on a dirtball full of trees in the middle of the river and just start a country."

"I've been told all my life I'd never get married," she says, kind of pissed lookin'. "And I'm just about to."

"But . . . ."

"I was also told I'd never walk without a walker. But I do and I was even a cheerleader. Briefly."

"Sal, you was put on this earth to take all the fun out of people's lives," says Guess Who?

Now Blondie says to me, "Did you ever think of starting your own country?" Like she been readin' my mind or somethin'.

"Well, everyone thinks about that sometime or other." Truth is, I been thinkin' about it all my life. Lately I been thinkin' it's easier to take over one that's already there. I got my eye on Costa Rica. All I got to do is get some kind of conglomeration together and . . . Shit! What am I thinkin' about Costa Rica for? "Listen. Your idea gets better the more I think about it." Truth is, I'm beginnin' to love it. I'll buy the fuckin' island from the city or state or whoever owns it and give it to 'em. Legalized gamblin' ain't far off in this state. I'll get Boombug and the broad to let me open a casino. That'll be part of the deal. "I got a boat and sleepin' bags and all the sort of stuff you gonna need. You want to go to Pilgrim that's your business."

"It's what we want," she says.

He nods.

"Okay," I say, "when you get hitched I'll take you there."

"No," says Blondie. "We have to go our own way."

"Hey, babe! You think there's a ferry service?"

"Well . . " She looks at Boombug. "Don't worry. This time I won't let anything slip out." Then she says back to me, "I can't tell you how, but . . . we have a way."

∘◖◗∘ ARNOLD

I'm running, running, man, like I did that third night at Pong Chu. Running 'cause the devil's on my tail. Feel like I'm running inside a balloon, man, up and around. There's got to be some way out. Where am I going? Don't remember. Run, man, run!

Come back last night on acid so cheap I didn't have to pay for it. Come back to the shithole I live in with Slim and the Mex and see this mother, I think—no, man, don't think—*know*, man, is the final fucking Cong. Must have come downstream in a cutout canoe and is ready to send up a flare. See that slant-eye in the hut sitting around the candle with Slim and the Mex and some little white chick and go berserking nearly off the edge of the globe, man. What in the fucking hell is going on?

"This mother paying you off or what?" I say to Slim.

He mumbles some oh-shit-he's-off-again talk to the Mex and next thing he and the Mex are trying to grab me.

"It's different now," I tell 'em. I try and point at the Cong, say,

"Ain't seeing things. Look at those eyes!" But they're spinning me around.

The Mex is mad as a bee. "What the hell you think you be sayin' to our guest?"

Guest! Now I know what is really up. Slim and the Mex are fucking spies! V.C. spies! They brought the Cong dog in to check out the territory. Bad shit! I start fighting off Slim and the Mex like I never did before. The Cong stands up. His chick is small but this dog is one big hound. In the candlelight he looks kind of white. Yeah, man, right motherfucking on! What am I, stupid? They aren't going to send no yellow-face. But they couldn't change the eyes. The eyes are the eyes of a Cong!

A lot of paranoia potential. I know that this morning, man. But this was last night.

Lupe and Slim swing me out of the hut and someone takes hold of my feet. Slim has my head tight and I can't look down. I start kicking, sure it's the motherfucking Cong. I yell. I yell real loud. I don't care if the blues hear me. Lot of those blues fought in the war. I yell: "Let go of me, you goddamned yellow-backed un-American son-of-a-bitches!" Shit like that. Loud as can be. That Lucinda bitch yelled from her carton, "Shut that crazy dog up! I can't get a wink of sleep!" Thing is, they drag me out of Reagan-ville, all the *way* out! Right to the end of that old factory building that's still standing. In my head I think, "These mothers are going to kill this marine!" No way I'm going to let that happen. I am going to make up for the shame of Nam the way I hear those beach-jumpers in Saudiland did. The Marines ain't taking any more shit! The Cong or whoever has let go of my feet so's they can drag me easier. I drop down and swing my legs, tripping Lupe and the Weed. Then I get up and run for light.

In a second I hear Lupe yell after me, "We been having a party for our guests! You be fucking it up, Arnold! Tomorrow they be getting married at the zoo! You be ruining it for them! You was being invited. Not now, Arnold! What's the matter with you?"

You think any of that matters to me last night?

Shee-yit!

I finish the night at the Green Halo Saloon where the yuppie dogs like to buy me free beers and listen to me tell them what it's going to be like when the Cong come. Last night I don't tell them the shooting and screaming is about to get underway. I am calm as a V.C. camp at midnight. "Hey, Vet, what's the latest word on the invasion?" one of them finally asks. I see their little crispy-mouth smiles moving like worms. Am looking at their bottled tans dripping down their faces. Am watching their skins get as smooth as a computer top. Just sit there and grin. They buy me a tableful of beer. Finally I speak. I say, "Tomorrow the shit's gonna fly." They laugh. Man, do they laugh!

There is no going back to the huts. Too much trouble and yackety-yack there. The Vet knows he has to find another place to sleep. Does that often. Sometimes in back of a Macy's truck. Sometimes under the phone company stairs. Used to sleep on the grate near the bus depot but they put a light over it and now robbers and thugs can see. Take turns coming down and kicking shit out of you. My left hip don't care. It went numb near Chu Lai. But the rest of me does. I end up between two rocks under the War Memorial Bridge.

I dream a lot of dreams. In one I am a mirror in a psychedelic barber shop.

Shee-*yit!*

Colors, man! There for a long time after I woke up. They phase up into the blue and I begin looking around. Am hearing strange tractor sounds. What the fuck is that? Don't know. Start climbing up the rocks to go to breakfast at All Night Hamburger across the river. Big Ham Dickson owns the place and was in Nam. Has got himself the "Hell on Wheels" insignia tattooed on the big muscle of his right arm. Got a little table at the back of the kitchen where he feeds me and some of the other vets around here. Feeds us the stuff left on the breakfast plates. If it ain't much, he'll cook us up some hashbrowns special. Lot of us sit there with him after breakfast and talk about the bad days. There's a bucket in the corner where he puts his tips. Is saving to take several of us to the Nam Memorial in D.C. I'm going, man. Want to look at the names of my buddies. One of them ain't dead yet but his name is there. May as well be. What's left of him is in a box on a bed in some VA hospital in Philly.

Start back over the bridge to do some grubbing and hear those tractor noises. Look down river and see shit going in. Must be halfway across when I realize what is going in is the huts. Holy shit! I start running. Don't know how long it takes me. Nearly ten minutes maybe. I come down Washington to see them. Bulldozers. Three big suckers. They're pushing all our poor peoples' lives and belongings into the fucking river. In Slim and Lupe's place is my commendation medal! Now it all comes piecing back together.

Last night! The Cong bastard! The Weed and the Mex! Fucking traitors. The Cong have stolen government tractors and are pushing the rest of us into the river. Didn't I see this coming? Didn't I warn them? Jesus! Where's the Weed and the Mex? The zoo. They're reconnoitering at the fucking zoo! Fuck this! Fuck it! Got no goddamn M-16.

I'm now thirty feet away. I start picking up slabs of concrete, ones I can manage, and fling them at the 'dozers. Can't see the drivers' faces. Know they're fucking Cong! "Stop, you bastards!" I shout. "Stop!" All the floatable shit, the crates and such, have been broken up and lie in a pile on the far side of the last 'dozer. Old Charles Feeblebrain's desk is there all smashed up. Did they make a grave out of his hole? Goddamn! No fucking M-16! Now the son-of-a-bitch in the nearest tractor turns it on me. I fling a couple of hunks of concrete but he keeps coming. The blade is scraping toward me, popping little stones and bits of concrete as it comes. I keep throwing. "You fucking murderers!" I can see the driver's face. He ain't a Cong. I yell. "You fucking traitors!" He keeps coming. He's going to have me pinned against a pile of brick in a few seconds, in the rubble they ain't got to yet. Shee-*yit!* It don't stop me, though, it don't. We backed off too soon at Pong Chu. This soldier ain't backing off this time! This Marine is going to do to the Cong what he been hearing the young ones did to the ragheads in Iraqville. *Can't.* He traps me inside a little curve in the bricks. I can see there's no way out. I try to scramble over the bricks and he's going to turn the tractor and plaster me into them. Fuck him! I pick up bricks and begin throwing. At his fucking head. I hit him with one. A few throws later I hit him with another. He revs down the tractor engine. This old Marine is fighting off a 'dozer singlehanded!

But I'm not.

What I don't see is what the tractor driver must have seen when he turned around to get out of the way of a brick. I don't see them 'til after the engine slows and someone yells, "Knock that shit off, lunatic, or you'll be eatin' .38 slugs!" And around the tractor comes this tall guy about my age with skin like engine oil and a black overcoat and white scarf and matching fucking hat. He's holding what is the biggest fucking sneezer I have ever seen. Alls I can think is I was in one losing war and I ain't gonna be in another one. No one's gonna blame me for not winning or trying to win this one. I let go with a sharp-edged stone which goes right for the bastard's hat. He ducks and delivers a shot between my legs. It hits a brick behind me—fssshinnnggggg!—and goes up. Fuck if I'm about to quit! I bend over and pick up two more bricks. I cock my arm and see the bastard waving the green tractor back with his pistol. The engine's now on idle and I hear the driver say, "We've got orders to get all this fill into the river." The mad dog with the pistol says, "You and your two buddies and the lunatic will be fill if you don't get those things outta here." Now he turns to me. "Put those fuckin' rocks down or the next one I shoot goes in your fuckin' mouth." He turns. "Hey Tony!" He waves his arm. "Bring the limo over here." I'm still holding the bricks. I see a big black car back up behind the tractor, then turn toward the pistol man and me. The tractor backs up and turns toward the river to get out of the limo's way. On the side of the tractor I read:

RED LUCK CORP.
REMOVAL & DISPOSAL
566-3312

Pistol man says to the driver, "Give you ten minutes to get these fuckin' things down the street and back on their rigs. Another five to be outta here. On foot. My guys and me are takin' the rigs."

"My boss ain't gonna like this. We got only half the job done."

"Your fuckin' boss already has a broken leg. And 'cause we didn't catch you in fuckin' time, he's gonna get two."

"Okay, okay. We're goin'." The 'dozer driver waves the other two drivers toward Washington Street.

As of that moment I had not given an inch of U.S. territory. I had failed to fire off my brick rounds only because I was reconnoitering what was going on. The end result of that was I didn't know.

Now I hear a voice from the car say, "What you gonna do about the looney bug over there?"

He jams his pistol back into his belt and wags his head. "C'mon. We'll stuff bricks in his pants and throw him in the fuckin' river."

Out of the back seat of the limo steps the biggest thing I would call human I have ever seen. He makes Master Sergeant "Big Mike" Murdoch, who was six foot six and weighed 285, look like a horse jockey. Ain't never been a Cong this big! I drop my bricks and take off toward Washington, passing the tractors like they were stopped.

Which way is the fucking zoo?

∘💬∘ SALVATORE

Into the cage comes this bent-over old nigger in a suit so worn it ain't black anymore but gray. In fact, when he turns around to close the gate I see his elbows shinin' through. He's carryin' a book old as the suit, old as him. He shuffles toward us so slow he's sandpaperin' the path with the soles of his shoes. He's wearin' a purple vestlike frock thing with a priest's collar on top. The pants, old as the threads are, is pressed as neat as the pants I get from Steinberg, the tailor. You can shave yourself with the creases. The guy comes past a puddle where the alligators are congregatin' and gets to the wide space where I'm standin' with Blondie and Maria. There he stops and cranks his head up 'til his eyes find Blondie. "Judging by the period wedding dress you're wearing," he says, "you are the bride in the partnership."

"Yes, I am," says Blondie, givin' the guy a tiny bow. "My name is Beatrice. Beatrice Dove. But it will soon be Flynn."

She was tellin' me about the dress just before the old guy came shht-shhtin' up the path. The old wrinkled lady sittin' on a rock over there that's about one alligator-hop from the biggest alligator pulled it out of a box last night and gave it to her. Said she'd offered it to her daughters for each of their weddin's and none would wear it. "I was standing there with Boombah and in the light of her candle," Blondie told me, "and I looked at it and looked at it. Then you know what I did?" I told her how could I know, I wasn't there. "I fainted with happiness," she said. Fuckin' fainted! Anyway, she took up the offer and has been fingerin' it all the time we been standin' here talkin'.

She also told me the black suit Boombug is wearin' was in another box Eleanor had. "It was Eleanor's husband's. She didn't have a shirt or tie which is why Boombah is wearin' his basketball shirt. I found him the flower when we were walking to the zoo." The flower is somethin' like an orchid only cheaper, like you see along the road and in vacant lots. "He wanted to wear his high school jacket but I told him I wouldn't take my vows if he did." She said Eleanor found the minister for 'em.

Eleanor's been lookin' at me with one eye closed. I don't think she likes me. Like I give a shit.

"I'm Reverend Jarmond Peabody Robinson the Third," the old guy says, holdin' out a hand nearly as big as my father, Mario's, which was big enough to hold a basketball. "I'm honored and grateful to be performing the nuptials. I preside at Ebenezer Baptist Church on the corner of Division and Washington where all gifts and gratuities go into my rebuilding program."

I pass his joint goin' downtown for Business and can say for sure it needs some kind of fixin'. It's at the bottom of one of those three-cornered buildin's in what used to be a candy or grocery store. Got whitewashed boards where the windows used to be with messages in sloppy red paint in words all different sizes.

"Eleanor told us she'd get you and . . . she did!" says Blondie. "I'm so grateful!"

"I'm going to be doing some invocating during the ceremony, Miss Beatrice, once upon the head of you, once upon the head of the other. Out of due repect for the lady, I always give her first choice. Would you prefer to be invocated on first or second?"

"What does 'invocatin' ' mean?" I whisper to Maria.

"I'm supposed to know?" she whispers back.

Anyway Blondie tells the Reverend she wants Boombug to go first. "I don't know why," she says. "It's just my choice."

"No need to know," says the Reverend. "And where is the fortunate fellow?"

"Over there." She points to where he's standin' with Wrinkles. "Boombah!"

"No need to interrupt their conversation. I'll wait beside them and introduce myself."

Off he goes: shuffle, shuffle, shuffle, shuffle.

"I'd go second like you, babe," I tell her. "Never know what he's gonna do. I heard of a guy puts a snake around people's necks he's tryin' to cure. Nearly fuh . . . nearly choked some lady."

"Oh, Mr. Mangione, you're a wonderful person!" Blondie comes over and wraps her arms around me for no good reason. "I hope Boombah and I will know you forever!"

"Isn't that nice?" says Maria.

I can't answer 'cause of the fist swellin' up in my throat.

The birds are squawkin' like they know somethin' important is gonna happen. Same as the crawly animals that are hoppin' around. Even the slimy alligators are twitchin'. I'm glad I brought Pistolino. One of us puts a foot in the pond and those creatures will go after it. I'm keepin' the Pisto ready in case someone steps over. One of those slimes even starts to open his mouth around a leg he's gonna get a slug in his head. "Don't bring your gun," Maria said. "Okay, Precious," I said. I brought it. Some people say bein' truthful keeps a marriage together. I say lyin' does. Anyway, last time I didn't bring Pisto I nearly got choked to death in a restaurant. If the cops hadn't of come I'd be dead. If I'd of had Pisto, the Gombino creeps would of been in garbage bags in the dumpster before the cops got there. The fucks still got my name on their list.

I kept thinkin' about that after Maria talked me into comin' to this thing. Said to myself, worse thing could happen is two nice kids end up havin' to remember their weddin' turned into a shoot up. The Gombinos been lookin' for me ever since they found out my guys took their cars. And they make a fuckin' specialty of knockin' people off at weddin's and funerals. What I'm tryin' to say in a nice way is the Gombinos are fuckin' pigs who would mess up even a First Communion. They wouldn't just come and do me in in a gentleman's way. No. Their fuckin' way would be to stand outside the cage, five or six of 'em, raise their Uzis and knock off not just me but everything that moves. Even them little chickadee-type birds would be nothin' but feathers. When it comes to style, they're slot machines.

I decided I got to take out insurance.

Which I did but I ain't sayin' how.

Pretty soon the musicians stop playin' and the Reverend goes to the far end of the wide space with B. and B. and tells us the ceremony is about to begin.

"Yippee!" says one of the audience boobies.

The Reverend explains that the rings were given him for the bride and groom by Eleanor. "They were hers and her late husband's," he says, "and one will be held by young Mr. Andy there—" he points to a kid about eleven—"and the other by Rosa." He points to a little chick no more'n eight or nine.

Now he puts his big ham slabs on Boombug's head and speaks:

"Oh, Lord, bring down into the skull of the servant I cup within my palms the voice he speak with in the deepest part of his sleep. Bring it down the way the Holy Spirit brought down voices for those eleven that were left around the table when the one called Judas went out and turned you in for cash money."

If I was there that fuckin' Judas wouldn't of had to hang himself. I'd of done it for him. Upside down by his nuts from that olive tree of his. Fuckin' traitor!

"Bring it down the way you brought down for your humble and vagabond servant—yes, truly, Lord!—Jarmond Peabody Robinson the Third's very own preaching voice which he presently uses."

Like listenin' to old Satchmo playin' the trumpet which I did when I was a kid and my old man brought me to Miami for my first lay.

Now he moves the hams to Blondie's head, which almost disappears in 'em and wigwags his own head around like it's an antenna to God and he's got to get it pointed the right way. Finally he says: "Let the beauty of this young lady, Lord, soak down into the fiber of her body and into her crooked legs so that she can glide upon this earth like the cranes and the ostriches and the deers of the forest."

The Reverend could have a great racket if he bought the right radio advertisin'. Puts his hands on people's heads and pretends him and Jesus is gonna fix 'em. Hey, who's gonna sue if it don't work? The people go home and, if it don't work, blame themselves. "I forgot to say my prayers Tuesday. The Holy Lord got pissed and decided to leave me blind." Can't fuckin' lose! You can sell anybody any fuckin' thing, you market it right.

I hear screamin'. I think it's the chimps or elephants. But this is more like human screams and is comin' from down along the river somewhere. Gettin' louder too. Maybe one of the boobs run off and cracked up. This long-legged broad Maria told me was the Boomer's teacher is lookin' around too. Everyone else is deaf or pretendin' to be like Maria. They're all watchin' the Reverend who's now givin' what he said was his oration:

"Hardest thing to find on this earth, as you know, Lord, is true freedom. However, people sometimes believe they've got it when they can buy a big-screen television or a brand-new Sheva-lay. Say, 'Lookee at those poor Africans who haven't got but dirt floors and outhouses and not even a mule. Man, *we* are free!' You aren't free, brother. You are a slave to your money. And so, Lord, I pray upon the heads of these two being here united today that they don't become like many of those other false servants."

The screamin' has been gettin' closer and now the screamer lets out a shout: "The Cong have landed!"

A guest, guy in torn jeans and a flannel shirt with the design washed out comes runnin' to the back where Maria an' me are standin' and looks out through the jungle plants and past the monkey cages.

"What's goin' on?" I say.

"It's our friend, Arnold. Keeps thinkin' he's back in the Vietnam War. I've got to stop him before he wrecks poor Evrett's wedding."

Hate those vets that whine all the time about the war puttin' 'em off their heads. You think they was the only ones in this country ever to be in a fuckin' war. I like the young ones who went over and wiped that greaseball Sad Damn's ass with his own face. If you went on vacation you would have missed it. "Hey," I tell the guy. "I'll help you take this bugger out."

Maria jabs me with her elbow.

I turn. "What?"

"You keep your nose out of those people's business, Sal. Slim knows how to handle him. Beatrice told me . . . never mind. He's gone."

I turn. The raggedy guy is now runnin' toward the monkey cages.

In a second I see why.

"They're kissin' now," Maria says, givin' me a nudge.

"Right."

But I'm watchin' somethin' else.

Comin' along the path by the monkey cages is another guy movin' even faster than Slim is goin' toward him, faster even though he's kind of stumblin' the way racers do near the end. People and their kids on the path are scatterin' the way they did the day Dondero the Prick had to chase down some Jap out in a crowd at Westland Shoppin' Center. Slim stops and crouches down like a defensive back gettin' ready for a downfield tackle. But the other guy—must be the vet—swivel-hips him and comes flyin' toward us. If it wasn't for Blondie and the Boomer bein' married now I'd take out Pistolino and point it at him.

"The Cong . . . are here!" he shouts, comin' right at the cage. "They bulldozed . . . the hovels . . . into the river!"

"Jesus Christ!" I shout.

"Salvatore!"

Louie fucked up. Louie fucked up so bad he's got to die! I myself will kill Louie. I start walkin' toward the gate. I can't wait to kill Louie.

"Sal?"

It won't be with Pisto. It won't be with poison. It won't be with a rag on the nose.

Who's got a fuckin' basement big enough?

Not us.

Dondero. Dondero the Prick is also Dondero the bachelor and has a duplex with a basement. He lives on top. Dondero can get rid of the boarders on the bottom for awhile. Have him tell 'em, "Take a vacation." Or just evict 'em.

I'm at the gate just as this vet screwball turns the corner and comes at us in the wire-mesh cage. But he ain't runnin' at the gate, which I'm waitin' to hold closed. He must know that. The fuckin' maniac is headed for the side of the cage. Full blast!

Oh, Jesus! Comes right through the mesh, stomps into the pool where the alligators are lyin'. I think they're gonna bite him but they don't. They slither away. He stands in the pool and points to the Mexican Slim was standin' next to. He points at her. "She and Slim betrayed us!" Now he turns and points to Boombug. "That bastard is a Cong spy!"

I take out Pistolino, turn it around backwards, handle up, and start after him.

"Salvatore!"

"Shut up, Maria. It's Business."

I creep as close as I can but I don't want to step in the fuckin' pond. If he takes one step back, I can pop him. I raise my arm.

"Momma! That man's got a gun!" some girl in the weddin' crowd shouts.

"Shut the fuck up!" I tell her.

I think the vet guy's gonna turn when he hears her, but he doesn't.

All of a sudden everyone's standin' still, bein' as quiet as Soft Shoe Sal del Vecchio. Sal works with a knife. Can take out a restaurant full of people without a peep. No one's movin' 'cept the guy named Slim, who must of hurt his knee 'cause he's limpin' back to the cage. Everyone stays quiet, like each one of us is tryin' to figure out what to do next.

First I figure it's 'cause I pulled out Pisto. But it ain't that. Somethin' else.

Even the animals are quiet.

What finally busts up the silence is this old boob woman with hair stickin' out and about two and a half teeth. She points to the big slit the vet guy left in the screen comin' in and says, "Look! We can efcape!" Like she has to live here all the time.

"Hey," I say. "You can walk out the gate."

She ain't listenin'. There's a lotta chirpin' from the birds and noises like loud yawns from the alligators and squeaks and clucks from the crawly things. There's also a lot of mumblin' among the people. I think I hear Maria say to the boob I jabbed, "It's time to go."

What's goin' on?

At the same time a bunch of creatures start goin' slow motion toward the slit in the fence.

I see Maria goin'.

"Hey, Maria!" I say.

She's deaf to me.

"Hey! Maria!"

She don't answer.

I look around.

The only ones not movin' are Blondie and the Boomer and the Reverend and Wrinkles. They're watchin' and smilin'. Except the Reverend. He's just standin' there. Prob'ly wonderin' when he'll get his moolah. Wrinkles is standin' up next to the rock she was sittin' on and starin' at me. What's *her* fuckin' problem? Maybe it's that I'm still holdin' the heat. Okay. I stick it back in my pants. She's still starin'. *Her* fuckin' problem.

Now somethin' even stranger happens. The birds start flyin' out through the hole, the little ones first, zoomin', and the big ones flip-flappin'. There goes a parrot with about four colors. Must be worth several grand. There go the alligators, one by fuckin' one, marchin' right along the pond and to the hole.

This makes me nervous. You got to have control and order. Got to depend on people behavin' and things bein' in place. That's why Louie's got to die a painful death. He didn't control the operation. That's the way a society has to work. Even the mob. Why ain't the cops here? Tomorrow I call the chief at his home an' tell him his boys fucked up. A lot of people and animals escaped. Where were you?

Bad shit.

All started because of Louie fuckin' up. No. Before that. Started when that fuckin' Public Works Garrity let the scrapin' job out to the Gombino company. No, no. Started before that. Started when the city let the poor fucks live down by the river. What in Christ's name they do that for? No money in it. Just fuckin' let it happen. Anyway, that's when it . . . Naw. That ain't when it started. Started when there was no rubbers distributed in the poor neighborhoods so the riffraff wouldn't have kids.

Somebody's tappin' my arm.

I turn.

It's the ancient lady. "It is time for you to depart." She's wearin' rags but talks like a fuckin' English broad. "Exit, Malvolio."

What's she talkin' about?

Blondie and Boombug have come up beside us.

Blondie gives me a hug. "I will always love you, Salvatore."

I feel my heart flip-flappin'. And the fist is back in my throat. All I do is hug her back and say, "Yeah, babe." What am I turnin' into, a fuckin' wimp?

"We come visit you sometime," says Boombug, grabbin' my hands and shakin' 'em like I'm a slot machine. "You come see us."

"Hey wait," I say. "I'm gonna take you over to your island. I got some campin' stuff I'll stick in the boat."

"No," says the wrinkled bitch. "That's just what you mustn't do."

I want to say, "Who the fuck are you to be talkin' to me like that?" All I say is, "Why not?" without openin' my teeth.

"They must do what they have to do by themselves, their own way, and mustn't be intimidated even by the feeling that they owe anyone a favor. No matter what the dangers or difficulties they face, they have to manage them by themselves. Do you understand?

"No. Everyone does favors. What the hell's wrong with favors?"

Her bony finger comes up between us and wiggles in front of my chest. "I speak of favors that are obligations."

"So do I."

"They corrupt politicians. Make lawbreakers out of businessmen. Cause doctors to prescribe when they shouldn't. Produce educators who can't teach. And let people like you control what they shouldn't. I'm not going on, though I could."

She ain't said a thing I don't agree with. So what's the problem? Favors get things done. It's the way the Business works when it's workin' best. The way the country works.

She's turned to Blondie and the Boomer. "You'd better hurry. It's a mile to your raft. Go along the side streets, the way we came."

Raft?

She turns to me. "I'm too old and experienced to be corrupted, purchased, whored, paid-off, or anything else. My legs are tired. You may therefore take me to my quarters."

What a spicy old broad! "I don't mind takin' you. We prob'ly got things we could talk about. But first I got to find my wife."

"From what I've heard and observed, I don't think you need concern yourself."

"What are you talkin' about?"

"I think she's out there finding herself."

I'll still take her home. Only maybe now I'll knock her off when we get there.

Why not?

∘👄∘ BRENDAN

Beatrice and I are being carried on a twisting current down the Indian River aboard a large and awkward raft to, we trust, our island, our place of love. It was Beatrice, not I, who foresaw the threats and troubles that lurked on the mainland, who began urging not only that we undertake the adventure but make it a bold public act.

"We've got to stand up and be free," she said.

"We do what *you* say, stand up in jail."

"No," she said. "Listen to me."

I listened.

We sat under candlelight in Eleanor's vault, the two of us on rattan chairs Eleanor said had been tossed into the street after another downtown department store had been shut down. She herself sat on a log about two-feet thick and three- long which another of the homeless, after snatching it from the river, turned into a bench.

Beatrice argued we'd get nowhere except back to the confinements we both detested unless we drew as much attention to our trip as we could. "My mother is in public relations," she said. "She once told me, 'Beatrice, you can't do anything effectively unless you project the right image.' She said nobody can, not even the President."

Momma read me a book about careers when I was fifteen and

a half or sixteen, and one career was public relations. After she read the description, I said, "Make things look good, Momma?" That was the point, she said. "Say lies?" I went on. She didn't answer right away.

Not answering on the moment was a characteristic of Momma. She might go a day without answering a question, but eventually she would. When I waited I learned to watch her think. To *see* her think. When she was thinking, as opposed to, say, vaguely listening to music or daydreaming, when she was really thinking, you could see her eyebrows rippling. Once I said, "See you think, Momma." She laughed. Oh, she thought that was a clever remark. I wanted to explain how I *could* see her thinking, but, you know, saying complicated things with a tripping tongue even to a Momma like mine, was all but impossible.

Finally she gave me her public relations answer: "People in the field would say they're putting the truth in a different light."

I laughed then.

And I laughed last night.

"What's funny?" Beatrice said.

"*No pub*lic relations. Okay, Be-ah-triss?"

"Why?"

Why! When you can't transport thoughts to mouth and board them on sentences which reliably carry them across rooms, over fields, through airports, up ladders, down stairwells, into crevices and to the far end of phone lines, you've got a seriously malfunctioning delivery system. Reverend Jarmon Peabody Robinson the Third's warm invocating hands haven't added a slender adverb or lazy adjective to my capabilities, haven't made the presentation of even those weightless indefinite articles any easier. It was the same last night, when I had to offer one of my standard replies:

"Can't say *that*."

Maybe I should have attempted more, but in my condition you have to choose carefully the replies you push beyond five or six words.

Clearly unsatisfied by my answer/guess, Beatrice turned to Eleanor. "What do *you* think about, you know, calling attention to ourselves?"

Eleanor, in candlelight, with shawl, resembled very much the woman Helga who was the subject of a series of paintings by

Andrew Wyeth that Momma took me to see at the Detroit Institute of Art before she died. I was fascinated to see presentations of the same woman in various lights and in various poses. We stayed the whole day. I stood in front of some of the Helgas for fifteen or twenty minutes each. Momma didn't rush me. She never rushed me. I'd look around and find her watching me study them. When I finally told her I was getting weary and wanted to leave, she wrapped her arms around me from behind and said, "You see so much in them, don't you?" I did. So much. About light and beauty and even thought. I wanted nothing more than to share my own thoughts with Momma. But there was such a bridge, such a great bridge, between what was in my mind and what I could say.

Now Eleanor turned and the flickering light instantly transformed her from an afternoon to an evening Helga. "I'm afraid, my dear," she said, "if you and Evrett want the freedom you absolutely deserve, you're going to have to make the decision yourselves. If I had anything terribly significant to say—a warning that your lives might be in danger—I'd say it. In fact, I thought of that, the danger of you two falling into the river and drowning. The river is muddy and the current swift. But the raft you describe is a sturdy one which can't easily be tipped over and you both claim to be able to swim. There are obviously dangers. You must weigh them against your needs, then choose."

Beatrice nodded. "*Real* choices," she said. "Not whether to watch HBO or Cinemax but, like, where to live and whether to have kids. Right now it's whether to take a raft to the island. *Hard* choices. That's what they are. And I want to take very big risks." She turned. "What about you, Boombah?"

When we were with Maria, coming to River City, Beatrice suggested we have our honeymoon on an island we saw from the car. She mentioned the raft by the plaza, which she'd seen on one of her home's field trips. "I saw a couple of men untie it and move it around," she said. "I know it comes away from where it is." I liked the idea of camping on the island for our honeymoon but, when she brought up the raft, I was sure I was running off with a woman who was dangerously impulsive. I gave her one of my "No way!" answers and spoke it so vehemently she didn't, until we sat with Eleanor, bring up the subject again.

"The raft," said Beatrice. "What do you think?"

I had been thinking. When I held up to myself the risks of the voyage by raft I kept picturing something else, remembering it.

"Long time ago," I said. "For me long, not you, Eleanor. I go in bus to special school. Guy come to me first day. Say, 'Take off your shirt.' Boombah do that. Say, 'Lift up your arms.' Do *that*. He raise up hand with tiny knife. Pumb! Ouch! He stick little hole in this part." I point to my right armpit. "Make me bleed tiny bit. Someone other take rag. Wipe off blood 'til I dry. Guy with knife say. 'Okay. Put shirt back on.' I do that. He say, 'We do that again soon. Every Friday. And when you don't do what *we* say. In some secret place on you. Better not show Mommy or Daddy.' Say, 'We do that 'cause we own you.' Big guys. I shut up. Okay? Things not always like those guys. But never good."

"Never?" said Eleanor.

"Momma and Poppa take me out of *that* school. Oh boy! Happy life, right? No way. No want be home all day. Want to be in real school. One. Can't be in Hartsville West. Two. Can't play in schoolyard. Three. Can't go in classroom. Four. Can't be in park! Okay. Just park. What *it* mean. Other friends there. Squirrels. Bugs. Birds. Trees. Mr. Farnsworth. Childrens after school. Baseball too. Hey. You name it. Now Boombah can't go *there*? Hey. Know what?"

Beatrice's mouth had been open and twisting to one side and the other as I spoke. Once she said, "Poor Boombah." Now her hands were clasped in the lap of the beautiful white dress Eleanor gave her. "What?" she said.

"Want to go to island. Want to go on raft."

Beatrice, who usually stands up slowly, catapulted right out of the rattan chair and landed—poof—on my stomach, knocking my chair and me onto the concrete floor behind the old carpet it had been on. We ended up with one of her breasts against my eye. She squirmed down and positioned herself for a kiss. "I love you to the stars and back!"

Smacko!

She inspired the voyage, but my tape-measure ego prompts me to speak of one of my own contributions, the oar now planted on the deck between me and the blanket we're going to sleep on or in tonight. I spotted it sticking out from beneath the canvas of a twenty-foot plus Chris-Craft as we approached the raft. "Oar!

Oar!" I pointed at it. "You're brilliant!" she said. "Boombah know."
I knelt on the dock, reached across and deftly plucked it away.

At the most advantageous moment I'll pull myself to my feet,
slide the misappropriated paddle from beneath the blanket and
navigate this bulky rectangle the last few yards to our destination.
For the moment we need only stay glued to the deck and each other
and, as Momma used to say when I grumbled about being on a long
trip, enjoy the ride.

The easy throb of the current is the easy throb of my thoughts:
plip plap, plip plap, plip plap.

Beatrice is humming to the same rhythm.

When she stops I say, "Be-ah-triss?"

"Yes, Brendan."

"You cold?"

"Wet. I hope you can make a fire and we can dry ourselves
when we're there."

"No problem."

As we moved from narrow street to narrow street through
near-abandoned neighborhoods, she suggested stopping for
matches. She wanted us to get the big wooden kind that would
light in a wind. We hadn't a cent. "Someone will let us have a few
free," she said, as though there were people standing around with
matches that went out of common use thirty years ago.

Oh, I could have had fun with her over that.

But, then, I couldn't. How much observation, wit, sarcasm,
humor, irony, *et al.* have had over the years of my life to be
buried under the two words I next spoke: "No way"? So frus-
trated was I that I resolved to convey the idea that would save us
in a world where even a well-stocked grocery store might not
have stick matches. "Stop!" She twisted to a stop. I stopped too.
I found myself on a slab of sidewalk a tree root had broken so
that one part angled toward the street and the other toward the
top of an old fence. From this precarious speaking platform I,
braggadocio, delivered what might have been my best speech of
the decade:

"No need for matches, Be-ah-triss. Momma read books on
Indian umm, ummmmm . . . *lore.* Yep!" Already I felt I'd walked
a mile uphill in a heat wave with Mr. Reed Stark on my back. But
I chugged pluckily on. "Give muh . . . *Boombah* hard stick. Soft

wood. Can be *no* rain. Oh. Leafs too. Le-uvvvs. Leevvzzuh. *You* know. Boombah can make fire."

"You can?"

"Did once. In backyard. Next door guy call fire trucks. Oh, boy! Boombah have to go in bed early *that* night."

"Know what?"

"What?"

"You're almost speaking in regular-sized sentences. Do you think you can, I mean will, ever?"

"Yep." I really didn't, but if, someday, late at night after a long argument between us, Beatrice, while trying to sleep, asks herself, "Why did I marry this guy?" she just might take hope in the promise, given a boost by Reverend Jarmond Peabody Robinson the Third that sentences will someday flutter from my mouth like freed butterflies.

"When?"

Why set up unrealistic expectations when none might be most appropriate? "Ummmmm, twenty-two years."

"Oh, Boombah!" Her arm started to come up but went down again. "I'm tired of striking you with my little fist. I'll have to think of something else. Let's get to the boat."

"Then island."

"Our place of love."

"Of moon and honey."

"That's good! Our home."

"Country too."

"Yes! What shall we call it, New America?"

New America? Pee-yoooo! Had I chosen a woman of no imagination? New America? God! How about New Zealand Two? How about New New Rochelle? How about New Old Spice? Heeyoww! "Be-ah-triss?"

"What?"

"Don't like *that* name."

"Then what's a better one?"

Mull mull. Think think. Ponder ponder. "Some Country."

"Are you serious?"

"Yep."

That is the most unromantic, the most uninspired, the most colorless . . . I can't go on!"

"Can't go on? Mean we got to moon and honey here on sidewalk?"

"Boob! Let's go."

We goed.

As we turned the corner toward the river, I said, "Know what Sal say *to* me?"

"What?"

"He bring two sleeping bags. In boat."

"I know. I talked to him after you did. I told him we need just one."

"What!"

"I know. I know. You hate to cuddle. Just *hate* to. I know about that from HBO. We're on our honeymoon and you want two sleeping bags. All men are the same. Well, no. But a lot of them. You're one of the same. Give you your momentary thrill, your—oh, I hate to say it but I will!—little piece, and you think you've done your job for the day. You just want to roll over and snooze. Am I right?"

The lip is zipped. She wants a traditional answer. Does she also want a traditional marriage? Oh, curses! Oh, curtains! But maybe that's what I want. I don't think so. Is this the first crisis, so-called? Suppose we have nothing but crises. Did I declare before Reverend Jarmond, "Forever"? Maybe I just said, "For a long time" or "For a long time, if possible." I know I thought of saying, "Or until one of us no longer wants to stay with the other," but for me to have articulated it as I meant it would have taken at least two and a half hours. Since I only remember saying "Forever" I must have said that. A commitment.

Yeek!

"Well? Am I right?"

"No way." A lie. (Did anyone hear me say I was perfect? Anyone?)

"I don't believe you. But I don't care. I mean I do but I'm not going to worry about it. You have a beautiful heart. You'll change."

Get out the leg-irons, man!

Joke.

Look. I'm changing, trying to, have changed a lot since I met Beatrice, but am, I guess, too much an old-fashioned male. Yet one in progress. Yes. There's a ticking ticker in here. An open mind.

Opening more. Bonnie Jean said, "You have a loving face." What a lift that was! For a short time I stopped worrying about people staring at me. One, here or there, just might be thinking what Bonnie Jean did. I felt better about myself. Then I remembered that she'd been looking at me upside down, realized that the only way she'd ever seen my face was upside down. Did that then mean I had a hateable face right-side-up? Curses! Yet I must try to believe in myself and I will try to see Beatrice as a person, not a wife. As a woman. A companion. Partner. Lover. Free being!

"I change, Be-ah-triss."

"I know. I said you would."

But cuddle? Yuck!

I love her.

Do I?

I must. She's the only one I ever let talk me out of wearing my Lancers jacket, the very only one. "You can't wear that filthy thing at your wedding," she said. Right. I'd started to carry it from the vault. She took it away, gave it to Eleanor. "We'll pick it up later," she said. If the Vet hadn't come maniacking into the wedding cage, we'd have gone back to get it. Now I've got to shiver at least one night in this tight-fitting tux, circa 1945. If Beatrice can make it in that flimsy wedding dress, I can make it in this. But I do want my jacket, ASAP.

We're passing under the Gray Bridge that binds East River City to River City.

One night, after Poppa had fallen asleep, I was listening to the Sis McGovern Talk-in Show on WRCC, River City, and a baritone-voiced man called in and said, "Why is the Gray Bridge gray?"

What questions it released in me, cousins to his own, the kind I often had but usually dismissed as stupid. That night they centered on dandelions. Why are dandelions yellow? Why are dandelions called dandelions? Why aren't they worn in garlands at weddings? You can make dandelion soup. Momma did. Can you, then, make a dandelion salad? Why not? Dandelion sandwiches? Is dandelion tea good with dandelion salad? What vitamins, minerals and herbs are contained in dandelions? Is it itself an herb? I'd be getting to the park late the next day. Many mornings I go—went now, I guess it is—to the library, especially when Momma was alive. I still did after she died, but too infrequently. She was much more demanding than Sarah. I would go the next day to the library and learn all I could about dandelions. I resolved to do that a moment after the baritone man spoke his question.

Now I waited for Sis's answer. Sis is a fantastic answer-giver, but this time she didn't know. "Why is Gray Bridge gray? If anyone knows, call us please." She didn't know! I'd been lying in bed ready to sleep. I was soon pacing the floor of my bedroom. Why is the Gray Bridge gray? No answer from radio. Why? I paced into the kitchen, back and forth there, waited, no answer. I then paced in both kitchen and bedroom. Still no answer. I turned up the volume knob and, on the verge of madness, paced into the store. Why did I choose to tune in Sis tonight? Too late to tune out. I hung on. Would I have to check on bridge paint at the library? Finally— finally!—someone called long-distance from the state capital and promised an answer, which, if satisfying, would let me and, I imagined, thousands of other "Work Radio" listeners get a few winks before tomorrow. "I worked in the Department of Highways and Transportation for near thirty years 'til recently," said a weary voice that carried its own static. "Reason the Gray Bridge in River City is gray is that's the only color of paint the State Department of Transportation has to give away. Any other kind we special-order and the city pays for it. Don't ask me why. Don't know why. They's this little bridge down in Grass Forks they keep paintin' chartreuse and I hear it's about bankrupt the town. So there you are." Sis thanked him and said, "There's always someone out there with an answer."

Questions, too.

I wanted to call in and ask Sis to survey her audience on the question of afterlife. I couldn't of course have gotten the word "afterlife" out of my mouth during the impatient seconds you're given to speak, and by the time I'd have mumble-stumbled it out in my own fucking characteristic Brendan manner I might have been cut off. Even if I hadn't been, I'd have worried about someone reading my condition from my voice and saying, "In answer to that retard-person's question . . ." So I listened and listened to myself listening but didn't pick up the phone, just remained mum and kept on listening, hoping some other bewildered late-nighter whose pop or mom had recently slid into the wherever would call in and ask the question.

No one did.

I don't want to believe she's altogether gone.

Listen. After Momma died, a purple-eyed professor who teaches abnormal psychology at Midland State University told Poppa in the store—get this—the retarded adapt to death more easily than normal people. "Don't worry about the young man over there." I wanted to shout at him my pain, my grief, but sometimes there's nothing left to say. You've just got to kick ass! What I did was try to bomb his foot with a large can of french-cut beans I popped off the shelf with my elbow when he passed out of the store. I swear I missed by no more than a quarter-inch.

Momma, if I'm in range, give me a sign. Give one to Poppa too. Perk him up. Love, Brendan.

Can a person put as loving energy in the world as she did and then just zip eternally away?

I wait.

No sign.

Maybe she's back in Hartsville working on Joseph.

Poppa.

I'm not going to bite into my guilt over him and that heart attack. Keep remembering Momma saying, "Joseph, I read that eating oats helps reverse heart damage." Poppa backlashed with, "My heart's ticking as strong as a woodpecker pecks." But Momma knew. When I was reading my books at the library she was reading books containing information about the heart and its functions because she was aware, I now think, that Joseph had some kind of malfunction. I remember her reading him a description of anginal pain. Afterwards he said, "I don't get pains in the chest." She read it again, hitting down on certain words, ". . . or *upper back, neck* and *arm*, particularly the *left*." All she could draw out of him was his weekly resolution: "I'll see Doc Grable pretty soon." My running off might have triggered the "event" or myocardial infarction, as the books Mother read to him called certain heart attacks.

So, okay, I'm, after all, biting into the guilt.

I know I shouldn't have run off, should have been patient. I'd have gotten my turn to speak in that mausoleum of a courtroom.

Hey. I was younger then. I've learned a little. Can I forget it? Can I please fucking forget it or am I going to have to scrub it off my conscience with the Lava soap? I'll get a message to Pop somehow. After we reach landfall.

How?

No phones.

And what *about* food?

No pizza delivery boats.

I'll use my slim knowledge of berries, herbs, roots, bark and even grasses. There are items on that island that can sustain us and, in doing so, inflict in us less damage than, say, the food Joseph was eating or that slop—mashed, squashed, pounded, or crushed—they serve at the county house. Bluckee-bloo! Further, while I easily make friends with birds and small animals (never had much of a chance with large ones), survival comes first and, if necessary, I mean *bottom-line* necessary, I'll snatch one, clean it with one of the Indian-style tools I intend to shape, roast it on our fire, and with a willing Beatrice, munch. If we aren't too soon bothered by the River Police or whoever patrols around here, I'll try to persuade Beatrice to let Sal or one of his hoods bring us a three-courser now and then. *Remember, sweet Bea,* I'll find a way to say, *the early Americans got help when necessary from outsiders.* I have a feeling that Maria will have Sal coming soon with a hot pan of big raviolis.

Holy God!

The island is coming quickly upon us. "Bee-ah-triss! Sit. Mean kneel." Has to be ready to jump off. In case raft bounces back into river.

"Brendan. Look!"

Look? Can't look. Am, uff, on knees, reaching for oar, trying not to let Eleanor's blanket or me slide into the river. "Can't. What?"

"There are a lot of people on the banks and walking along the street above it. Some of them are waving. Oh, this is wonderful!"

"No . . . uhhh . . . wave back. Make you fall."

"I won't. But I want to."

I have the oar. I look ahead.

The current breaks at the head of the island. Bits of wood and such are parting with it. There's a little eddy of water behind the parting water. I must get through . . . here we go . . . now row row . . . not gently down the . . . but through it! Way to go, Boomer! Whoops! We're still in the eddy. It's like a little whirl-pool. Row row . . . through it.

Fwump!

There.

"Boombah! You did it!" She turns toward me, obviously about to pounce on me.

"No!" Into the whirlpool we'll fall, kissing while we drown. "No! No! No!"

"You don't *have* to keep saying it."

Oh-oh. The raft is slipping from where it planted itself on the muddy bank, back into . . . "Up!" I take her hand. Together we struggle upward. In my other hand is Eleanor's blanket. The raft is slipping away. Off we go, together, so together both of our feet, right and right, land simultaneously in the virgin mud.

"Know what?" I say as we plop down.

"What?"

"The Dove . . . has landed."

She screams out a laugh, tucks up her fist and lets me have one right on the heart.

°☉° DANA

We didn't go home, Angela or me. I mean we did but now we're back, the only ones from the school tour who came back. We were together on the bus, going and coming, and not once, I swear, did either one of us say to the other, "I'm coming back." Or even that we wanted to. But we did. I decided to the second after Miss Carroll said to Mr. Constanza in that totally bitchy voice of hers, "We're in scheduled lunch period right now. Don't you think they ought to be taken back to school?" Like something really bizarre, really interesting, is happening, and she's just waiting to shut it off.

This morning the bus caught up with the raft and followed it along, thanks to Mr. Constanza, who told the driver to keep it in sight if he could. Mr. Constanza seemed just as excited as most of us. Not all. Like Greg Martin. He and his girlfriend go off the school grounds and have lunch together every day. He wanted to get back for lunch with her and kept saying, "What time are we leaving, Mr. Constanza?" God, I could have choked him! *Never!* I answered in my head. *You have to stay in the bus forever.* Some people have no curiosity. None, Greg and Miss Carroll included.

Anyway, suddenly the two people on the raft knelt up. It was Mr. Constanza who first saw them move. He was sitting two seats in front of me and said, "Well . . . well, I'll be darned," and sort of half-stood up in his seat. We all rubbernecked out the windows on the right and, sure enough, the pudgy one was trying to do two things at once, get something out from under him and help the other one to her knees.

I had been half-sitting up and then kind of weakly slipped back and turned to Angela, who was in the aisle seat.

"Wow! You were right."

"Not exactly," she said. "I really wasn't all that sure they were dead."

She's cool.

Some on the bus were laughing. The reason is the male who was rowing had a kind of jerking way of moving that made him look like people in those real old movies. The female had her head tilted like she was looking at something in the sky, even though you were kind of sure she wasn't. From where we were you couldn't tell until they stopped whether they were going to go around the island or stop on it.

The raft hit the island and started to twist and go back into the river. They had to jump at the very last second. That was so exciting, how close it was that they both almost didn't get off in time. I mean one second after they landed that raft got caught in a little tide and went spinning around, like if they'd been on it, it might have thrown them off. Then, still turning, it went around the other side of the island and disappeared for a few seconds.

When you could see it go past at the bottom-end of the island it seemed to be going a lot faster. I think they were lucky because there are really fast rapids a few miles below, where my dad fishes for walleyes.

Then we rushed off the bus with everyone almost getting squeezed in the door at the same second but we made it and headed for a fence that maybe wasn't the best place to watch from but was the easiest to get to. Right up next to it was parked a small yellow bus which had on the side: CLEAVER COUNTY SPECIAL SCHOOL. I've heard them called "retard buses" all my life and now wish I knew another name. Anyway I soon figured out that others by the fence had come off the bus. I was glancing at them when one, a girl about nine, said, "Look, Beatrice is waving!" I looked to the island and, sure enough, the female was waving her hands and looking right in our direction. I moved away from my class and stood by the one who had spoken.

"Do you know them?"

"Oh, yes," she said proudly. She was holding the hand of an older lady who wasn't much taller than her. "The boy is Brendan and the girl is Beatrice. I guess I shouldn't say boy and girl. They just got married."

"Really?" That made sense of what they were wearing. Kind of. "But why did they take a raft to that island? In fact, why did they go there at all?"

"Oh, they're having their honeymoon and then are going to start a new country," she said as calmly as if she had just said she'd had Cocoa Puffs for breakfast. "Sarah—that's Brendan's teacher— is trying to get a court order so they can't be taken off the island."

The older lady pulled her hand out of the girl's and said, "Yippee!"

Some kids from my class laughed at that but none of the ones who were with her did.

"That's just what she does," said the girl.

Then she put her hand back in the lady's.

"My name is Rosa and this is Miss Goss." She held up Miss Goss's hand.

I told them my name and asked how the ones on the island expected to live there. "I mean there's no house or food or anything."

"They just will." Rosa was looking at them all the time she was talking.

I looked out.

The islanders were walking around among the trees near the middle of the island. You could see parts of them moving behind the branches, exploring, I guess. The way everyone was staring out made me think it was like we were watching little kids when you bring them to a new playground.

Rosa tapped me and pointed to a young black lady at the far end of the fence. "That's Delia. After we left the zoo she said one of Brendan and Beatrice's new friends is going to try to buy the island and let them stay. It's just a rumor."

I nodded. But I thought, then it won't be their country. I hoped they would just sort of claim the island. I mean I don't think anyone else uses it.

We turned to watch.

Brendan and Beatrice came out of the woods part with handfuls of little sticks and put them down near where they'd landed. The one named Brendan turned and looked at us and then made a signal like a baseball umpire when someone is safe.

Many of us laughed.

He clasped his hands together and shook them at us.

I think if someone had yelled across they could have been heard. No one did. It was like the two out there were in their own sacred place and shouldn't be disturbed by voices or anything. In fact, to me it was almost like a different time.

All the time we'd stood there, Miss Carroll and Greg had been buzzing in Mr. Constanza's ears. There could have been a volcano on that island and they wouldn't have looked out. And then, of course, they got their way. Mr. Constanza said, "All right. Guess we've got to go back." You could tell he really didn't want to. I bet he was worried Miss Carroll would fill out a report on him that started like, "Mr. Constanza wouldn't let the students return in time for lunch." I know I should be more tolerant of dodo-heads like her. But I don't know why. In class she sometimes talks about how her father withheld privileges and made life hard on his children. Right. So now she can be obnoxious.

Okay. That was earlier.

Later, around eight, when it was starting to get dark, I told my

mother I was going to the library which, I swear, I did do. But I
stayed only fifteen minutes, long enough to return a biography of
Harriet Tubman and find a novel by a writer named Ana Castillo.
Then I took a bus downtown and transferred to another one that
stopped near the island. I walked down a long like-hallway below
the fence and sat just above where the bank was muddy. I was as
close as I could get to the island without being in the water.

"Dana? Hey, Dana?"

It's about ten seconds later and guess who's running down the
long alleyway? "What are *you* doing here?" I said.

"I was at that carry-out near the bus stop, watching them,
then I saw you get off the bus."

"This is great! This is just great!"

We didn't ask ourselves why we came back. Why should we?
Someone should ask why the others didn't.

She said when she stopped to get a candy bar before going
outside to watch, there was a man in a tan overcoat asking the
cash-register man if police had come by and asked about the islanders. The cash-register man said they'd been here when the
crowds were here but then had left. Angela said, "What was
strange is, he gave the man a card and held up a hundred dollar bill
and said, 'You the owner?' The other one said, 'Yes, sir.' Then the
overcoat man said, 'Take this. It's so's you'll check the island every
hour. Call if anyone, even police, stops there or shines a light there
or does anything to bother the people on it. Got it?' The owner
nodded. Then the other one said, 'If you can't do it right, give me
back the paper now. Understand?' The other nodded. Then the
overcoat one said, 'My friends and I will treat you nice if you do a
good job. If you don't . . .' He shrugged at the owner. 'Know what
I mean?' 'Oh,' the other one said. 'Know what I mean?' said the
first one again. Then the owner said, 'I do know. I been here
before.' 'Good.' The one in the overcoat made his hand into a little
pistol and flicked it at the owner. 'We're gonna be friends, okay?'
he said."

I was totally impressed. I mean things like this don't happen in
my dull neighborhood. Angela lives somewhere near here and
maybe wasn't as impressed. "What do you think all that meant?"

"I don't know what it meant," she said. "I'm still thinking
about it."

We watched the islanders.

I won't tell you everything else we saw, but I'll tell you the best part.

Nearly the whole time we sat there they were kneeling and their heads were down over the little pile they'd gathered together. The heads were in a silhouette against the lights in East River City, and you could see them bobbing up and down, one then the other, like when they were talking. Once he put both hands to his head and then threw them up in the air like when my dad thinks he fixed something in our car and then finds out he didn't. She moved her head more than her hands when she was expressing herself and once looked straight up into the sky, I mean right up to what was just above her head. I looked up and saw a huge white star. Maybe she was looking at that, but I think she was sort of expressing some feeling like, how long is this going to take? Or maybe praying. Although the weather had gotten a little warmer and it was more like spring the way it should be, the air was still chilly. Anyway, he kept working. You could see him bent over and his hands moving back and forth and he worked for a long time, a very long time, stopping hardly at all. And then there was a little spark of light. That made him move his hands faster. Faster and faster they went. Now she picked up something and scattered it or them in the pile and then a little flame appeared. He dropped whatever he was holding and bent down lower, and they both went lower until their faces were on the ground, or nearly. They were blowing on the fire and the flames got larger and you could see smoke coming up and then an even larger flame. They pulled back and their faces glowed in the light.

"That's fantastic," said Angela.

It really was.

They huddled together on the far side of the fire looking into it.

Angela and I watched them for a long time more.

ABOUT THE AUTHOR

PHILIP F. O'CONNOR founded and directs the Creative Writing Program at Bowling Green University. He has written two critically acclaimed novels, *Stealing Home,* which was a National Book Award finalist, and *Defending Civilization.* He is also the author of two award-winning short story collections, *Old Morals, Small Continents, Darker Times* and *A Season for Unnatural Causes.* He lives in Bowling Green, Ohio.